BLEMISHED BEAUTY

Brenda Hodnett

Crystal Publishing LLC
Fort Collins, Colorado

BLEMISHED BEAUTY

Blemished Beauty

2016 ©COPYRIGHT Brenda Hodnett
2016 ©COVER COPYRIGHT Crystal Publishing LLC
Edited by Keri De Deo and Bonnie Walker
Cover design by lotusdesign.biz

Published by Crystal Publishing LLC
Fort Collins, Colorado
ISBN 978-1-942624-09-7

To Danny Lee, for always believing in me

Contents

Prologue

Daphne Zollinger shifted with discomfort in her cold, metal chair. She rolled her rigid shoulders and circled her stiff neck. The blank walls of the stale clinic room echoed the raw emptiness inside her.

"Stop fidgeting, Daphne," said her best friend, Laurel, who was sitting in the corner. "Everything will be fine."

Daphne wanted to roll her eyes. *Easy for you to say.*

Just then, a dermatologist entered the room after a soft knock at the door. Daphne stared at her with anxious anticipation.

Dr. Willow sat in a chair opposite Daphne and crossed her lengthy legs so her purple skirt hung just longer than her lab coat. Her curly, black hair framed her solemn face. She leaned toward Daphne when she spoke. "You have a condition called rosacea. It's a treatable condition, but also a chronic one."

Daphne shook her head as if to clear it. "Are you saying I'm going to have this red-colored, acne skin for the rest of my life? I'm twenty-two. I thought I would have grown out of this by now."

The doctor frowned in understanding. "This is different. Sometimes rosacea can go on through your forties, even beyond. Each case is different. In the meantime, you will continue to have some flare-ups and remissions, but if we stay on top of your treatments, it can be manageable."

Since when has my skin ever been manageable? "What are the treatments?"

"I'll give you oral and topical antibiotics. You'll need to manage your stress. It will also help if you stay out of the heat, which shouldn't be a problem this winter." The doctor smiled as if this made everything better.

"Will the burning ever go away?" Daphne asked as she put a subconscious hand up to her cheek.

"It shouldn't bother you all the time," Dr. Willow assured her. "Rosacea can affect your eyes, too. Make sure you see an ophthalmologist right away if you notice any swelling."

Daphne inhaled deeply. She glanced at Laurel who continued to sit in silence. She threw Daphne a sympathetic look.

"I'll write you a prescription," the doctor said, standing up. "Don't worry yourself too much over this," she said with a polite smile and then left the room, closing the door behind her.

"'Don't worry,'" Daphne quoted sourly. "Fat chance of that." She stood up and walked across the clinic room where a small, oval mirror hung on the wall. She peered at her reflection in disgust. Her cheeks were near crimson, scattered with small pimples, as were her forehead and chin. *Will I really look like this forever?*

"I know what you're thinking," Laurel announced, now standing behind her. She placed a comforting hand on her shoulder. "It won't be this bad all the time."

Daphne glanced at Laurel's reflection. Her light hair was tied back in a high ponytail and her face was perfect—the smoothest, creamiest complexion one could have. Daphne's cheeks burned all the more as she swallowed hard. If only she could swallow her resentment.

Chapter 1

On the Edge

Daphne Zollinger wiped the heavy, wet snow from her goggles. Not that it helped much. Every time she did so, her icy, soggy gloves left streaks on the lenses. Her ski mask was starting to freeze to her face, and every deep breath blurred her vision further. She pressed her hands hard against her ears to warm them. Her head ached as the bitter, icy wind bellowed down the mountain. She adjusted her goggles to get a better look at what lay ahead. A deep sigh made its way through her dry throat. The blinding snow continued to fall furiously from the dark Alaskan sky.

Daphne could not keep up with Laurel, an avid skier, on this terrain in such a terrible blizzard. *Oh, why did I ever let Laurel talk me into this? This is crazy!* Every last inch of her was numb to the bone. She realized her feet no longer had any control over her skis as she collided very clumsily into the trunk of a tree. Her entire body throbbed from the small accident.

"Daphne!" shouted a distant, muffled voice.

Daphne lifted her head to see Laurel a few yards ahead of her. Laurel looked like a big, puffy strawberry, powdered with sugar from head to toe.

"Come on!" Laurel yelled into the blustering air. "We have to move faster if we're going to make it out of here!" She then swiftly poked her poles into the ground to spin herself around. Gracefully, she glided across the snow past the thick, red cedar trees, despite the falling sleet and circling wind blowing against her.

Ignoring her tired arms, Daphne quickly pricked her poles into the snowy ground to follow her friend. As she gathered sufficient momentum, one of her poles cracked a patch of ice and brought her to a jolting halt. She lost her balance but caught herself before she collapsed. She frowned as she realized the small delay would put her even farther behind Laurel. She could hardly see her anymore. The dreadful snow and wind mercilessly pelted her face. Daphne reached the top of a slope and spotted Laurel at the bottom of it.

The hill was quite steep, and Daphne usually would have skied down it with a little caution. However, fear of losing Laurel triggered her to be a bit braver, so she headed straight down without trying to slow herself. Daphne leaned over her knees to put her weight into her toes, keeping her skis together and her poles jutting out behind her.

She zoomed down the slope, faster and faster. The thrill of such speed coursed through her veins so swiftly she felt as if her heart would leap right out of her chest and fly off with the wind. She felt daring and powerful as she kept her feet and knees in control.

Her confidence left as instantly as it had come, however, once she saw the perilous sight in front of her. How it got there, Daphne couldn't imagine: just beyond an oversized cedar was a cliff. She didn't know how dangerous a cliff it was, and she was suddenly strangled with terror at the thought of how treacherous it could be. Daphne shrieked involuntarily and desperately tried to whip herself around to avoid the drop. In her attempt, she crashed to the ground. She vaguely noticed one of her skis flying through the air. Her poles were no longer in her hands because her fingers were clawing futilely at the icy ground. It was too dark, and she was moving too fast to see anything clearly. Daphne heard screams in the air and wondered if they were her own. Her heart throbbed in her ears as she stared, petrified, at the cliff's edge skyrocketing towards her. She *had* to stop herself! Daphne struggled with all her strength to dig the ski that was still attached to her toe into the icy slope, but there was no way of it catching while she was at such a twisted angle.

And then, she knew she was done for. This was it. This was the end.

Unmercifully, the cliff seemed to increase its slippery surface, and Daphne plummeted over the edge, shrieking in panic. Her eyes desperately searched for a branch, a root, anything to grab ahold of. She saw several and grappled at them all, but they immediately slipped from her grasp. Daphne went tumbling down the untamed mountain. Branches and rocks cut her at every move. With each roll of her body, her stubborn ski had an evil mind of its own and smacked her in the knee, the head, the face. A sudden wrenching tear in her leg lashed through her. She heard herself scream again. And then, finally, she was still.

***

Tom Multon was busy hauling some freshly chopped wood into the lean-to shed adjacent to his two-bedroom cabin. A blizzard was screaming through the mountains. The black evening sky, which was usually clear and beautiful and scattered with sparkling stars, had quickly turned ominous. He shuddered at the thought of another long winter. Gathering his precious wood together, he turned toward the cabin. Mid-step, he thought he heard yelling off in the distance. *What the devil?*

Out of curiosity, he pointed his flashlight towards the high cliff above him, about a quarter of a mile away. The lofty mountain rose majestically—massive boulders bulged out of its surface, giant pines feathered across the tree line, and red cedars plumped at the bottom. Even after all the months he had been here, this impressive beauty still filled him with a sense of wonder and awe.

Then, he heard it again—that strange screaming. *What is going on?* Tom used his flashlight to scan the nearby field and woods this time. He saw no one.

He shrugged. It was probably his imagination. His long-term solitude might very well be bringing him close to insanity. Tom let out an enormous sigh and continued heaving the chopped wood into organized piles.

Still, an eerie feeling crept over him. Was it another "fellow hunter" who would try to kill him again? Tom shivered as he tossed another log onto the pile.

Now the screaming sounded more like a cry—a sad, piercing cry. *That's definitely a person.*

Tom clicked on his light again and walked briskly towards the desperate cries, suddenly quite determined to discover whoever it was. The knee-deep snow was quickly getting even deeper. Tom waded through the snow longer than he had expected. He wasn't worried about getting lost, but the mystery person probably was. They would need shelter soon since this storm was intensifying swiftly.

"If you're out there, make a sound!" Tom shouted. "I can't see you!" It was strange to hear a voice again, even if it were his own.

"I'm—" croaked a voice, followed by a loud, hacking cough.

Tom pointed his flashlight towards the sound. He saw a lone figure standing next to...to what? He quickened his step but slowed as he moved into deeper snow. Then he saw the object was a ski standing upright in the snow. A figure was leaning against it.

"Do you need help? Are you lost?" Tom asked, moving closer.

"Y...y...yes," a trembling voice faintly whispered.

A girl just a few years younger than Tom. What was she doing out here alone? *Well, at least she probably won't try to kill me. I think.*

***

Daphne was barely aware she had fainted again, but she figured she must have because she didn't remember this man picking her up. However, at the moment, she was very aware she was in his arms with her head against his chest. He felt like a furnace next to her frozen body. Now that she could feel herself breathing, she could also sense the breathing of the man, slow and even. A new shock of alarm shot through her veins. *What kind of man is this? And where is he taking me?* Suddenly, she wasn't so sure being lost and forsaken was all that bad. Unless...unless he really would help her. *Country folk are always friendly, right?* Daphne continued to hope as the man balanced her on a lifted knee so one of his hands could open the wooden door of a cabin. He pushed the door open with his foot and carried her across the threshold and then down a few stairs.

A newer sense of warmth and light swirled all around her as her stinging eyes strained to see her surroundings through her ice-covered goggles. With one clumsy effort, Daphne attempted to pry the wretched things off her face. The man gently put her down on a padded bench and promptly took them off for her. Then he stepped aside to close the door. Daphne sighed in relief since she no longer felt the wind in her ears.

Trying to be discreet, she glanced at her surroundings and discovered she was in a very small mudroom. She assumed they had come in the back entrance. A large moose head was mounted on the wall directly in front of her. Adjacent to the door they had just entered was another open door on her right . Daphne could see a washing machine in there. To her left, she saw nothing but an entrance to a hallway that ran parallel to her. Instinctively, Daphne knew this cabin was larger and more modern than she had expected. She groaned at the possibility of more strangers.

"I bet you want to warm up," the man presumed, turning to face her. However, the only thing that registered in Daphne's ears was the man's thick Texas twang.

Daphne moved to nod but wasn't certain she had succeeded.

"Um, I'll take that as a yes," the man said. He walked past her and poked his head around the corner, into the hallway. "It looks like the bathroom is in okay shape." He turned to face her again without moving his stance. "Feel free to take a hot bath, or whatever you need."

A hot bath! Oh, to be in one of those again! Daphne told her lips to say "thank you," but she didn't hear a sound. She tried again, but her frozen chin was unable to move a single muscle.

The man pursed his lips. Seeing him in the light, Daphne noticed for the first time he had red hair. It didn't detract from his face, however. In fact, it complemented it quite nicely.

"Uh, can I help you with your coat or anything?" he asked as he moved towards Daphne. She flinched involuntarily. Well, at least now he knew she wasn't made of stone.

The man's eyes bulged in surprise at her movement, and then an expression of sympathy crossed his face. "It's okay. I...I'm not insane or anything." He swallowed hard, looking a little embarrassed. "Er, what I mean is, you can trust me."

Daphne sniffed. Just because he said those words didn't make it so.

The man slowly moved closer to her and helped her stand. Daphne now realized she was just three or four inches shorter than he. He couldn't be more than 5 feet 10 inches. For some reason, she found this surprising. She had imagined him to be taller considering how strong he was. She studied him a little further and decided he must be somewhere in his mid-twenties. *If Laurel were here, she would be all over him.*

And then, an impulsive panic seized Daphne's heart. "Laurel!" she gasped out loud.

"What?" the Texan asked, looking startled.

"My best friend is still out there!" she cried.

The man put his hands on either side of Daphne's arms and looked directly at her as if he were deciphering something difficult. "Say that again," he said.

Daphne spoke slow and deliberate. "My best friend is still out there."

The man's eyes bulged, and he cursed under his breath. "Does she have a cell phone with her?" he asked.

"Yes!" Daphne exclaimed. For the first time she was grateful Laurel never left her cyber friends behind.

The man quickly disappeared without a word. Not moments later he was back with a phone in hand. "You're in luck," he declared. "Cell service returned a few hours ago after being out for a week."

Daphne reached for the phone but was unable to grasp it with her gloved hand. The man took the phone back and said, "What's the number?" Daphne barely noticed. He pulled off her glove and placed the phone back in her naked hand.

Before Daphne could even register a dial tone, Laurel had answered on the other end. "Hello?" Laurel said in a hurried voice. Instant relief flooded through her at the sound of her friend's voice.

"Laurel?" Daphne replied. She moved her jaw up and down as she began to feel her nerves tingle.

"Oh, Daphne! Where are you? Are you okay?" Laurel inquired, sounding anxious.

"Yeah, I'm fine. A guy found me and brought me to his cabin. What about you?"

"Oh, I'm good. I made it to the highway. I called Brian, and he picked me up. We've been driving back and forth trying to spot you. Where is the cabin?"

"I have no idea. Don't risk coming after me. I'm sure the man will help me get back after the blizzard is over." Daphne glanced up at her host, silently asking for this favor. He nodded in return.

"Okay, then. I'm so glad you're safe!"

"You, too," said Daphne. "Bye, Laurel."

"Bye!"

Daphne ended the call and handed the phone back to the stranger whom she was trusting with her life.

"Is she okay?" he asked.

"Yes, thank goodness."

"Why don't you take off your snow gear, and I will start running some hot water in the tub?" He didn't wait for her to respond but just walked out of the mudroom and around the corner to where she assumed the bathroom was.

The warm cabin was slowly bringing back her senses—and it hurt. Her fingers and toes tingled with pain. Her face felt raw and withered underneath her thick, fleece ski mask. Her ears were still numb, and she was instantly aware her heart, which an hour or so ago she thought would stop from the chill, was now beating rapidly. This was too frightening. However, it was also too wonderful. The fact that she had seen the light from the cabin and then had actually seen the man outside was a direct answer to her prayers! Even though it was a little terrifying to be with this stranger, she would not give up on this miracle.

She moved to unzip her coat but was clumsy with the zipper. She pulled off her second glove and examined her hands. They were so painfully dry they were bleeding through cracks in her skin. With a trembling effort, she finally managed to maneuver the zipper. She looked up, and the redheaded man was by her side again, assisting her in taking her arms out of her coat. He hung it up on a hook near the door. Daphne leaned over to take off her boots. After a couple of futile yanks and heaves, she slumped against the wall to catch her breath.

"Let me help," said the man as he crouched in front of her and began to unbuckle her ski boots. Daphne realized she liked this man's voice quite a lot. It had a pleasant deep pitch, almost lyrical, with no hint of self-importance. Daphne smiled to herself. A southerner, no doubt.

Amidst Daphne's speculations, she was now aware this southerner had also unzipped her snow pants and was sliding her legs out of them as well.

"Do you have any, uh, clothes under these?" he inquired, looking up at her cautiously.

"I have long johns on if that's what you mean," said Daphne. Her voice sounded dry, crackly, and strange.

The man raised his eyebrows. "Yeah, that's what I meant." Before she knew it, the man was helping her peel out of the rest of her clothes, right down to her long johns. Without notice, he picked her up and carried her to the bathroom. As awkward as this was, Daphne was grateful not to have to put weight on her injured leg again. The pain of it was beginning to increase much faster than her thawing body.

The man gently set her down on her feet, and Daphne leaned her back against the tiled counter, supporting herself with her hands.

"Um, you'll be okay now?" he asked, looking worried.

Daphne nodded. "I'll manage," she muttered, although she was certain she couldn't since she could barely move her muscles even with his assistance.

"Oh, we forgot this," the man said as he reached to take off Daphne's ski mask.

"No!" Daphne snapped, batting his hand away. Fortunately, she was with it enough to refuse that offer. No way would she allow him to see her face right now. This situation was already embarrassing enough.

The man staggered and took a step back with his hands up in surrender.

She frowned under the fleece. "I'm sorry," she mumbled. "I'll manage," she said again.

***

Wow. Strange, strange girl. But then again, if he had just been lost in the darkness on a vast, dangerous mountain for who knows how long, fainted, and then found himself in the arms of a stranger who had just helped him undress, he would probably be a little on edge, too.

Tom hoped the girl wouldn't get too sick while she was here. He made his way to the kitchen to make some hot soup. She would need something to eat. He already had leftover cooked potatoes and chicken.

While he was slicing some carrots, he heard a sob come from the bathroom. *Poor girl. I wonder why she's out here.* Well, whoever she was, he was glad to have someone else with him in the cabin. Yesterday, loneliness had overwhelmed him so much he had almost hugged his most recent moose kill.

Although he would never admit this to the girl, he was secretly glad she would have to spend some extra time with him. Considering how much snow was coming down, there was no way that girl could go anywhere, and there was no way any rescue team could come in either—for who knew how long.

Tom smiled to himself as he recalled how lovely his visitor had looked in her long johns. *I bet she has a pretty face, too.* He began whistling a nameless tune as he dropped some vegetables into the simmering broth. He had company.

Chapter 2

Red in the Face

Daphne leaned back in the oversized tub and allowed herself to breathe the steam from the hot water. She couldn't remember the last time being warm felt so nice. She tried to focus on the soothing water and not worry about the pulled muscle in her leg. She remembered a time when her mom had pulled a muscle during a run. After a couple of weeks of taking it easy, she had been back to normal. Right now, Daphne was grateful to be alive and safe. At least, she was almost sure she was safe.

Daphne glanced at her soaked long johns hanging over a towel rack. They slowly dripped water onto the floor, forming a puddle she would be hard pressed to explain. She hadn't planned on getting into the tub with them on, but how was she supposed to get them off when her frozen muscles wouldn't cooperate? Granted, it was also hard to get them off while they were wet, but not by comparison. Daphne cringed when she remembered how she had cried in frustration with the task, hoping the redheaded man hadn't heard.

Oh, how was she going to get out of here? And when? She hoped it was soon. She couldn't bear to look at that handsome stranger's face for too long. She already owed him so much for rescuing her! How could she ever repay him? Daphne bonked her head against the back of the tub in frustration. The piercing pain in her leg was throbbing all the more. She inhaled slowly and closed her eyes. *This too will end.*

***

Daphne woke up, startled.

"Hello!" The man was banging on the door. Instant relief rushed through her as she remembered she had locked it.

More banging. "Hey! Are you all right?"

"Yes," Daphne croaked and then cleared her throat. "Yes, I'm fine!" she called out loudly.

"You've been in there for over two hours," the man exclaimed.

Daphne sat up in the water, wincing at the pain. "I'm sorry. I fell asleep," she admitted.

"Oh, well…do you, I mean…I made some food for you."

Food did sound good, but how was she going to get out of this tub? "Oh, that's…very thoughtful." Daphne cringed at the thought that not only would she have to pay him back for his kindness but also for food as well. She wouldn't let herself owe anybody anything, even if she couldn't really afford it. She could barely afford to feed herself, what with tuition, books, and dorm expenses.

"Um, well, I'll be in the kitchen," the man called through the door.

"Thank you," she muttered. "I will…get out now." *If* she could get out. Carefully, she stood up on one foot, steadying herself with one hand on the wall. She moaned when she realized there was no way out but to step on her crippled leg. Well, it had to be done.

Cringing the entire time, she lifted her stinging leg over the edge of the tub. Now she wished she had her ski to use as a crutch. Anticipating the pain of having to shift her weight onto a leg that could not support her, she braced herself for the torture. Even though she tried to step onto the bathroom floor quickly, a sharp jab of pain left her woozy. Her good leg slipped out from under her, and she went crashing to the floor, knocking over the small towel shelf. Luckily, she caught herself so she didn't hit her head, but now her hip and knees were throbbing, too. Daphne pressed her lips together hard to force herself not to cry out. Footsteps rushed down the hall.

"Are you all right?" the man called through the door.

Daphne wanted to answer, but she was still fighting against the sharp, piercing pain.

The man was pounding on the door again. "Hey! Tell me if you're okay!"

"I'm fine," Daphne gasped.

"It doesn't sound like it," the man disputed loudly. "Are you hurt?"

"Yes," she said a little too harshly.

"Do you need help?"

"No," Daphne groaned. *Please, no.*

She heard the man sigh heavily and then pause before he spoke again. "I set some dry clothes for you outside the door. They'll be way too big because...they're mine. Uh, anyway, just holler if you need help."

"Okay," Daphne squeaked. *This is beyond mortifying.* She would never live this down. Never. Clumsily, Daphne stood up on her good leg and quickly wrapped herself in a thick, olive-colored towel she found hanging up on the towel rack. She glanced at her face in the mirror above the sink. She grimaced with repulsion at the deep red blotches flaring across her face. She could easily tell the nasty bumps within them were starting to form. Daphne put her palms to her cheeks. Yep, they were already burning, all right. She closed her eyes tightly. Those were burning now, too, but she didn't know if it was because of what she had seen in the mirror. Tomorrow would be worse as her skin would get drier and drier without any antibiotic cream to remedy it. Cold weather burned her skin from the inside out; by the time it reached the surface, it was parched with blisters or acne or just cracked skin.

Of course, she had no one but herself to blame for this. She knew her skin would flare up if she went skiing with Laurel in such freezing temperatures, but Laurel had pestered her to death about it! "Come on, Daphne, you need to get out. You're acting depressed. Let's go have some fun." Never mind Laurel was number one on her cross-country ski team and Daphne wasn't good at all. Never mind a blizzard was coming. Never mind it was Daphne who would get stuck with a stranger all alone! Never mind her skin was going to burn itself to pieces! And never mind she had no cream to help!

Daphne took a deep breath and ducked her head. She focused on breathing in and out. "And never mind that stranger will have to see my face at sometime," she mumbled out loud. She sighed again and looked back up at her awful reflection. *Oh, well, it is what it is.*

***

Tom sighed heavily as he tromped away from the bathroom, across the hallway, and into his small bedroom. The window opposite him brought no light into the room, so he flipped on a nearby switch. He plopped himself down at his writing desk, which sat under the dark window. He needed to do something but didn't know what!

He glanced down at a pad of paper in front of him where he had begun sketches: his plan for a new dresser he was building for Ma. He opened the desk drawer to find a pencil and resumed the sketch from where he had left off. As he was drawing a rose petal he intended to carve into the top of the dresser, he pushed his pencil too hard into the paper and broke the lead tip.

"Drat," he muttered out loud. He began flipping his pencil up and down on the desk while at the same time his nervous leg was bouncing up and down under it. *Why didn't she tell me she was hurt? Why else would she have fallen?*

Just then, he heard the bathroom door creak open, followed by some very distinct hopping. Tom got to his feet, tiptoed to the hallway and peeked around the wall. The girl had just hopped around the corner into the kitchen. Quietly, he followed suit.

To Tom's surprise, the girl was standing at the far side of the kitchen facing the wall with her back to him. He could hear her stirring her soup and then slowly sipping it.

Why doesn't she sit down and eat it? It was obvious she was favoring her left leg as she attempted to put all of her weight on it. She had pulled up the long sleeves of his green sweater, and he noticed his pants hung quite loosely around her thin waist. Her wet, brunette hair hung long and straight down her back. She did not turn around at his approach. He found that odd.

"I warmed that up again a few minutes ago, but if it's still too cold, the microwave is right over there." He gestured with his hand to the counter on the right side of him, but again she didn't turn around.

"Thank you," she said in a soft voice. "I appreciate it."

"No problem," Tom replied. "After you finish eating, why don't you let me look at your leg. I'm no doctor, but I've seen a lot of injuries. I might be able to help."

"Thank you," the girl said again. "I'm sorry to put you out so much."

"Not at all," Tom countered.

The girl let out the smallest of sighs. "Well, I'm very grateful."

"So...what's your name?"

She hesitated for a brief moment. "Daphne."

"I'm Tom. It's nice to meet you, Daphne," he said to her.

"It's good to meet you, too," she said to the wall, taking a few sips of her soup.

"Would you like to sit down?" Tom offered.

"I'm good for now. Thank you," Daphne declined.

I guess she needs space. Surely he could do something else for the girl. *Ah, I know something.* He walked out of the kitchen and into the bathroom where he grabbed all the clothes Daphne had left there. Puzzled, he glanced at the leaking long johns and the massive puddle on the floor. *Did these fall into the bathtub?* Tom shrugged and meandered to the mudroom where he picked up all of Daphne's snow clothes. He pushed another door open and entered his tiny laundry room.

***

Tom must be all right. Anyone who can make soup like this can't be dangerous. Daphne savored each spoonful as long as possible. She sloshed the broth around in her mouth, amazed at the delicious taste. The canned soup she ate in her dorm room could never compare to this.

After she had sipped every last drop in her bowl, she hopped to the kitchen sink and washed her dishes with a sponge and the Palmolive she found by the faucet. She would love to explore the cozy cabin, but courtesy—and her aching leg—demanded she first find a place to sit. So, she hopped into the living room, merely an extension of the kitchen. The breakfast bar was the only thing that divided the space. She didn't bother to find a light to turn on, but the light from the kitchen provided enough brightness for her to spy a rocking chair next to the small glow of a fireplace. She was elated to see there was also an ottoman to rest her feet on. She plopped down into the chair, cringing as she lifted her injured leg onto the footrest. She smiled to herself as she realized the ottoman moved with the rocking chair. Perfect.

She glanced around the dark living room. It was larger than she had originally thought. From the kitchen, it formed an L shape, and at the far end of the room was what looked like a tiny movie theater. A large widescreen TV was the center of a large, wooden entertainment center. Sofas were a few feet away from the TV, also forming an L shape. They separated the room into two distinct areas: the movie theater and the living room by the fire.

Daphne rocked herself back and forth as she made a list in her head of everything she owed Tom. If she stayed here two days, that would be six meals. If she paid him $5 per meal, that would be $30, plus, say, $50 extra for all his trouble? Yes, she could manage that. Daphne smiled and leaned back on the headrest of the cozy chair.

She wished she could keep Tom from seeing her face until she left. Oh, if only she had her cream with her! Or at least some makeup! A stream of bitterness crept into her heart as she recalled prior, cruel observers. "We still know what's underneath," one boy had said. Daphne flushed with anger just at the thought of it. She wasn't under any delusions about her complexion—rosacea, she thought with bitterness. Makeup made her coloring more even, rather than blotchy. Daphne grimaced as she imagined what Tom's face would look like when he first saw hers.

"Are you in pain?" Tom asked. Daphne hadn't noticed he was standing in the kitchen drinking a glass of water, peering over at her.

"Um...well," Daphne stammered.

"You don't have to hide it, you know," he said with a warm smile.

Oh *lands*, he is handsome! *Do I really have to endure face-planting into a rock, tumbling down a mountain, getting lost, AND a handsome man?*

Tom walked out of the kitchen light and into the darkness of the living room. When he reached her, he kneeled next to her raised leg. "This is the injured one?" he asked.

Daphne nodded.

"Oh, well let me turn on the light so I can see better."

"I like the dark," Daphne blurted out.

Tom looked up at her, but she couldn't see his expression. Good. That meant he couldn't see hers. She smiled at that.

"Um...okay," he muttered. "Well, I will probably be able to feel if it's broken." He put his hands on her ankle. "May I?"

"It's not my ankle: it's my calf," she informed him. "I'm pretty sure it's just a pulled muscle."

"Let's try something else then," he suggested. "May I?" he asked again.

Daphne hesitated, knowing this would probably hurt, but she also wondered what his hands would feel like on her cold skin. "Sure, go ahead," she agreed.

Tom put a palm to the bottom of her bare foot and pushed it back slightly.

Daphne grit her teeth to keep from calling out in pain, but a cry escaped her lips nonetheless.

"Drat! I'm sorry!" Tom exclaimed, letting go quickly. Daphne clutched both sides of the armrest tightly.

Tom squeezed around her ankle and her tendon. "Does any of that hurt?" he inquired. Daphne shook her head quickly, still trying to catch her breath.

Tom rested his elbow on his knee and looked in her direction. "I'm so sorry about that. You're right about the pulled muscle, but your Achilles and ankle seem fine. At least we know what the problem is now."

"What can I do for it?" Daphne questioned.

Daphne saw Tom's shadow rub his chin. "Not much," he said.

Daphne grimaced and leaned back into the chair, inhaling deeply.

"Hey, but I have something that might help," Tom said, quickly getting to his feet. Moments later, he came back with a large ice pack and a small, blue towel. "This should help reduce the swelling."

"Oh, thank you," Daphne said politely.

"Why don't I help you to your bed?" Tom offered. He cleared his throat. "Uh, you know, since you can't walk very well."

Daphne was dead tired. She thought she trusted Tom, so she nodded in consent. Tom carried Daphne down the hall, past the kitchen, past the bathroom, past the mudroom, and into a large guest room where the light was already on. Daphne was surprised to see this room was just as long as the entire living and movie room. Right in the middle was an over-blanketed double bed, with a rosy red comforter and matching decorative pillows. The long back wall had three bay windows spread out evenly. Tom headed to the rosy bed and laid her on top of it. Daphne sat up slightly so her back was against the pillows. She scanned the room further and spotted another glowing fireplace in the corner. She flipped her head around the other way and saw three single beds along the opposite wall, perpendicular to her rosy bed. To her surprise, Tom dragged a lone wooden chair next to her and sat in it before placing the wrapped ice pack under her calf.

"Thank you," said Daphne. "How much do people pay you to stay here?"

"What?" Tom sounded surprised.

"It looks like you often house...um, families." Daphne pointed to the other beds.

"Oh, this was my grandpa's cabin before he passed on. He put in a lot of beds so he could have all his grandkids come visit him."

"Where's your family now?" Daphne wondered.

"In Bangater," Tom answered.

"Is that in Texas?" Daphne asked.

"Oh, no. It's here in Alaska, about an hour away from Brocksville. My family moved there from Texas when I was about sixteen. My pa is in the oil business," Tom explained.

"So, what do you do? I mean, how do you live all the way out here?"

Tom let out a strained laugh. "Good question."

Daphne waited for a response that made sense.

Tom sighed. "I'm a hunter. The Wildlife Association pays me to hunt animals and package them during the winter and then bring them back in the spring for sale. I also have a contract with a taxidermist to bring them animal skins."

"Oh, okay. Well, do you ever get any visitors?"

Tom fell silent for a short moment. "Occasionally I get lost drifters like you who need shelter and food. But not very often," he clarified.

"I...I hope you know I'm grateful."

Daphne could hear a smile in Tom's voice. "I do know that, Daphne. You're very welcome."

With sudden alarm, Daphne realized she had been having a conversation in a very well-lit room without her face covered. She let out a heavy sigh as she felt her cheeks burn with humiliation. Too late now.

Chapter 3

Checkmate

Daphne knew she was asleep, but she still couldn't stop the dream. She was skiing down a snowy mountain at a rapid pace. Her skill didn't escape her now. She glided through trees and under branches. As she caught sight of her boots, she realized she was wearing downhill ski boots instead of cross-country skis. She glanced up to see a long, steep stretch of moguls. She skied in and out of them with no trouble at all, spraying mists of snowy powder behind her. The sun was shining brightly, and she smiled, basking in the warmth of it.

Then she sensed someone coming up behind her. It was danger; she knew it. She forced herself to ski faster and faster. Then, she spotted Laurel at the bottom of the hill. Three men surrounded her, and they all had their undivided attention on her. Laurel smiled and laughed and touched every one of their arms.

Then, Daphne heard someone behind her.

"Where are you headed, Daphne?" came the rough voice of a man. He was so close she could feel the sprays from his skis.

"I'm going to catch Laurel!" she cried into the wind.

"You'll never catch up with Laurel," the voice leered. "This hill never ends."

"I will catch up with her," Daphne insisted. The man was right. The harder she tried to reach the bottom of the hill, the longer and longer it seemed to stretch. Daphne smacked her lips in frustration and moved her legs harder and faster.

"What are you running from, Daphne?" the man mocked again.

"I'm running from you!" she yelled.

"No, you're not running from me," he noted. "You're running from yourself."

And then, the scene changed, and she was suddenly on the edge of a pool, ready to dive into a butterfly stroke. Laurel was standing beside her ready to do the same. They were wearing matching purple racing suits like they always had as children. Their features had also been so similar back then everyone called them the "twin goddesses." But standing next to Laurel now, Daphne knew they looked nothing like twins. Although they were both thin, Laurel seemed to be stronger and more mature. Even though their hair was about the same light color, Daphne couldn't help notice how the blonde streaks in Laurel's hair glistened with every turn of her head.

The most excruciating difference between them was Laurel's smooth, tan complexion. Instinctively, Daphne touched her cheeks only to feel her red, bumpy sores. To her great horror, she saw them spread rapidly down her neck, arms, legs, and even her feet. Daphne gasped as she stared at her infected toes.

Just then a whistle blew, and Laurel did a perfect dive into the water. Daphne dove in a second later and was determined to catch up. Adrenaline pumped through her veins as she swam as hard and as fast as she ever had, but Laurel still won the race.

Breathing hard, Daphne walked towards her locker room but instead found herself in a recital hall. Laurel was standing on the stage dressed in an elegant red gown with her viola in hand. She was performing a magnificent piece with a beautiful vibrato and lovely smooth bowing. People were walking past Daphne, who, for some reason, was still drenched and dripping. They gave her disdainful sideways glances before they turned towards Laurel and cheered.

When Laurel finished performing, Daphne scampered up to meet her, but three guys beat her to it.

"Look, boys!" Laurel cried, pulling out a piece of paper from her breast pocket. "I'm an honor student."

"Oh, wow! Ooo!" The boys ogled Laurel and admired her paper.

"I'm an honor student, too," Daphne announced. But no one turned around to acknowledge her. "Hey!"

Daphne woke startled, gasping for air. She found herself lying on her back on top of the rosy bed. Although she had never actually gotten into the bed, she discovered two extra blankets were spread out on top of her. Even in the darkness, she knew it was morning.

She inhaled deeply. "Just a dream," Daphne breathed. Although Daphne hated to admit it to herself, that dream was fairly indicative of her life. She would never catch up to Laurel.

There was a soft knock on the door. Daphne saw the brass doorknob turn slowly, and Tom peeked in.

"Oh, good, you're awake now. Do you feel any better?" He switched on a tall lamp close to him.

Daphne stretched her arms and legs. Her calf didn't have the same piercing pain as before, but it certainly had not healed. "Yes, I feel better. Thank you."

"I brought you some crutches in case you need them," Tom said, motioning to the right side of Daphne's bed. Daphne turned her head slightly to see some tall crutches padded with some kind of tan foam leaning against a tall, shiny oak dresser.

"Oh, yes, that will be very helpful." She sat up a bit as she spotted her clothes, dry and folded on top of the dresser. "Did you wash my clothes?" Daphne asked, surprised.

"Oh, yeah. I figured you might want clothes that fit you," Tom explained with a small smile.

"Wow, that's very nice," Daphne muttered, blushing again at the sight of his gorgeous self. "You didn't have to do that."

Tom shrugged. "No big deal."

Daphne glanced at Tom's face in the brightly lit room. He was looking at her, too, and she noticed he didn't even look abhorred to see her, nor did he appear surprised. "Why are you so nice to me?" Daphne wondered out loud.

Tom raised his red eyebrows and then smiled a little shyly. "Well, first of all, you need the help right now. And second of all, it's nice to have something else to do besides the same old stuff, you know?"

Daphne sat up and nodded. "I can understand that. I'm not accustomed to people doing things for me."

"I bet you're also not accustomed to getting lost in a blizzard, either, are you?" Tom said with a warm smile.

Daphne smiled back. "That is definitely true."

Tom was still grinning as he left the room. Now she had her mind made up. If he could look at her without reproach, then she wouldn't shy away either. She would feign confidence. She would make sure to look him in the eye. After all, in a couple of days, she would never see him again anyway.

***

There we go, thought Tom, as he scooped a hot waffle out of the waffle iron. *I finally got her to smile a genuine smile.* Tom piled the waffles on top of each other and poured some of his homemade cinnamon syrup into a small, glass pitcher. He was placing some thawed strawberries on a plate when he heard the loud clunking of crutches coming down the hallway. He turned around to see Daphne smiling wide at him. Tom smiled back, mostly because of how much her smile, as well as wearing her own clothes, improved her looks.

"Want some breakfast?" he offered.

"I would love some. It smells wonderful."

The two of them sat at the tall breakfast bar and began to dig into their food. "Is this made from scratch?" asked Daphne with admiration in her voice.

"It is. Do you like it?"

"Mmm, hmm," she murmured, her mouth still full. She chewed some more and then swallowed. "It's amazing."

Tom smiled at that. "Thanks. It's nice to have someone appreciate my cooking." *He thought of the last meal he had cooked for Tanya, his ex-fiancée. He had spent hours cooking a delicious crab rangoon. She had taken one look at it, turned up her nose, and said, "Yuck! Get me some fries."*

"Well, it's certainly better than anything I've had lately. I usually eat cold cereal or pry open a can of soup for my meals," Daphne noted. Then suddenly she turned towards Tom with a big grin. "Speaking of which, the soup you made last night was delicious!" she exclaimed.

Tom let out a brief laugh. "It's good to see you take pleasure in the small things."

"Well, how else are you going to enjoy life, you know?" Daphne paused, taking another bite.

Tom nodded, chewing his waffle. *Hmm. She is kind of insightful.* "So neither of your parents cook, huh?" Tom asked.

Daphne looked at him with surprise. "Oh, I don't live at home. I live in the dorms at Brocksville University. And actually, my parents are in Afghanistan right now running an orphanage."

Tom was quite surprised by both of these explanations. *She was in college?* "Oh, wow! I didn't realize you were, um...have your parents always had big ideas like that?"

"I think so," answered Daphne.

"How long have they been away?"

"Three years."

Tom's eyes opened wide, but he couldn't speak with his mouth full. Daphne smirked at him and drank some more orange juice.

"How have you been with them being away for so long?"

"Well, I do feel kind of..." Daphne shrugged. "It's fine."

Tom could read through the lines on that one. She wasn't fine with it.

"I'm sure glad you got a hold of your friend," Tom said. "It's more dangerous than you can imagine out there."

"Is the blizzard still going on?" asked Daphne, instinctively turning around to look out the windows but instead saw the curtains still drawn.

Tom forced himself not to laugh, but he couldn't keep the smile off his face. "Let me show you something, Daphne," he offered as he made his way to the window next to the fire. He slid the maroon curtains open with one movement to expose the outside view. "Come here," he directed, motioning her towards him with his hand.

Daphne frowned, grabbed her crutches, and hobbled over to him. Tom frowned, too. He wouldn't have asked her to come if he had remembered she couldn't walk.

Daphne stopped next to him and stared out the window. Tom watched her changing countenance as she observed the huge snowflakes falling from the sky. Her dismay increased as she saw the snow on the ground already piling halfway up the window. She moaned softly, looking like she wanted to cry.

"Do you know how long the storm is supposed to last?" she asked softly.

"Until next Tuesday," Tom informed her.

"So I can leave in five days," Daphne assumed.

Tom tried to sound matter-of-fact when he spoke. "Well, we are expected to get six feet of snow by the time the blizzard is over. We won't be able to get out the doorway for at least three weeks after that. Maybe longer."

Daphne's expressions varied from shock to deep disappointment to worry. Her eyes were wide and her mouth slightly open.

"How about we sit down before you faint, Daphne?" Tom advised. Daphne agreed rather absentmindedly. Tom followed her to the cushioned rocking chair a few feet away. He took her crutches and extended a hand to help her sit while she tried to maneuver her injured leg onto the ottoman. Then he sat down on the sofa across from her on the other side of the coffee table.

Daphne put both palms on either side of her face. "I have to find a way out. I just have to." She sounded convinced.

"You might be able to work on some of your classes online. Is that what you're worried about?" Tom wondered as he settled into the sofa.

Daphne let her hands fall. "No. I mean yes. I'm worried about that, too, but..."

"But you're worried about staying with me for that long," Tom assumed.

"Well, yes," she confessed.

Tom pursed his lips together and glanced over at the fire as he recalled a biting insult from Tanya: *"No girl would ever want to live with you in that horrible, forsaken place!"* The memory still stung.

He looked back at Daphne, who was looking at him with concern. He cleared his throat. "Come on, I'm not that bad. You liked my food, didn't you?"

Daphne raised her arms and started gesturing as she spoke. "Yes, that's just it! All the food!" she cried. Then she put a hand up in front of her. "I will pay you back for it all, I promise. I'm going to keep track of everything: room and board, water and...and...and power, and laundry soap, and..." She glanced at the fire. "And wood, and..."

"Whoa! Good *night!*" Tom interrupted. "You won't owe me anything, Daphne. It's all free of charge."

"I can't let you do that!" Daphne exclaimed.

"Of course you can. Even if you try to pay me back, I won't take a penny." Tom smiled with amusement as he leaned back and put his hands behind his head.

Daphne attempted to look stern, which made Tom smile more.

"You don't know me very well," she pointed out. "I'll pay you back. Besides, your food might be gone by the time I leave."

Tom laughed out loud. "Right! That entire waffle you ate is sure to break us!" Tom leaned his head back and laughed some more.

Daphne looked half flustered, half delighted at his amusement. "Those were really filling!" she exclaimed.

Tom couldn't stop chuckling. "You're not an imposition, Daphne. You're probably the easiest guest I've ever had. We could live here for two years on the food storage I have."

Daphne was staring with perplexed admiration. "You're so nice. I'm *still* going to pay you back."

Tom leaned forward in earnest. "Consider your good company payment."

Daphne took a deep breath but said nothing.

Then Tom slapped his thighs. "How about a game of chess, Daphne? I've been dying to have a partner."

Daphne raised her eyebrows. "Oh, um...okay."

Tom pulled the game out from the low shelf under the coffee table and set up the pieces quickly.

"Ladies first," he announced.

Daphne moved a knight.

"Oh, starting bold! I like that," Tom said with a smile.

Daphne blushed and smiled back shyly.

"You're not a cheater, are you?" Tom teased as he moved out his knight as well.

Daphne shrugged. "Only time will tell," she said with a grin.

"Ah, I bet I can figure it out before you even do it. How about we play a second little game as well? Tell me three things about yourself and make one of them a lie. I will try to guess which one it is."

Daphne grew thoughtful with a slight look of amusement.

Tom was discovering Daphne's face was very expressive, even from moment to moment. Her emotions were easily detected. This was going to be easy.

She moved a pawn. "All right, I have it. I was named after a Greek goddess, I won first place in a swim meet, and I've been kissed twice." She looked up at him with a brilliant smile on her face.

Tom couldn't help but smile back. "Did you just dare me to guess if you've been kissed?"

Daphne's smile broadened.

Hmm...she is tricky. It's like one of those wicked-woman traps. He thought for a moment as the two of them moved pieces across the chessboard, each occasionally losing one.

"Are you giving up?" Daphne asked with a mischievous grin on her face.

Tom smiled a little. "No," he countered. "It's the first one. The first one isn't true."

Daphne raised her eyebrows. "You didn't know Daphne was a Greek goddess? I thought that would be the easy one to guess."

Tom groaned. "No, I didn't know. That one was true?"

Daphne nodded. "Now you have a 50/50 chance."

Tom shook his head as he moved his bishop diagonally across the board. "No. Just tell me."

"Oh, come on, Tom," she teased. "You're the one who wanted to play this game."

Tom looked up at her, scrutinizing her expression for a clue. She had a pronounced smirk on her face. Now he knew. "Number three," he guessed. "You've been kissed three times, haven't you?"

Daphne looked surprised at his response, but she grinned and shook her head.

"Really? How many, then?"

Daphne laughed. "No, number two was the lie. I got second place at the swim meet."

Tom threw back his head. "Oh, drat! That one was the trick! I was sure it had something to do with the kissing."

Daphne laughed some more.

Tom pointed a mock scolding finger at her. "That is totally cheating."

"Not at all!" she exclaimed, looking delighted.

"Well then, it's a good thing I just won our chess game! Checkmate!" Tom exclaimed as he knocked over Daphne's king.

"Oh, *lands!*" Daphne cried. "How did I not see that?"

Tom chuckled. "You were too distracted with that other little game."

"So, that's how *you* cheated," Daphne concluded.

"Not at all!" Tom mimicked the same look Daphne had given him. They both laughed and began putting the chess pieces back into the box. "You know, I knew you wouldn't be a cheater, anyway," Tom said seriously. "My pa always taught me how naturally honest and purely good most women are."

"Only women?" Daphne asked, raising her eyebrows.

Tom shrugged and nodded. "More so than men, anyway."

"Really? That's what he taught you?" Daphne questioned, looking curious.

"Yep," Tom said with one short nod. "And I should always treat them that way or I would be a worse man for it."

Daphne put the lid on the chess box and leaned her head back on her headrest and gave him an amusing look. "Well, he sounds like a very good man, but I would venture to say you are every bit as good as I am."

Tom shook his head at the floor, smiling to himself. *If only she knew.* "I don't think so, Daphne."

"Really," she insisted. And then she grew earnest. "When I was lost, I prayed hard I would find someone to help me. And here you are—doing everything possible for me."

Tom's heart pounded at her deep, sincere gratitude. "Daphne, you just solidified my point," he said with a smile.

***

Daphne could not stop blushing when he smiled like that! It was so unfair! He made it worse with his next question.

"So, why don't you tell me about those two guys you kissed? I love a good story."

Daphne blushed as she rolled her eyes. "Not a story I want to share, Tom."

Tom gazed at her with a teasing look, but he shrugged and let it go. "All right, then. Tell me the story of Daphne, the Greek goddess."

Tom shifted so his arm was stretched out over the backrest of the sofa. Daphne felt her eyes bulge as she was able to make out the muscles on his chest and arms. She looked at his gorgeous face smiling at her. This was too much. How was it possible for one man to be so handsome and so sweet? Daphne suddenly realized she was beginning to have feelings for Tom. Just as quickly, she knew he would never reciprocate. Not ever. Guys always fell for beauty, no matter what the other girls had to offer the world. Daphne definitely was not beautiful, and her life was certainly not like those dumb movies where the girl thinks she's not pretty but is actually super gorgeous.

A crushing rush of sadness washed through her at this honest revelation.

"Daphne? Are you okay?" Tom asked.

"Oh, yeah." Daphne blinked. "Um, the goddess Daphne was chased by Apollo so aggressively she petitioned the gods to help her. By doing so, they changed her into a laurel tree. Then all Apollo could do was gaze at the beautiful tree and wish in vain."

Daphne didn't mention she wished *she* could change into a laurel tree. Or in other words, she wished she could turn into her friend Laurel or at least be like her. However, Daphne was not a Greek goddess so desire was hopeless.

"Why did your parents give you that name?" Tom wondered.

"Wish I knew the answer, Tom. It doesn't make a whole lot of sense to me."

Tom leaned forward now and rested his forearms on his knees. "What's bothering you, Daphne?" Tom asked softly.

Daphne batted a hand at him. "Oh, I'm fine."

He didn't look convinced. "I've occasionally been known to have a very open mind, you know," he said, smiling a little.

Daphne shook her head.

"Is there something I can do to help?"

What did Tom want her to say, "Sure. Can you make me gorgeous like you?" Oh, this maddening man was so nice to her! The fact Tom even made an effort to talk to her at all while she looked like this was a miracle. Granted, she was the only one to talk to, and that was probably the only reason he was doing it.

Daphne was suddenly determined not to give Tom any hint about her feelings for him. Then, they could at least have a friendship.

"Do you mind if I email my professors?" asked Daphne, desperately wanting a subject change.

"Oh, no, of course not," Tom responded, pushing himself off the sofa. "The Internet is in my room. The wind really messed with everything this week. I wasn't able to get a connection up and running until just before you woke up this morning. Believe it or not, the satellite connection is better than you can imagine out here."

Daphne smiled. "I believe it."

Tom held out a hand for Daphne to take. Ridiculously, her heart beat faster as she put her hand in his and stood up on her good leg. Tom leaned over to grab Daphne's crutches that were lying on the floor and handed them to her.

"Thank you," said Daphne. "You're very thoughtful. You know that?"

Tom smiled a bright smile. "And your gratitude is like a breath of fresh air, Daphne."

Daphne blushed deeply at his compliment and then beat herself up about it as she followed Tom past the kitchen and into a bedroom just a few steps farther.

This bedroom was much smaller than the one she had slept in last night. It had a single bed covered with a dark blue comforter against the wall on the right-hand side. A wooden computer desk stood directly beside the bed, with a bay window behind the desk. On the opposite wall, there was a tall closet with closed wooden doors. Daphne started noticing a stylistic theme throughout the cabin: almost all the furniture was either oak or pine. Daphne liked the simple beauty very much.

Before Daphne was done admiring her surroundings, Tom was already sitting in the desk chair checking some of his own messages online. She stopped when she saw his hand was covering his mouth.

"What is it?" asked Daphne. "More bad weather?"

Tom didn't move, so Daphne thumped her way towards him so she was standing beside him. Now she noticed his chest was moving up and down with deep breathing, and he was shaking his head slowly with an expression of utter dismay as he stared at the computer screen.

"Tom, what is it?" asked Daphne. She glanced at the screen to see what he was looking at, but he had shut it off completely.

"I can't—please, no," he whispered.

"Tom," Daphne whispered in return. "What happened?"

Abruptly, Tom stood up, causing his chair to tip over backward as he briskly walked out of the room.

What on earth? Daphne slowly thumped her way with her crutches out of the bedroom. She spotted Tom facing the window, his hands pressed against the glass with his arms stretched out and his head bowed low.

"Tom?" Daphne called cautiously to him.

"I need a minute, Daphne," he said rather curtly.

"Oh…okay," Daphne stammered. She clumsily turned around and clunked down the hall to her bedroom. She plopped down on her bed, wondering what could possibly have happened to turn Tom's world upside down in only a matter of seconds.

She didn't dare leave her room, but just as she thought she might die of boredom, Tom opened her bedroom door. She noticed his eyes were red and a bit puffy, but other than that he looked calm.

"My pa was killed," he choked out.

"What?" asked Daphne, shocked.

"A drunk driver on ice," he explained.

Daphne inhaled a slow, silent breath. "Oh, I'm so sorry, Tom," she said softly.

"The viewing is tonight. I'll have to leave soon," Tom sniffed. He pursed his lips and inhaled a shaky breath. Daphne knew he was trying to hold back a sob. The whole thing was so heartbreaking! She thought of reminding him it wasn't safe to travel, but she knew if she were in his shoes, she would go anyway.

"Why don't you come sit down for a minute," Daphne suggested, patting the bed next to her.

Tom shook his head. "No, thank you." He inhaled another forced breath. "I know you want to get out of here, Daphne, but it wouldn't be safe to take you with me, especially since you can't walk well. My snowmobile has a good chance of getting stuck out there." Tom rubbed his eyes with his arm. "I promise I'll come back in two weeks when the storm has cleared and take you home. I'll show you where I keep all the food storage before I go. Do you think you'll be all right?" Tom sniffed.

"Don't worry about me, Tom," Daphne insisted. "Let's get you out of here before the storm gets worse."

Tom nodded but did nothing except step back and lean against the wall. He stared at the ceiling in silence.

Poor Tom. What a good man he was! He had rescued her from a deserted wilderness and life-threatening temperatures. He had fed her, clothed her, sheltered her, and on top of that, he was kind to her and looked her in the eye without flinching. Yes, she owed Tom big time. Now he was the one in need, and she had no idea how to help him. "Um, I...I will go pack you some food for the trip so you can get your other things together," she said.

Tom glanced at her with a weak smile. "Thanks, Daphne."

Daphne smiled a little in return. "Of course," she said. "I'm so sorry this happened."

Tom stared back at her with a tortured look in his eyes.

Chapter 4

Facing the Music

Tom slowly pulled on his stuffed, Gore-Tex gloves as he stared out the window at the never-ending, falling snow.

"Tom?" Daphne spoke behind him.

Tom turned to face her.

"Be careful out there," she said politely.

"I will."

Without warning, Daphne embraced him in a warm hug. Tom was certainly surprised, but he returned the gesture. "Thank you for everything, Tom. I hope you'll be safe. I'll say a prayer for you." Her voice was soft.

Tom took a step back. "You're a bit of a believer, aren't you?"

Daphne raised her eyebrows, looking startled at his question. "Of course."

"Well, that's refreshing," he acknowledged. "Take care, Daphne."

"You, too, Tom. Goodbye."

With that, he rushed out into the wet wind, snow, and freezing air. He could feel Daphne's eyes on him as he sped away on his snowmobile. How endearing she had been with her sincere concern. How nice she had been to give him the space he needed after hearing the news. Tanya had never given him space; she had hovered like a hawk. He recalled one day when he had just been denied a job. All he had wanted was to be alone, but Tanya kept wanting to talk about it. Finally, when he told her what had happened, she did nothing but rub salt in the wound. "That's what you get for dropping out of college," she had said vindictively.

Tom burned with resentment at the memory. "How do I get rid of those bad feelings, Pa?" Tom asked out loud.

Tom was out of the thicket now and on a trail. As he sped along, he couldn't help but imagine Pa's fatal accident. *That daft drunk driver!* Tom shivered. He could have been that very driver just two short years ago! A deep depression seeped into his soul and seemed to drown him—not only sadness his pa was gone but also shame for the son Tom had turned out to be. "Oh, I'm so sorry, Pa," Tom whispered out loud again. "Why did you have to go before I could show you I can be a man like you? Why, Pa? How could you leave Ma like this? How could you *do* that? It's not right!" Tom was yelling into the wind now. He didn't know why he was risking his life to go to this viewing. The thought of Pa lying motionless in a casket left him with nothing but raw emptiness inside.

***

Tom raced from his parked snowmobile to the entrance of the church building. His backpack hung off one shoulder. He yanked his helmet and face mask off and shook as much snow out of them as possible. He opened the heavy door leading into the church, stamping his feet hard on the mat just inside. Wiping the snow off his watch, he glanced at the time: 6:20. The viewing had started twenty minutes ago. He stepped to the side and took off his coat and hung it on the rack next to him. Fortunately, a bathroom was right around the corner. He dashed inside and into a stall.

As quickly as possible he pulled out a new set of clothes from his backpack. He was happy to see they had stayed dry in the mini trunk of the snowmobile, but they were still plenty wrinkled. Oh well. It was better than his sopping snow pants. He grimaced at the muddy puddle his soaking boots had created on the linoleum floor. He stuffed his wet clothes into his backpack and stepped out of the stall to grab some paper towels. Quickly, and a bit sloppily, he wiped up the puddle.

He came to a sink and washed his hands under warm water, clenching and unclenching his fists to get some feeling back into them. He glanced at his face in the mirror. The new, warm air inside was causing his runny nose to drip all the more. He snatched a paper towel from a dispenser and wiped his nose furiously. His face was beet red, even redder than his hair, which was sticking up in most places and matted in all the others. What a mess he was.

He leaned over the sink and splashed some warm water over his face and head a few times. After drying himself, he grabbed a comb out of his backpack and did his best to smooth out his hair. He rolled up the sleeves of his white, button-up shirt and smoothed down his collar. His shirt hung loose and low around his black corduroy pants. He frowned and decided to tuck it in. He groaned to himself as he realized he had forgotten a tie. Oh well. He pulled his shirt straighter. *Pa won't care. He's just glad I'm here, I bet. And it doesn't matter what people think right now.*

Leaving his backpack on the bathroom floor, Tom looked at himself one last time, took a deep breath, and pushed his way out the door. *Time to face the crowd.*

Before he entered the viewing room, Tom stopped to look at the display just outside. A long desk was set out with a white lace tablecloth on top. A large picture of his father stood upright. He was happy to see it was a recent picture. His father had the same wrinkly smile he remembered. He read the neat writing engraved into the matting at the bottom:

JEFFERY THOMAS MULTON
5 MAY 1949–15 JANUARY 2016.

A smaller picture of his mother and father, much younger, sat next to the first. At the bottom of the frame were the gold-printed words: Jeffrey and Diane Multon, married 29 August 1970. Tom began to scan the other scattered, framed pictures of his pa. He was looking closely at one from his Navy days when his ma nearly toppled him over with her abrupt embrace.

"Oh, I knew you would make it! I just knew it!" She sobbed into his shoulder. Ma was a good three inches shorter than her son, about the same height as Daphne, Tom noticed.

Tom tightened his arms around his mother. "You know I would never miss it, Ma," Tom whispered into her ear. The two pulled back to look at each other. "I didn't get your message until this morning. The Internet connection was completely down for a good five days straight."

"Then it's a miracle you're here," said his ma, smiling through her tears.

Tom ached at the sight of his mother. Her purple blouse matched the purple circles under her eyes. She had painted her eyebrows to be as dark as her dyed, chocolate hair. Her round face was as red as a tomato, and black streaks of mascara were already streaming down her cheeks. Tom hated to notice it, but at the moment, his ma looked twenty years older than her actual age.

"I love you, Ma," murmured Tom, placing a gentle arm on her shoulder. She smiled up at him as fresh tears streamed down her face.

"Tom!"

Tom turned around to see his sister Jenny walking towards him with her arms outstretched. Tom met her halfway and wrapped her in a gigantic bear hug.

"We were so worried!" Jenny exclaimed, burying her face in his chest.

Tom held her head close to him, lightly kissing the top of long, blonde hair.

"Where's Sammy?" he asked.

"I'm right here," said a small voice.

Tom let go of Jenny and turned to see his little brother standing beside him. Unlike the women, Sammy looked like he had not shed a single tear.

Tom crouched down so he was the same height as Sammy. "Wow! You've grown! Are you sure you didn't just turn twelve instead of eight?"

Sammy stood up taller and smiled but then frowned just as readily. "You missed my birthday party," he sulked.

"I know. I'm sorry, Sammy. I wish I could have been there. Did you get my present?"

Sammy's face lit up again. "That was so cool! All my friends say they want their very own helicopter, too!"

Tom laughed. "I'm glad you liked it."

"Did you really make it yourself, Tom?" Sammy asked.

"I sure did. I only do my best work for my favorite brother."

"Thanks, Tom!" cried Sammy. He leaped into Tom's arms.

Tom held him close.

"I wish Pa could fly it with me again," said Sammy. Suddenly the poor little boy burst into loud sobs.

"Shh," soothed Tom, rubbing Sammy's back. "Shh."

Sammy's sobs only got louder. Tom could feel all the heads in the room turned in their direction, but he didn't look back. He just held Sammy tighter. Tom felt a hand on his shoulder. He shifted his head to find his mother's head right beside his. "Come here, Sammy," she coaxed, reaching for her youngest son. Sammy left Tom and fell into his mother's embrace, but he continued sobbing. "You go on and pay your respects to your father, son," she said to Tom.

Tom nodded once as he stood up. Jenny was still standing beside them, crying silently. Tom grabbed her hand. "Come with me," he whispered in her ear. "I can't do this alone."

Jenny followed her brother to the front of the room where their father lay in a beautifully adorned casket. Tom walked slowly, taking in the white lilies cascading over and around the open box where his father lay. Ma must have spent a fortune shipping those fresh flowers here. He made a mental note to give her whatever money she had spent on them.

He couldn't see his pa's face yet. He was afraid to see it. He stopped in his tracks and turned to face Jenny. "I can't do this," he protested.

"Yes, you can," she assured him. She pulled on his hand lightly and led the way to the casket.

Tom didn't let go but dreaded every step. When they reached the casket, he laid his eyes on his pa's face. Nothing could have prepared him for the shock of seeing his father lying there lifeless. His skin sagged in an unnatural way, and his eyelids drooped. Tom rested his gaze on his pa's hands folded across his stomach and reached down to hold one of them. It was soft to the touch, rather than the firm, hard grip he was accustomed to. Upon seeing this hand, Tom could see his pa alive again with his wide grin and twinkling brown eyes. He could still feel his complimentary slaps on the back, and he could still hear his voice as clear as anything: "Good work, son."

Tom held his breath to keep in the tears. He gripped his pa's hand harder, wishing more than anything for Pa to respond.

No response. He was gone, and Tom couldn't do anything about it.

Beside him, Jenny's shoulders shook with silent sobs. Tom put one arm around her and hugged her tightly as they both stared at their father's lifeless body. Tom managed to keep his body still, but Jenny's sobbing made it impossible for him to hold back the tears any longer. She made no move to leave his side. He was grateful for that. Jenny was in dire need of some tissues, so Tom wiggled out of their embrace to find some.

In a matter of minutes, Jenny had emptied the entire tissue box. At that point, some distant relatives began making their way towards them, offering sincere condolences and hugs. Tom replied as politely as he could manage, and that's when he saw Tanya.

He cursed her mentally when he saw she was still as beautiful as ever. *Why is she here at the worst time of my life? Doesn't she know she makes everything worse?* Tanya's silky black hair ran perfectly down her back, with a few tempting, loose curls framing her face. To match her hair, she wore a black silk dress that flowed with elegant ease all the way to the floor. Her ruby red lips taunted him with the memories of all the tender kisses they had shared.

But worse than all of this was the ugly man standing next to her, his arm around her slender waist. He pulled her closer to him with his massive hands in what Tom thought was an overprotective gesture. His black suit was pressed perfectly as was his blond, glued-together hair. Tom imagined himself slapping that arrogant smile right off his face. What imbecile smiled at a viewing?

Then, what he had feared the most happened. The two of them, hand-in-hand, started walking towards him. *Oh, no! Please spare me.* Their thoughts did not coincide with his since they kept getting closer to him. Tom shifted and looked for an exit. With a sudden wave of intense desire, he wished with all his heart he were in the same place Pa was. Pa always knew what to do. He always made things better, but Tom was on his own now.

Tanya's face lacked the angry contention he had grown accustomed to seeing their last few months together. Instead, she looked gentle, sympathetic, and even a little sad. He recognized this face, too, but it had been awhile. "I'm so sorry for your loss, Tom," said Tanya as the couple approached him. "Your father was a good man. The best of the best."

Tom cleared his throat. "Thank you, Tanya." Suddenly Tom realized he was glad she had come. He was happy to remember a soft, caring part of her. The thought only made his heart ache more.

"This is Guy," Tanya shyly introduced her companion.

Guy released Tanya's hand as he offered Tom a handshake. "I've known your father for only a few months now. He made quite an impression on me."

Slowly, Tom lifted his arm and gripped the hand of Brad Pitt's clone, but he said nothing.

"You should be proud to be part of such a family," Guy continued.

"I am. Thank you," Tom said in a rather raspy voice. He cleared his throat again.

Then he looked at Tanya. "Thank you for coming. It means a lot." As those words came out, Tom could feel he meant them. As much as he hated it, it was good to see Tanya again. This way they could say goodbye on good terms. Now he could have a little more closure. His heart didn't stop aching; it just ached differently.

***

Tom lay down on his single bed in his small childhood room. What fond memories he had here! He glanced around at the same old blue and white wallpaper. He smiled to himself. His ma was so old-fashioned, she probably thought the decor was still in style. The same off-white curtains hung in front of an old rectangular window. Tom couldn't help but chuckle when he thought back to the day he had learned off-white was a color. He argued with all the seven-year-old wisdom he could muster to his ma that such a color was ridiculous and impossible. His ma had laughed and laughed at his refusal to believe it was true.

Then Tom looked straight to where his very first deer head was mounted to the wall. He had shot that deer as a fourteen-year-old while hunting with his pa. Tom bit his lip, knowing the memories would soon bring unwanted tears. He forced his sight elsewhere in the room, but everywhere he looked he was reminded of his pa somehow. The short table in the corner reminded him of a train set he had as a young boy. While he played with it, his pa would tell him all about the days when he used to ride a train every day to work. In later years, the table became a place for Tom and his pa to build small things, like wooden cars or boats. Even the circular, navy rug lying in the center of the room brought back memories. How many times had he and his pa wrestled on that thing? Pa had always let him win until he was older, and then Tom really did win. Tom chuckled out loud when he thought of how many times Ma had come in to chastise them both. When that happened, Pa would just grin at his wife and say, "I'm sorry, dear," and kiss her on the cheek. Tom smiled at the memories as a pesky tear escaped the corner of his eye.

"You know you're supposed to give the eulogy tomorrow at the funeral, right?" asked Tom's mother, interrupting his reverie. She was standing in the doorway, looking at Tom with a worried expression.

Tom groaned in the darkness.

"Don't you want to do that for your pa?" she questioned.

"Of course, I do, Ma," muttered Tom. "He's the only one I want to hear it."

"Then do it for him and no one else."

Tom nodded a little reluctantly. "I'll try. Will you come talk with me a minute, Ma?" he asked.

His mother walked towards him, her soft pink nightgown swishing along with her. She sat on the edge of the bed by Tom's side. She grabbed his hand in hers and kissed it firmly.

"How are you doing, Ma?" he asked.

"I'm doing fine, son," she assured him. "Your pa hasn't left me, you know. I can still feel him close by."

"Really?" Tom asked.

His mother nodded. "Don't you feel him, son?"

Tom thought about that a moment. "I don't know, Ma."

His mother rubbed her hand over his with her rough, gentle fingers. "Your pa is proud of you, son, and so am I."

Tom sniffed a bit and shrugged. "I wish I could believe it, Ma."

"It's true," his mother said sternly. "How can you say that, Tom?" Her trembling voice threatened more tears.

Tom sat up to look at his mother more fully. "Ma, you know I want nothing more than to be like Pa. I'm so far from it. I've made so many mistakes. How am I supposed to come back from all that?"

"You are more like your father than you think," she said, looking Tom straight in the eye. "Do you really think that man was always perfect?"

"He was as close as you can get, I think," Tom said resolutely.

His mother smiled, taking a slow breath. Tom could see new tears overflowing her eyes. She wiped them gently away. "Yes, I think you're right."

Tom took a deep breath and rubbed his mother's hand. "I love you, Ma."

His mother patted his knee with her free hand. "I know that, son. You show more love on your sleeve than many people feel in their hearts."

"I don't know about that."

"Oh, yes, you do," she said, giving him a slight slap on the knee. "You always think the best of people."

Tom gave her a baffled look. "That's definitely not true," he countered, thinking of all the horrible thoughts he had had about Tanya.

His mother waved a hand at him. "We're getting off topic. What you need to remember, son, is that you make your parents proud."

Tom scratched his head. "Why are you saying this, Ma? I have done nothing but disappoint you these past few years."

His mother pressed both her palms on either side of Tom's head and looked right into his very soul. "A real man isn't one who doesn't make mistakes," she said firmly. "A real man faces his mistakes and fixes them as best he can. You have done that, Tom. You have done it with more humility than anyone I have seen. You're a good boy. You need to start believing it."

He bit his lip hard as a burning hope grew in his chest. "Do you think that's what Pa thought, Ma?" Tom asked, choking on his words.

His mother grabbed his face again. "You know it is, son. You know it is." With that, the pooling tears behind his eyes spilled over. His mother reached out and hugged him close until he felt as if their bodies ached as one.

Chapter 5

Fantasy Girlfriend

Tom woke up to Jenny's singing. She sounded like an angel, her voice as clear as crystal. Tom lay awake for a few minutes, staring at the ceiling and listening to her voice. Then, the smell of eggs and sausage tempted him so much he abruptly jumped out of bed. He opened his small suitcase to retrieve a shirt but found it empty. He slid open his closet and saw his shirts hanging there. Had Ma stayed up late to iron his clothes? He must have been quite the sight last night.

He changed quickly because the delicious smell from the kitchen lured him down the long staircase. He paused as he passed the family room where Jenny was still practicing. He leaned against the wall until she stopped to look at him.

"Do I sound that bad?" she asked him.

Tom laughed once. "You sound beautiful, sis. Are you really going to sing for the funeral?"

"Well, I'm on the program, but I don't know if I'll get through it. I always lose it when I get to the words, 'when we shall be forever with the Lord.'" Jenny choked on the last word.

Tom stepped towards her and hugged her closely. "You know Pa would want you to sing," he said softly.

"What if I can't?" she wept. "What if I cry the whole time?"

"I'll say a prayer for you," said Tom.

Jenny pulled back to look at him. "Did you just say that?"

Tom pulled his eyebrows together and stared at his sister.

"I'm sorry...I," Jenny stammered. "I just...I'm sorry."

Tom licked his lips. He knew he was messed up but did his sister think he had given up praying? "It's fine," he finally said. "So was it you or Ma who ironed my shirts last night?" Tom asked.

"Wasn't me," said Jenny, wiping her eyes.

"It was Aunt Mira."

Tom and Jenny turned to see their mother coming down the stairs in her nightgown. "I went to bed right after we talked, Tom. Aunt Mira has taken care of almost everything this week. Now, let's not allow the breakfast she made for us wait any longer," she urged, motioning for them to follow her into the kitchen.

"Good morning, Diane," Aunt Mira said to Tom's mother. "Tom, it's good to see you again. I'm sorry we didn't get a chance to talk last night," she said, pulling him in for a hug.

"No need to apologize," Tom said. "Thanks for everything, Aunt Mira," he said, giving her a kiss on the cheek.

"Of course. Y'all have enough to worry about right now," she commented sympathetically as they all took their places at the table. Sammy was already sitting down, his eyes fixed on the steaming sausages.

After a few minutes of silent eating, Tom decided this was as good a time as any to announce his plans: "I'm going to go back to college next year."

Forks stopped moving, and all eyes fell on Tom. He scanned each of their faces and looked back to his plate, buttering his toast. "They probably won't give me a scholarship again, but I'd like to go back."

Ma spoke up first. "That's an excellent plan, Thomas."

"I'll be living at home now so I can help take care of things."

Ma spoke up again, but this time sternly. "Son, you can't break your job contract. It's not over until the spring."

"I know that, Ma," Tom calmly said as he dished up some more eggs and set the serving bowl down in the middle of the table. "I also can't leave you here alone right after...you're my priority. Besides, I'm twenty-five. It's about time I stepped up to the plate."

"You mean sat at the plate?" Sammy interjected.

Tom flashed his brother a grin. "It's just an expression," he clarified.

"She's not alone; I'm here. I can help," Jenny noted.

"You're in school, and you have your dancing and music and twenty boyfriends. So...I will stay. Someone needs to be here to chop wood at the very least," Tom declared, taking a bite of his toast.

"We have a heating system, Tom," Jenny announced. "Pa hasn't, or didn't...I mean, we haven't needed wood for a year now."

"Yes, Tom," Ma confirmed. "You're very thoughtful, but we will be fine. No need to forfeit your employment."

Tom took a drink of orange juice before he spoke. "Pa is gone. It's my responsibility to take care of you now. I'm staying."

Tom could feel his mother's gaze on him; it was one of those severe expressions, so he refused to look back at her.

"Son, you look at me," Ma demanded.

Here it comes. Tom turned to look at his mother.

"Do you really think I am so old and decrepit I cannot find a job or cook and clean and shop and drive or even chop wood by myself?" she asked, trying to keep her voice even.

Tom swallowed. His ma worked harder than any person alive. "I'm not saying that, Ma, I'm just—"

"You will *not* lose this job and all that money because of me," Ma said firmly, pointing a finger at him. "Do you hear me?"

Tom grimaced. His mother was serious. He could find no way of changing her mind, but he had to try. "It's not right, Ma. I won't be able to live with myself knowing you and Jenny and Sammy are without..."

Ma took a shaky breath and put a comforting hand on his arm. "You don't need to save the world, Thomas," she told him, "especially since we don't need saving."

Tom bit his lip and sighed heavily. "Well, I do need to go back to the cabin after the storm is over so I can bring Daphne back, but then—"

"Who's Daphne?" Jenny cut in. "You have a new girl-friend?" she exclaimed, her face suddenly lighting up.

"No, Jenny," Tom shot back as he stabbed another sausage with his fork.

Jenny just grinned. "Is she pretty? What does she look like?" she asked, leaning toward him from across the table.

"She's...I barely know her. I found her two nights ago a few yards from the cabin. She was hurt and lost. After the storm clears, I'll take her back to the university."

"Brocksville University?" Jenny wondered.

Tom nodded.

"So that's why you want to go back to college!" Jenny assumed. She was nearly bouncing on her chair.

Tom opened his mouth to deny it, but he remembered it *was* Daphne who sparked his interest in it again. So instead, he filled his mouth with eggs.

Tom looked up from his plate; he could see the load of questions on every face.

"Why didn't you bring her back with you this time?" questioned Ma. "I'm surprised you left her alone."

"I didn't want to risk both our lives in the blizzard. Daphne pulled a muscle in her leg, and she can't walk on it yet. She's not very heavy, but I wouldn't be able to carry her fifty miles if the snowmobile got stuck," Tom explained.

"How do you know she's not that heavy? Have you danced with her?" Jenny asked with the same excited grin.

Tom chuckled and shook his head. "She looks like you; that's how I know," he told her.

"Ah, so she's pretty," Aunt Mira interjected with a smile, giving Jenny a wink.

Tom glanced at his sister's truly pretty face. "Nobody's as pretty as my sis."

Jenny just scowled. "That means you're not in love with her."

This time Tom laughed out loud. "I highly doubt that's in the future, Jen. I'm just helping the poor girl out."

"Why do you want to go back for her if you don't—"

"Because he's a nice boy, Jennifer," interrupted Ma. "Now leave your brother alone."

"Why was she out there all alone anyway?" asked Sammy.

Tom turned to look at his brother. "She made a not-so-good choice to go cross-country skiing," he explained.

"Oooh!" Jenny exclaimed slowly, drawing out the word. "A tomboy! Or should I say a Tom-girl? Get it? She's a Tom girl!"

Sammy let out a guttural laugh, showing all the sausage in his mouth. Jenny joined in the laughter, and the others couldn't help smiling, including Tom. It had been a long time since he had heard that terrible joke.

***

The quiet was unbearable with Tom gone. How did he stand this dreadful, lonely silence all the time? What would she do here for two weeks all by herself? She wanted to do something for Tom, but what? She could clean and do the laundry, but standing up became very painful after a few minutes. She wanted to write in her journal. Maybe she could find an empty notebook somewhere. Daphne hobbled down the hall with her crutches and into Tom's bedroom. Surely some extra blank paper was around here somewhere.

She scanned the room for something spiral bound, and her eyes rested on some large photo albums. Curiosity got the best of her, and she clunked her way over to the shelf where the albums rested. She tilted her head to read the titles printed on their spines: *Family Pictures 2008-2013*. Was Tom a memory keeper? She found a few more albums with the same title but different dates. Then she spotted something more interesting: *The Life of Tom Multon*. Daphne quickly snatched the album from its place and opened it to the first page.

Dear Tom,
I hope you like this.
Your loving sister,
Jenny

Daphne flipped through some more pages. The book began with Tom as an infant. His hair was already a curly red. Holding him was a beautiful brunette with big brown eyes, and standing behind them was a man with red hair like Tom's but with a little more brown in it. Daphne smiled at the lovely photo. She flipped through more pages and found an abundance of pictures of Tom's childhood. She was surprised to see how short he had been for so many years. Many of the pictures were of Tom and his father doing carpentry work together. She was astounded at all of the beautiful furniture they had built. She recognized some of the pieces from the cabin. She also found some photos of Tom and his dad fishing and some very thrilling photos of Tom jumping off a cliff into a lake. Daphne grinned at the picture of Tom doing a spread-eagle into the water with what looked like a wide, open-mouthed scream. Then there were some more subdued photos of Tom sitting with his mom on a porch swing. The older he got in the book, the more pictures of friends there were, and the very last page was Tom with another woman. They were facing each other, arms around each other and heads together. The background was a beautiful orange sunset. It was quite breathtaking, actually. Beneath the picture was Jenny's handwriting again:

And now you are on to your future life. Make it as good as your life before!

Tom is engaged! What on earth was he doing here without his fiancée? Would he bring her back with him? Daphne stared at the bedroom wall for a long moment. She flipped back through some more pages. Suddenly she knew what she could do for Tom. She hopped to his computer and did a search to see which software programs he had. Yes, he had it. Daphne sat down at the computer desk and got to work.

***

Tom sat in an oversized, cotton chair in the living room of his mother's home, listening contentedly to Jenny's music on the shiny black baby grand piano, which filled much of the space in the room. He was holding a picture of his mother and father in his hands. His father was wearing a Navy uniform, and his mother wore a deep purple blouse. Her dark hair was curly as it flowed just past her neck. His ma must have wondered if she would see him again before he headed out to sea.

"We will see him again, you know."

Tom looked up at his mother, who had been watching him from the entryway. *How does she know what I'm thinking?*

Tom tried to smile but failed. "I know that, Ma. I can't stop thinking of his casket stuck in that memorial facility."

Ma nodded and walked over to sit in another large chair next to him.

"You've been wonderful to me this past week, Tom. You've done everything your father would have done and more."

Tom smiled and put a hand on his mother's knee. "Good to be home, Ma."

Ma smiled back and clasped her son's hand in her own. "I think you should head back to the cabin today. There's a lull in the storm. Look how beautiful it is outside."

Tom glanced out the window into the dim light that would only last the hour. Every white branch and bush outside looked as calm as could be. "It will be safer to go when the snow goes down, Ma," Tom noted.

"Yes, I know, but another blizzard is due tonight. News reports say once the storm hits, all the roads headed north will close for another month."

"What? I thought the storm was supposed to have passed by now."

Ma shook her head. "The weather changed its mind."

Tom sighed and began rubbing his mouth in thought.

"You should leave today," his mother pressed. "You'll miss out on a lot of money if you don't hunt anything until then."

Tom sighed again and leaned back in his chair. His mother was right.

"Your girlfriend might worry about you," Jenny teased as she continued her Chopin prelude. Even with her music playing, Tom had almost forgotten she was in the room.

"I do need to get some things for Daphne before I go," Tom said, ignoring Jenny's comment.

Jenny's fingers suddenly stopped. "I'll go with you!" she cried excitedly. "I'm sure you have no idea how to buy for a girl."

"No way! You will pester me the entire time," Tom protested, only a tad sarcastically.

"Please, Tom." Jenny begged. "I need the diversion. Please."

Tom glanced at his sister a moment. She did look somewhat troubled. "All right. I'd love the company," he said with a small smile.

"You two better hurry so Tom can beat the blizzard," Ma advised.

***

Tom was in the checkout line waiting to buy a load of girl items. He was sure it would be the talk of the small town, but he still felt too empty inside over Pa to even give it a second thought.

"What color of skin does Daphne have?" whispered Jenny.

"I don't know. Why does that matter?" Tom inquired.

"Just tell me—light skin, dark skin?"

"Um..." *Is it rude to say her face was mostly red?* "Sort of in between. So what?"

Jenny gave him a brief, puzzling look and then ran off in another direction. Tom sighed. Jenny was part of the reason he had bought so much. What was she getting now?

Jenny was gone a few minutes, but it didn't matter as the checkout line was taking an eternity. Tom had just made it to the register when Jenny came back with tiny plastic circles in her hands and two small brushes.

"What is that?" he wondered.

"Foundation and powder," Jenny replied.

"Are you...sculpting something?"

Jenny laughed at that. "It's makeup, Tom, for your girlfriend."

Tom saw the cashier look their way and raise her eyebrows. Tom groaned out loud. "Jenny, I don't even know if she likes makeup!" he said to her in hushed tones.

Jenny slapped him on the shoulder. "Ah-hah! So she *is* your girlfriend!"

Tom huffed in frustration. Normally, he liked to play this kind of game with her in front of a small-town gossip, but not today. "Jenny, I've only known her for a week," he muttered. The cashier's eyes widened, and so did Jenny's grin. Tom rolled his eyes. That was definitely the wrong thing to say.

"Come on," Jenny pleaded. "Why wouldn't she like it? I think I got a good color."

"It's not about the color," Tom argued. "She doesn't need it and may not want it." And possibly be insulted by it.

"Is there anything else?" asked the cashier.

Jenny promptly placed two small tubes on the counter top—one black, one pink.

"Now, what are those things?" Tom asked, feeling more irritated by the moment.

"Mascara and lipstick, Tom. I'm sure you've heard of *those things.*"

"Jenny," Tom chided as he ran a hand through his hair.

"I'll pay for it if that's the problem," claimed his sister.

"With your money or Ma's?" Tom questioned, scolding her with his eyes.

Jenny shrugged. "I don't have a job. Show choir takes up all my spare time."

Tom groaned under his breath. "How much is it?" he asked the cashier.

He didn't even hear what she said as he slid his debit card through the slot.

Tom ignored Jenny's bouncing steps on the way to their pickup.

"Pa would be proud of what you are doing for this poor girlfriend of yours," Jenny said after they climbed into the truck's cab.

"Jenny, stop calling her my girlfriend," Tom reprimanded, "and don't insult me by saying such a small thing would make Pa proud."

Jenny slammed her door shut, suddenly mad. "How dare you! You said in that eulogy of yours it was all the small things that made Pa great. Are you going to insult our father by preaching the opposite?" Jenny was nearly shouting.

"Whoa! That's not what I meant, Jen," Tom said, baffled.

Jenny ignored him and continued her case. "Pa was amazing! And it was because he didn't care about doing huge, stupid things! He cared about me! That's why he was amazing." Jenny was suddenly crying.

Tom turned on the ignition, not knowing what to do with this unexpected outburst. He hadn't seen behavior like this in his sister for years. Jenny was now sobbing while Tom drove out of the store's parking lot. He kept his voice soft when he spoke. "Jen, I would never insult Pa on purpose. All I meant was no matter what I do, I'll never catch up to being as good as he was. That's all I meant."

Jenny took a few slow, shaky breaths. "I know. Whenever I had a little problem, I would talk to him about it. Now he's gone. He's not here to talk to and that's a big problem."

Tom blew out a gush of air. "I think I should stay home," he professed.

"No!" Jenny blurted out. Then she calmed herself. "I'll be okay. I want to help Ma through this, but I don't know how because I can't deal with it myself," she explained. "That doesn't mean you should stay home," she said in a rush. "We need the money you'll make."

Tom turned his head sharply to look at his sister. "You do?"

Jenny nodded. "Pa lost his job last summer and—"

"What!" Tom interrupted, shocked by this news.

Jenny nodded. "He didn't tell you because it was the first time you were on your own two feet in a while and he didn't want to rock the boat. He thought he would have a new job by now. Obviously, now he...anyway, we've been living on savings ever since then."

Tom sighed heavily. "I'm glad you told me. I'm definitely going back now. I'll write a check before I leave."

"Good," said Jenny, wiping her eyes. "Don't tell Ma I said anything. She doesn't want to worry you because she worries about you enough."

"No need to worry about me," Tom said flatly.

"Ma will be Ma," Jenny shrugged. "I'm sorry I yelled at you. Ever since Pa died, I've been...I don't know."

"You don't have to explain it to me," Tom sympathized. "I understand the feeling."

Chapter 6

Helpless

Daphne woke with a start. She could have sworn she heard the sound of breaking glass. Looking around the dark room, she saw nothing. She rested her eyes on the red, glowing numbers of the alarm clock next to her: 2:30 am. Suddenly, the angry wind bellowed so loudly she could have sworn it had come inside. Daphne sat up straight, her heart accelerating to double its normal tempo. *What was that?* She heard a loud slam followed by footsteps thumping hard on the floor down the hallway. Someone was here!

Daphne hopped out of bed and crawled to the bedroom door, opening it just a crack. The light was on in the front room, and snow was scattered all over the floor. A harsh coughing and wheezing reached her ears. A stranger was here. *Even if I called the police, they probably wouldn't even be able to get out here!* Daphne limped down the hallway and into the well lit room. Lying on his side and facing the fire was a man bundled in a large coat and hat; every last inch of him was covered in snow.

"Excuse me!" Daphne called to him, trying to sound stern. "You can't barge into someone else's place like this!"

The man tried to speak but coughed instead.

Daphne crossed her arms, waiting for him to finish. He tried again. "You can when it's your own place, Daphne."

Daphne was so shocked at the sound of her name she stepped back. "Wha—is that you, Tom?"

Tom just coughed in response. Daphne hobbled around him to see his face. He still had his snowy face mask on, but she did recognize his brown eyes. "How did you get inside? The snow is almost five feet deep!" Daphne exclaimed.

Tom pointed upward with his finger. "I broke a window in the attic," he grumbled.

"Oh, that's...clever. Well, you're going to be sick, Tom," she accused. "Why did you do this to yourself?"

Tom folded his hands under his head. "Later, Daphne," he said, closing his eyes.

"Wait, Tom. Don't go to sleep in those wet clothes. You probably already have hypothermia; you don't need pneumonia, too."

"Can't move," Tom mumbled.

Daphne stared at him for a moment. This was her just a week ago. She knew exactly how he felt, except Tom looked worse.

Daphne knelt down beside him, slipping the large fur hat off his head. "You look soaked to the bone, Tom. We've got to get you warm."

She pulled and tugged at his clothes. It was exhausting. Tom's clothes were soaking wet, and his limp body was no help. Finally Daphne got him down to his boxer shorts and helped the shivering man stumble, along with herself, to the bathtub. Daphne turned the hot water on, letting it run until she found the perfect temperature and then plugged up the drain.

"There you go," she told him. "I washed the towels today so they are nice and fresh for you. I'll bring you some dry clothes in a minute. Get warm and call me if you need anything else."

Tom was hugging himself and shivering violently. "Thank you, D—Daphne."

"Of course," she said with a smile and left the room.

As Daphne set Tom's dry clothes on the counter of the vanity, she heard the wind howl violently again. Now she understood it was coming from the broken window in the attic. What was she supposed to do about that? Tom must have been thinking the same thing because he suddenly spoke up to her in a raspy voice from behind the bathtub's curtain. "In the a-t-tic, Daphne, you will find a s-square board that is larger than the w-window. Will you cover the window with it and j-just hammer it into the w-wall? That way the wind won't ruin everything up there. I'll install a new window when I c-can."

"Sure. Will I find a hammer and nails in the attic?"

"Yes. Thank you, Daphne."

"Of course," she said as she closed the bathroom door behind her and scurried into the mudroom. There she discovered a rope hanging from the ceiling attached to a metal ring. She yanked on it, and a hatch opened with an attached, retractable ladder. She climbed up the ladder as the temperature around her rapidly grew colder.

"Whoa!" she cried out loud when she reached the attic. A lot of half-made furniture was up here. No wonder Tom wanted it protected. Every piece was already dusted with snow. Daphne spotted the square board Tom had told her about and rushed to it. She saw there were already holes in the wall above the window. How many times had Tom done this? At any rate, she had a lot of work to do to clean this place up.

***

Once Daphne was finally back in bed, her alarm clock told her it was 4 am. The moment she closed her eyes, she heard some fumbling in the bathroom. Tom was finished. Quickly, she hopped out of bed and staggered to the kitchen where she heated up some cornbread she had baked herself for dinner the prior evening. Then she warmed up some hot cocoa and set it next to the bread. When the bathroom door opened, she stepped out into the hallway to find Tom walking towards his bedroom, holding onto the walls on his way. Daphne quickened her uneven step and put his arm in hers and led him to the kitchen. "Have an early morning snack," she suggested. "Your body needs it."

Without a word, Tom complied and sat down on a bar stool and ate and drank. Daphne didn't like that he was still coughing through it all. "Thank you, Daphne," he said when he had finished.

"No problem."

"Good night," he muttered while getting to his feet. And then he smiled. "I mean, good morning. I'm going to bed."

Daphne smiled. "Have a good sleep."

Tom slept almost the entire three days afterward. Daphne tried to get him to eat toast, crackers, anything, but he would shake his head, cough a lot, and go back to sleep. She did, however, successfully get him to drink a few sips of water with assistance. Other than occasionally getting up to use the bathroom, he stayed in bed and slept and coughed. Daphne checked on him often to refill the humidifier or bring him more tissues, water, decongestant, and blankets, but otherwise she tried to leave him alone and spent the days working on some new sketches. She found it hard to concentrate, however, since she was so worried about Tom and his low temperature. She had done all she could do to keep him warm, so she prayed Tom would return to good health.

Upon awakening after a short catnap in the rocking chair, Daphne saw the fire was dying down, so she walked over to light it. Only then did she realize Tom's two suitcases were still lying on the floor from when he toppled in from the blizzard. Hadn't he only taken one suitcase to the funeral? Daphne shrugged as she began lugging the heavy things to the laundry room.

As Daphne carefully began piling clothes into the washing machine, she discovered most of the clothes were for a girl. *Did Tom bring back all of these things for me?* Daphne stared at a deep green, fleece sweater in confusion before dropping it in. Underneath all the strange clothing was a tiny, purple plastic bag. Curious, Daphne peeked inside: an entire collection of makeup. Daphne gasped. *Is this also for me?* Of course, she knew Tom was probably just trying to be nice, but it was still outright humiliating her poor skin was so apparent that a *man* would think of this.

She sighed heavily as she slammed the door to the washing machine and twisted the dial to the cold cycle. She could do nothing about it, and she wouldn't let Tom know it bothered her so much. She wasn't going to wear the makeup.

***

His stomach woke him up first. Tom couldn't remember the last time he had felt so hungry, but he also didn't want to move. He ached everywhere. His lips were dry and cracked, and his nose hurt from wiping it so much with tissues. The entire length of his throat burned with a stinging pain.

Even though it was quiet in the cabin, Tom assumed Daphne was awake since he could see the light from the kitchen streaming into his room. He felt a little guilty she had sac-rificed so much of her sleep to take care of him. She didn't even seem to mind. And yesterday—checking on him all the time, making sure the humidifier was still going. She was so...caring, and he had barely lifted his head to say thank you. Then Tom thought of something his pa had said once: "A woman who sacrifices herself for you is a woman you better hold onto. You better sacrifice for her, or you'll have no grip to keep her." This thought about Daphne was a little strange since he had no intentions of holding onto Daphne in the way his pa had meant. She was a great person, and while she was here, he would do all he could to pay her back for what she had done for him. One thing was certain—Daphne was special. And he was sure, regardless of anything else, they would be good friends. He put his hands behind his head and smiled at the ceiling.

"Good morning," said Daphne from the doorway.

Tom looked her way. "Good—" he cleared his throat. "Good morning, Daphne. How are you?"

"I'm all right. The real question is how are you?"

Tom smiled weakly. "I'm feeling better. Thanks to you."

Daphne walked over to the desk where the thermometer lay and quickly took Tom's temperature. She sighed in relief and gave Tom a big smile. "You're finally back to normal. I was praying for that."

Tom smiled wider. "Praying I would no longer be weird?" He frowned at his bad joke, but Daphne obliged him by laugh-ing a little.

"You know what I meant. You were at ninety-six degrees all day yesterday. I was getting really anxious."

"I was?"

"Yes, I told you that yesterday morning. Remember?"

Tom shook his head. "I don't remember much of anything except that you took care of everything I needed."

"I was happy to return the favor," Daphne said simply.

Tom raised his eyebrows. "I guess you were cold and helpless not too long ago."

"Yes," said Daphne. "So are you hungry?"

"I'm starving, actually," Tom admitted.

"Great. I'm on it," she said with a grin and spun around to the kitchen.

Just a few minutes later, Daphne came back with a plate of dried peaches and a bowl of hot oatmeal. A cookie sheet posed as a bed tray. She patiently held it in her hands as Tom had another coughing fit. When he finally finished, she placed it on his lap.

"How did you know I like raisins in my oatmeal?" Tom croaked.

"I guessed."

Tom took a bite. He could feel its trail of warmth all the way down to his stomach.

"Thanks, Daphne," Tom croaked again. "It's been a long time since I've had breakfast in bed."

Suddenly, Daphne looked uncomfortable. "Tom, does your fiancée know you are here alone with me?"

Tom felt a shock rush through him. "H-How did you know I was engaged?"

Daphne's face blanched. "Well, I looked through some of your photo albums."

"Oh, I thought I had gotten rid of all the pictures of her." Tom scratched his head.

A confused look crossed Daphne's face.

"We're not engaged anymore," Tom explained.

"Oh, I'm so sorry. When did that happen?" Daphne asked hesitantly.

"Last spring," Tom declared.

"Oh!" Daphne breathed. "I...I'm sorry."

Tom shrugged. "It's okay. I saw her at the funeral," he confided, folding his arms. "We're…we're good. She has a new boyfriend now."

Daphne sat down on his bed below his feet with a sympathetic look on her face.

"I would like to change the subject, though," Tom said with a small smile.

Daphne nodded, understanding. "Tell me why you came back so early. I wasn't expecting you for at least another week."

"The weather forecast changed. There was a lull in the storm, or at least there was when I started out. If I had waited until next week, another blizzard would be on its way and would have made it impossible for me to come back for another month. I didn't want you to think I wasn't coming back. Plus, I would hate to waste all that hunting time."

"So you risked your life?" Daphne was shocked.

Tom swallowed and cringed with the pain of it. "I would have been fine, but there was a road blocked off. I had to take a detour, and my snowmobile got stuck. I really don't know how it happened since I know the mountain well. Just trying to be careful. I guess I was…distracted. Anyway, I had to walk the rest of the way."

"You walked?" exclaimed Daphne in the same shocked tone.

Tom finished chewing his peaches before he spoke again. "It was only a couple of miles, but even with my snow shoes it took me forever with the wind blowing against me."

Daphne sighed heavily. "Well, I'm glad you're okay," she finally said. "I'll let you be now. Call me if you need anything. When you're feeling good enough, I have something to show you. Two things, actually."

"What is it?" asked Tom, instantly curious.

"A surprise," said Daphne with a smile.

"Oh, just tell me," Tom insisted.

Daphne laughed. "Not a chance. Just eat your breakfast; I'm going to take a shower," she said as she spun around toward the door.

"Oh, hey, that reminds me," said Tom, his mouth still full. Daphne turned to face him again and waited while he finished chewing. "I brought you some clothes and things. They're in my suitcase," he said, his mouth empty now.

Daphne hesitated a moment. "Yeah, I saw them when I went to wash your clothes."

"Ah! You did that for me? Thanks!" Tom interjected, stuffing his mouth again.

"Sure," said Daphne. "All those things are for me?"

Tom swallowed as he nodded. "What other girl is there in this cabin? They certainly won't fit me," he said with a grin.

Daphne smiled shyly. "You didn't have to do that, Tom."

"Yes, I did. You don't have anything else."

"How much did you spend?" she inquired.

Tom shook his head. "It doesn't matter," he said, taking another bite of oatmeal.

Daphne gave him a pleading look. "Please Tom, just tell me. It had to have been at least $300. That makeup alone was probably close to $60. Am I right?"

Tom shrugged. "I don't remember, Daphne. My sister is the one who picked everything out."

"She has classy taste," Daphne noted.

Tom nodded in agreement. "Look, don't feel like you have to wear anything, I mean…" Tom stopped and scratched his head as he felt his cheeks turn ruddy. *Oh, good night.* "What I mean is, uh, don't feel obligated to…to wear…to wear anything I got you because I…I don't know what you like." Tom grimaced to himself. He had totally botched that one.

"Okay. Well, I appreciate it, Tom," Daphne declared. "You're very thoughtful, and generous, too—more so than I could ever imagine."

Tom rolled his eyes.

"What's with the eye rolling?" Daphne questioned.

Tom smiled as he dropped a peach in his mouth. "You're just so gracious with compliments, Daphne. Don't know that I deserve them."

"You absolutely do," Daphne countered.

"Why don't you stay and talk to me for a minute," Tom suggested. "Your shower can wait."

Daphne stared at him with a blank look. He actually wanted her company?

"Come on," Tom persisted. "Pull up the chair there."

Almost mechanically, Daphne obeyed and sat in the desk chair beside the bed. Tom probably did need to talk as he was still grieving over his father. "How are you, Tom? How's your family doing?" Daphne asked sincerely.

Tom looked directly at her as he spoke. "As good as can be expected," he replied. "I want to talk about you. Tell me a story about you."

"What would you like to know?" Daphne wondered.

"Start from the beginning. Where did you grow up?" Tom asked.

"Stonebrooke. It's about an hour south of the university."

"And you are a...sophomore now?" Tom wondered.

"A junior," corrected Daphne.

"How is college going for you?"

Daphne took a deep breath. "It's okay," she muttered.

Tom gave her a speculative look. "Does that mean it isn't going well?"

"No, it's fine. But on holiday weekends my roommates always go home, and I'm stuck by myself because I don't have a home to go to. Since I was the only one in the world on campus over winter break last year, I didn't find it much fun." Daphne tried to keep the frown off her face, but she didn't succeed.

"Didn't your parents have a home before they went to Afghanistan?" Tom wondered.

Daphne smiled sadly. "Yes, but they sold it before they left. They figured I'd be living in the dorms during the school year and with my grandmother in the summer. She lives only a half hour from Brocksville."

Tom had finished his breakfast and set his dishes on the stool by the bed. "Well, that's one thing I can relate to."

"What? Rooming with your grandma?" Daphne said wryly.

"No, being alone. It's terrible, isn't it?" Tom pointed out.

Daphne shrugged. "Not always, but sometimes it is."

Tom nodded. "Did you know that the night I found you outside I literally wondered if I was going crazy?"

A slow smile crept on Daphne's face. "Why? Because you actually saw another person?"

"That was part of it, but mostly I was sure I was hearing things. Was that you yelling?" Tom questioned.

Daphne nodded. "Yes, it was definitely me. I was desperate to find some help."

Tom smiled with understanding.

Daphne returned the smile graciously. "I was elated when I saw you outside your cabin. When you found me, I was suddenly terrified you were mean or loopy or crazy or something."

"Well, it was kind of crazy to help a complete stranger," Tom said with a smile, leaning back on his pillows.

Daphne's heart leaped at the sight of his perfect grin. She smiled back shyly. "Well, I'm glad you did."

"Me, too, Daphne. It would be a shame not to have met you."

His sincerity was melting Daphne's heart. She tried to wrap a shell around her soul, knowing Tom didn't mean the compliment in the same way she wanted to take it.

Daphne cleared her throat. "I'm happy to have met you, too, Tom," she said. "I've been thinking about how remarkable everything has been."

Tom cocked his head to one side. "What do you mean?"

"Well, you would have headed home to your father's funeral much sooner if the Internet hadn't been down and you had received that message from your mom when she sent it. Am I right?" Daphne inquired.

Tom nodded. "Yes, I would have."

"Well, if that hadn't have happened, you wouldn't have found me, and I might not have survived out there."

Tom grew thoughtful and slowly nodded his head once. "I still would have come back when I did to get more hunting done even if you hadn't been here, and I probably wouldn't have recovered from...whatever that was."

Daphne grinned. "I hadn't thought of that."

Tom grinned back. "It looks like we were both in the right place at the right time."

"Who knew it would be in a cabin in the middle of nowhere?"

Tom chuckled. "Who knew?"

For a moment, all Daphne could do was just gawk at Tom's brilliant face. She was shocked to see he was staring back at her. She didn't quite know what to make of it.

***

In a moment of utter chagrin, Tom realized he was staring at Daphne like an idiot. He cleared his throat. "So, are you going to show me that surprise of yours or are you going to make me suffer in wonder for the rest of the day?" he asked.

Daphne grinned again. "I would love to show you, but it's in the other room. Are you up for a walk?"

Tom noticed his headache was gone. *What a relief.* "I think so," he said, moving his legs from under the covers and climbing out of his bed. The moment he got to his feet, a sudden head rush ran through him. "Whoa," he muttered, bringing a hand to his head.

Daphne caught his elbow before he could topple over. "Can you walk?" she questioned.

"Yes. What about you? Is your leg better?" Tom wondered.

"Sure," said Daphne, leading him out of the room. "It still hurts a bit, but I can get around without the crutches now. I appreciate your letting me borrow them."

Tom shook his head. "I wish everyone in the world were as grateful as you are, Daphne."

"I wish everyone in the world were as giving as you are." Daphne smiled as she returned the compliment. She led him to the couch in front of the big-screen TV and flipped on the lights.

"You found a movie you like?" Tom assumed.

"Yes," said Daphne. "I hope you do, too."

"I have seen every movie I own about a billion times. What else is a lone man going to do when he can't get out of his own bunker?"

Daphne cracked a grin. "Stare at a movie screen, I guess."

Tom chuckled. "Or a computer screen or a phone screen. We humans have awful habits of all kinds of staring it seems."

Daphne laughed at that, and the two sat down next to each other on the sofa. Tom looked curiously at the menu on the screen for a movie he didn't recognize. A picture of his pa was to the left, and two menu options read "My Life with Pa," and "Music Play List."

"What is this?" Tom asked, confused.

"Just watch," Daphne said as she clicked the first option.

Some music started playing, and Tom saw his pa holding a baby with dark reddish hair whom he knew was himself. As the song went on, different pictures of Tom's childhood flashed on the screen. He watched himself grow up, his red hair getting redder and brighter the older he got. He saw pictures of his pa helping him walk, his pa throwing a baseball with him, his pa teaching him to ride a bike and to read a book. He saw pictures of himself and his pa fishing, boating, sawing, building, and hiking. Daphne had picked songs that went along exactly with the pictures—songs that were his favorite. Twenty minutes later, when the movie was over, Tom couldn't take his eyes off the last image of him and his pa sitting on the porch swing at home with both of their faces lit up with laughter. He felt as if his pa were in the room with him, or at least the memory of him was so strong it was almost tangible. He blinked rapidly to keep the moisture in his eyes.

Daphne pointed the remote at the TV, and it clicked off. Tom didn't know what to say or do.

"Did you like it?" she whispered.

Tom turned to face Daphne. Her big eyes were peering at him with intense curiosity. How could a near-stranger come up with something so remarkable and personal? He nodded slowly and very softly added, "I can't think of a better gift. Thank you, Daphne."

"You're welcome," she said simply.

"I didn't know you were so skilled," he added casually. "That was very well done."

"Thank you." She handed him one of his sketchbooks.

"Is there something inside you want me to see?" he asked.

Daphne nodded, looking a little shy. Tom opened the sketchbook to the first page. Instantly, his mouth dropped, and for a moment, he merely gasped. The drawing was in pencil with a very exact, artistic hand. His pa had his arm around him in a friendly gesture. His eyes seemed to glow the same way Tom remembered them, and he had the same subtle smile. What surprised him the most was the look on his own face. It *did* look like him, but the replica made Tom appear a lot happier than he felt.

"Do you like it?" Daphne asked again, but this time there was doubt in her voice.

"Oh, yes, of course, I do!" Tom exclaimed, giving her a reassuring smile. "I just can't believe how...how good it is." Tom shifted his gaze back to the drawing. "It's incredible," he said as he continued to stare at it in awe.

"You're very talented, Daphne," he said, looking back up at her, "and very thoughtful."

Daphne blushed at his praise. "Well, you're welcome," she replied.

Tom stood on his feet. "I think we need to hang this up! I'll be right back," he said with a grin. He hurried to his room and dug through the bottom drawer of his desk. Yep, the picture frame was still there. After he had dusted it off with his fingers, he grabbed a small hammer and nail out of the top drawer and rushed back to Daphne. She was standing up now. "How about right there?" she asked, pointing to a spot next to the front door.

"My thoughts exactly," Tom agreed. He slid the perfect drawing behind the glass of the frame, quickly hammered a nail into the wall, and hung up the picture. "There! It's perfect!" he exclaimed as he turned towards Daphne again. He paused as he looked at her friendly face that appeared elated at the moment. "This is exactly what I needed," he said more solemnly now. Then, he took her in his arms and squeezed her tightly. "Thank you, Daphne. Thank you so much."

Chapter 7

Snake Charmer

Tom was throwing darts at his dartboard. Daphne, who was sitting behind him in her new favorite chair, looked up from her sketches to watch. Each one of the darts pelted the red center.

"You're really good at that," Daphne noted.

"I get lots of practice when the weather is bad and I'm tired of working in the woodshop."

"Oh, yeah, I saw that in the attic," Daphne remembered.

"I'm sorry you had to clean up all that mess with the snow," Tom said, tossing another dart. "Bull's-eye!"

"You made all the furniture in this cabin, didn't you?"

Tom turned around to face her. "Yeah, with the help of my pa."

"I thought so! The craftsmanship is far too intricate and unique to be from a department store. It's all very beautiful, Tom," Daphne said, looking down at her hands.

A grin split Tom's face. "Do you want to come see what I'm working on now?" he asked.

"I would love to!" Daphne exclaimed. She uncrossed her legs and set her sketchbook down on the coffee table.

Tom placed the darts in his hand into a small box next to her sketchbook and continued to grin at her. "Perfect. Follow me."

Daphne followed Tom to the mudroom where Tom grabbed the hanging rope that opened the hatch and retractable stairs. He climbed up and pushed open the heavy door. Daphne climbed up after him. Once she reached the top, Tom held out a hand to help her over the ledge. She tried to ignore the way her heart sped up a bit at his touch.

"What do you think?" Tom asked.

Daphne glanced all around her. She saw two tables with strips of boards across one of them and a large saw on top of the other. Handmade shelves full of every kind of tool imaginable covered the walls. A few random small furniture items were scattered on the floor. Tom must have fixed the window he had broken into because there was only one, and it was intact. Then she spotted something she liked very much standing in the corner.

"Oh, is this it?" she asked, walking over to a half-finished dresser.

"Yes," answered Tom. "It's mahogany. Do you like it?"

"What's not to like?" Daphne ran her fingertips over the maroon drawers. "How in the world did you carve these flowers into it?"

Tom walked over to where she was and stood behind her. "I used a small tool," he said simply, "and a lot of patience."

"I would say so. Looks like you are also quite an artist." Daphne turned to face him with a smile.

Tom grinned back, and his face turned ruddy. "I've never been called that before."

"Well, it's true," Daphne affirmed as she ran her fingertips over the engraved petals. "Who is it for?"

"My ma," Tom said. "I wish…"

"You wish what?" asked Daphne, turning to face him again.

Tom shrugged. "I wish my pa would have been able to see it."

"I'm sure he sees it now," Daphne pointed out.

Tom gave her a thoughtful smile and nodded. "Speaking of artists, have you ever entered your work in some kind of contest?" he wondered.

Daphne shook her head. "No. I only have time for home-work and my part-time job. In high school, I was on the swim team so–"

"Really? You were on the swim team?"

Daphne nodded. "All four years."

Tom gazed at her with a strange admiration in his eyes. "That's right. You told me you took second place in a meet. That's incredible."

Daphne blushed at his praise. "Um, thanks."

Tom smiled broadly at her for a long minute with a twinkle in his eye before he cleared his throat. "Well, would you, uh, would you like me to show you how to make something or carve something?"

"Yes! I would love that!" Daphne exclaimed, suddenly excited.

Tom gave her a scrutinizing look. "Really?"

"Of course! Does that surprise you?"

Tom smiled and raked a hand through his hair. "Yes, it does, actually. Nobody has ever wanted to before."

"Well, it's a good thing you're stuck here with me then, isn't it?" Daphne asked with a grin.

"Absolutely," Tom said, his smile persistent. "Absolutely."

***

"I did it! Tom, come look at this! I finished!"

Tom set down his tools and rushed over to where Daphne sat cross-legged on the floor next to the stool she had been carving.

"A snake, huh?" Tom murmured as he crouched down to look at the engraving more closely.

"Well, I couldn't figure out what else would fit on the legs. Don't you like it?"

Tom chuckled. "Daphne, it's gorgeous. I've never seen a better-looking snake. Of course I like it."

A blushing smile crossed Daphne's face. "Well, it should be. It took me six entire days to do it."

"Have we really been coming up here every day for a week?" Tom questioned.

Daphne nodded. "While you've completed a dresser and a bench, I've only carved one snake."

Tom placed a hand on her shoulder. "But it's a beautiful one. And guess what?" he asked, looking at his watch. "It's 9. I've got to go to bed so I can go on a hunt in the morning–now that I can get out of the cabin."

"My eyes could use a rest as well," Daphne agreed.

Tom switched off their lantern. The two of them stood up and sauntered their way over to the ladder and descended. Downstairs was completely dark except for the tiniest glow from a dying ember in the other room.

Surprisingly, Daphne felt Tom whisper in her ear. "I've had a great week with you, Daphne."

She shivered at his closeness. "M-me, too, Tom."

"Goodnight," he whispered again.

"Goodnight," she replied. In an instant, he was gone from her side.

Chapter *8*

Flying Blind

"Daphne! Hey, Daphne, come here!" Tom called from the front door. He sounded urgent, so Daphne quickly put down her sketchbook and scurried to the sound of his voice. She had just turned the corner into the entryway when Tom shouted again. "Daphne!"

She jumped in surprise and then immediately froze in place at the shocking sight of Tom. Blood smothered his entire coat and pants. There was even blood splattered on his chin.

"Good *night*, Daphne. What's wrong?" Tom asked her, looking at her with alarm.

"Wh...what happened to you?" Daphne whispered, her eyes fixated on his bloody neck.

Tom looked himself over. "Oh, honey, I'm fine. I was just carrying a caribou I killed. That's what I wanted to show you."

Tom was not a walking corpse, then. Daphne sighed heavily with relief. She noticed his expression now and saw he was smiling kindly at her.

Daphne inhaled deeply. "Honey?" she questioned, raising her eyebrows.

Tom suddenly looked embarrassed. "Uh, sorry. That just...slipped out wrong," he explained, shaking his head. "Well, do you want to see him?"

"See who?"

"The caribou. Come on. He's just outside. "Tom grabbed Daphne's hand and led her up the stairs and out the door.

Tom turned his headlamp on so Daphne could see the animal in the dark. And there it was—a gigantic, bloody caribou with horns three times the size of its head. "Wow!" exclaimed Daphne in total awe. "He's massive!"

Tom beamed brightly at her. "He's a beauty, isn't he?"

"How did you carry him so far?" Daphne questioned.

"Well, that's the other thing I wanted to show you. Look!" Tom pointed his finger and turned his headlamp in another direction.

Daphne squinted a moment before she could make out the new shape. "You found your snowmobile!" she cried happily.

Tom laughed a bit. "Yes, I did!"

"Oh, I'm so happy for you! What good news!" Daphne turned to Tom and saw his expression was more excited than she had ever seen. He clapped his hands together once. "Tell you what, Daphne. Why don't I put this lovely beast in a safe place? Then I'll get out of this bloody mess, and you and I can go on a little adventure?"

"Oh? What kind of an adventure?" Daphne was curious.

Tom shrugged. "How about a snowmobile ride?"

"In the dark?"

Tom nodded eagerly. "It makes it all the more exhilarating."

Daphne felt a sudden thrill rise within her. This was just what she needed. Tom looked pleased at her excitement and smiled in return. "I hoped you would approve...honey," he added with a wry smile. Daphne smacked his bloody chest, but Tom just laughed. "Sorry, I couldn't help it. I'll take care of the beast," he declared.

"Don't you have to...you know, pull it apart and package it?"

"I'll do that later," he murmured. "I have plenty of time to myself with all the drawing you do."

"Oh, I'm...sorry."

"That wasn't an accusation, Daphne," Tom said kindly. "Now get on something warm."

***

Although it was 1 pm, it was still fairly dark outside, and Daphne found herself clinging to Tom with all her might as they sped way too fast on Tom's snowmobile. Daphne tried to peer around his thick arms so she could see the narrow path lighted by the single headlight. She felt a little safer this way. Tom moved his arms in and out so much while steering it was difficult for Daphne to see much of anything. Instead, she rested her head on his back and watched, wide-eyed, as passing trees suddenly came into view and disappeared just as quickly. The cold air lashed at her ears, threatening to slice through her woolen hat. Occasionally, a branch or a bush would whip within an inch of her face without her even realizing it was there in the first place. Going so fast and seeing very little in the dark, Daphne felt she were part of the wind itself.

"We're almost there, Daphne!" Tom called to her over his shoulder.

"Almost where?" she called back to him.

"The jumps!" he yelled into the wind.

"The wh—" Before Daphne could finish, they were suddenly airborne. Daphne let out a high-pitched cry before they landed hard and sped along again.

Daphne laughed out loud at the thrill of it, and then they were in the air once more. Although Daphne couldn't see, she could feel they were higher off the ground this time. Daphne's breath seemed to leave her lungs altogether and then abruptly push back inside her when they hurtled to the ground. Daphne couldn't anticipate when the jumps were coming or how high they would be or how they would hit the ground. It was all terrifying and exhilarating all at once! Daphne couldn't stop her excited cries of fear or her constant, gasping laughter. She could hear Tom laughing heartily as well.

After one particularly high jump, Daphne felt them hit the ground a little lopsided. The two of them were thrown from the snowmobile onto the freezing, snowy earth. Daphne rolled a little ways before she was able to stop herself. For a long moment, she just lay on her back, trying to catch her breath.

"Daphne!" She heard Tom call loudly. He couldn't have been more than an arm's length away.

"I'm right here," she answered.

Tom reached out and touched her arm. "Are you hurt?"

"That was so awesome, Tom!" She laughed breathlessly. "Oh, my *lands*! I have never been so terrified in my life!" She laughed out loud again.

Daphne saw Tom's figure kneeling over her now. "You're not hurt?" he asked again.

Daphne shook her head against the snow and continued to laugh, although her sides ached from the excitement and cold.

Tom was laughing now, too, and collapsed beside her on his back. "Oh, I loved that, Daphne," he laughed. "I loved hearing you scream like a—" and then Tom let out another sharp burst of laughter.

"Like a what?" Daphne chuckled back at him, trying to see his face in the dark.

"Like a preying eagle!" He tried to mimic her by making a ridiculous, obnoxious, high-pitched birdcall.

"I did not!" Daphne protested through her laughter.

Instead of responding, Tom just laughed harder than Daphne had ever heard him laugh before.

Daphne tried to protest again, but all she could do was laugh hysterically. Tom held his stomach as if it hurt. The two laughed and gasped in the cold air for another long minute.

"How are we going to find the snowmobile?" Daphne asked once their chuckles had subdued.

"Oh, I'm sure it's not too far. We're in a cove right now, and," he said, "I have a flashlight." They both sat up on their knees as Daphne saw a small stream of light appear on the white ground.

"Look! There it is."

Daphne followed the stream of light to the abandoned snowmobile resting with its front skis buried in the snowy powder.

Tom then brought the light back so it was shining between them. Daphne could see Tom clearly now. Snow nearly covered his black face mask. His russet eyes stared back at her, and Daphne found she couldn't look away.

"I can't believe how green your eyes are," Tom said, also staring at her. "They're really pretty, Daphne."

Daphne gulped, feeling like her tongue was now frozen along with the rest of her.

Tom finally broke the moment. "Let's get going," he said, standing up and extending a hand to her.

Chapter *9*

Brewing Desires

"This is great, Daphne," announced Tom. "You implied earlier that you weren't a very good cook."

"I'm not," she said.

Tom held his fork full of enchiladas up to his mouth. "This dish clearly proves otherwise," he disputed, before taking a bite.

Daphne was standing opposite of Tom with her hands on the edge of the counter. "It's the only thing I can make. I would love you to teach me some of your tricks."

Tom swallowed his mouthful of food. "That sounds great. After dinner, let's make caramel popcorn."

Daphne's face lit up. Tom loved that look.

After they stuffed themselves to the brim, Tom began his cooking lesson that, for some reason, he was ecstatic about. Perhaps it was because Daphne was such a smart pupil.

"All right, the popcorn is popped. Now we come to the tricky part. First, melt the butter in the pan and put in the rest of the ingredients. Make sure you constantly stir so nothing scorches."

Daphne nodded, and Tom watched her as she followed his directions. She took a long time measuring the cups of sugar, so Tom assisted her by stirring the butter in the pot.

"Sorry, I've never done this before," Daphne apologized.

"No worries. We're doing this together." Tom placated.

When Daphne resumed stirring, Tom said, "All right, now we want to boil it to death."

"Okay," said Daphne with a grin. "Where did you learn how to cook?" she asked, still looking at the caramel liquid.

Tom was leaning one hip against the counter, facing Daphne. "Trial and error, I guess," he speculated. "Kind of like life."

"I doubt your life has been too full of error," Daphne assumed.

Tom laughed at that. "You don't know me very well, Daphne."

"I know you love your family," Daphne noted.

"It would be senseless not to," Tom replied.

"I also know you have a good enough heart to take care of a stranger in need even to the point of spending a ridiculous amount of money on her."

"I...but that doesn't make up for other stuff."

"Like what?" Daphne asked, looking at him curiously while her spoon still moved round and round.

Tom took a deep breath. "Never mind. Besides, no matter how good you think I am, I don't even compare to you."

Daphne rolled her eyes. "I'm no better than you are, Tom," she assured him. "We went over this when I first arrived, remember?"

Tom smiled broadly and folded his arms across his chest. "You are, Daphne. I can sense it in you by the way you talk and how thoughtful you are. You know, most people in your place would take advantage of the situation and milk it for all it's worth. But you...you do everything you can to give back. It's not normal."

Daphne smiled and blushed for some reason. "Well, I will be the first to agree I'm not normal, but I think you're wrong about the general world. Most people do want to give back."

Tom laughed lightly again. "You just proved my point once more, Daphne. You naturally think better of people than I do."

Daphne shrugged. "I suppose if you want to think badly of yourself, then you can," she told him, turning her eyes back to the caramel that was starting a rolling boil.

Tom chuckled. For no reason he suddenly felt a stirring feeling for Daphne. Was it just gratitude? "Daphne..." Tom hesitated.

Daphne turned her head to look at him. He inhaled a nervous breath. "You've done more for me than anyone has in a long, long time. I...I don't know; you're just so ..."

Tom had no idea what his expression looked like, but Daphne stopped stirring and just stared at him. A deep rosy color touched her cheeks.

Tom lifted a hand to stroke her hair, but before he could, Daphne flinched and quickly shifted her gaze back to the caramel. *What am I doing anyway?*

Surely this crazy feeling for Daphne that had come over him must be because he'd been so emotional since Pa had died. Then again, Daphne was different somehow. How grateful he was she had not pushed him into disclosing why he wasn't that great of a guy. Tanya wouldn't have done that. Even in the beginning, she would have harped on the issue so hard it would have driven him mad. As a matter of fact, she did.

But Daphne. Daphne was observant and respectful—Ah! He was thinking about Daphne again! *What is wrong with me? Do I have feelings for her?* It seemed nearly impossible, yet there they were, right inside of him. His emotions had never been so whacked and messed up. He would have to get rid of them.

"Okay. Has it boiled long enough?" Daphne asked.

Tom abruptly came out of his reverie. "Oh! Let's check its temperature." Tom pulled out a candy thermometer and stuck it into the boiling liquid. "Yep, it's perfect. Let's pour it on the popcorn now." Daphne brought over the bowl of popcorn, and Tom dumped the caramel into it while Daphne stirred the popcorn around to coat it evenly.

While Tom was snitching and burning his fingers, Daphne was already washing dirty plates. "Oh, no, no. You cooked dinner; I'll do the dishes," Tom offered.

Daphne smiled at him. "I like that rule, but I don't mind helping."

Tom took hold of her shoulders and gently pulled her away from the sink. "You've done enough today, Daphne. I'll finish."

"Okay, if you insist," she agreed with a laugh in her voice. Tom resumed washing silverware as he watched Daphne take a seat in the recliner by the fire. She stretched her legs onto the ottoman and grabbed a notebook sitting on the end table next to it. She did have nice, long legs. *Oh, good night.* Tom sighed and turned toward the sink to do some rinsing, reminding himself he wasn't interested in Daphne.

"What are you drawing now?" Tom called.

"Oh, I'm actually writing. I hope you don't mind I borrowed two of your notebooks. I will pay you back for them."

What is it with her and wanting so much to pay me back for every little thing? "Daphne, it's just a notebook. What are you writing?"

"Um, it's a journal."

Huh? Is she writing about me? Of course, she is. She's probably writing about that bozo move I just made. He decided he would let her be so she could write about how stupid he was.

Once the pans were clean, Tom turned in Daphne's direction once again. "Ready for popcorn? I bet it's cool enough now."

"Absolutely!" Daphne cried, getting up from her chair.

"How about an old western movie to go with it?" Tom suggested.

Daphne looked at him in surprise. "Well, sure. I love westerns."

"Yeah? Okay, then. Let's make a date of it."

Tom swallowed. *What did I just say?* Daphne didn't give him any hint it was out of the ordinary, so he let it go.

Tom turned on the movie. The two of them immediately sat down and began eating the delicious caramel popcorn eagerly. "This stuff is amazing," Daphne announced in between bites.

"I know. Nice job, chef," Tom replied.

Daphne gave him a sideways glance. "It's because of you, not me. We really should make this every night."

"I agree," said Tom. "Tomorrow we'll do it again."

Tom was already excited about it. He was also excited to be here with Daphne. He was losing it. Simply losing it.

The popcorn disappeared quickly, and Tom and Daphne were now quietly watching a gunfight.

"Hmm, this is very romantic," Tom said sarcastically.

Daphne nodded. "Extremely."

"Well, in that case," he declared, and without any prior contemplation, Tom watched his arm lift up and over and around Daphne. It was as if some invisible hand had moved it. His heart was beating with adrenaline and confusion. He had to stop this insanity of his.

Daphne leaned her head against his shoulder: it felt too good to stop, so he didn't.

Chapter 10

About–face

Tom rubbed his barely open eyes and glanced out his bedroom window into the pitch-black morning. Why had he picked such a dark place to live? Tom put his hands behind his head and stared at the blank ceiling. Despite the dark world, Tom was smiling, and his heart was pounding with excitement. He couldn't kid himself any longer. He wanted Daphne. He cared for her. Although the depth of this surprised him, he couldn't deny it. He had to do something about it. He knew he would need to move slowly with Daphne, but he would be patient. Daphne was worth it.

***

"What's all this?" Daphne asked as she entered the kitchen. In front of her, she saw an entire display of scrambled eggs, sausages, toast, dried fruit, and orange juice. Tom had even folded napkins neatly around the forks sitting next to his nicest Corelle.

"Breakfast," Tom said casually. He was wearing a wide grin, and there was an energy about him Daphne couldn't explain.

Daphne eyed him suspiciously. "Let me guess. You make me a gourmet breakfast, and I have to tell you some secret about me. Or is this going to be another truth testing game?"

Tom smiled broadly. "No catch," he said as he placed two tall glasses that were way too fancy for breakfast at the head of their plates. "Although," he continued, turning to give her a wry smile, "I have plenty of secrets I would like to know about you, Daphne." His eyes gleamed at her.

Daphne felt her cheeks redden. Tom was flirting with her! "What has come over you, Tom Multon?"

Tom grinned again and shrugged. "I'm tired of the ordinary things, so I thought I would make today different for us. You know, more exciting."

Daphne put her hands on her hips. "Am I so boring sausage seems exciting by comparison?" she teased.

Tom raised his eyebrows, looking amused. "Oh, no! I would say this sausage is much less spicy than you, Daphne," he said with a wink.

Such a ridiculous line. Why was she blushing again? Daphne quickly smacked him on the shoulder with the back of her hand to hide her embarrassment. "Stop that!"

Tom flinched unnecessarily as he laughed out loud at her reaction. "You're hitting me right before we need to say grace," he complained.

Daphne scowled at him and then casually walked around the breakfast bar to sit in a chair. After she was comfortable, she glanced up at Tom again who was staring at her with subdued amusement and a renewed feeling of another kind.

"Why are you staring at me?" Daphne exclaimed, completely unnerved by this new side of him.

"I'm sorry," Tom muttered as he dropped his eyes to his hands. "I'll say grace," he offered.

Daphne was impressed by how Tom could go from flirting to reverence in a moment. He thanked God for their safety, for their warmth, and for Daphne's goodness and said amen.

"Thank you for that," Daphne said when they lifted their heads. Tom, who had already put an entire sausage into his mouth, turned to give her that teasing look again. He was too polite to talk with his mouth full, so he just winked again.

Daphne's eyes widened. "Stop doing that!" she cried. Tom laughed and then coughed as he nearly gagged on his food. Daphne stabbed her eggs a little forcefully, deciding to ignore him.

"I'm taking you on another adventure after breakfast," Tom said nonchalantly.

"Oh, really? What are we going to do this time? Build a snow cave with the bears?"

Tom looked at Daphne with sudden enthusiasm. "That's a brilliant idea! Will you do that with me, Daphne? Build a snow cave?"

"Are you serious?"

"Yes! Doesn't that sound like fun?"

"It sounds most invigorating," she agreed, matching Tom's broad smile.

"Excellent!" Tom said, his eyes wide with anticipation.

***

"You know, I haven't the first clue how to build a snow cave," Daphne admitted as she and Tom trudged through the snow in the dim light.

"No worries there," Tom boasted. "I was a boy scout. I know everything." He turned to look at Daphne, and she could see, even in the low light, he had winked at her again. She almost smacked him for it but decided she liked being winked at. She grinned in return, grateful her blush wasn't visible under her face mask.

"Why are you carrying that thermos of water, and why am I dragging this ice?" Daphne asked.

"The water is to pour on top of the cave when we finish so it freezes hard. The ice block in our doorway will keep the heat trapped in the cave," Tom explained.

"Ah," said Daphne.

They stopped in a nice open space where Tom set a lantern on the ground. Daphne was surprised to see how much surrounding light it provided.

Daphne began packing and shaping the snow as much as possible, but it was difficult to avoid staring at Tom while he dug deep into the snow with his shovel and heaved up great mounds of it. For a moment, Daphne wished it were summer so she could see him without all of his snow gear and watch his muscles flex and unflex. Tom sensed her eyes on him and stopped for a moment. He stuck his shovel in the ground so it was standing up and rested his forearm on the top. "What are you doing?" he asked pleasantly. "Do you like watching a man sweat while you just stand there?"

"Oh, I'm sorry," Daphne muttered as she continued molding the snow.

"I'm teasing, Daphne," Tom said, grabbing his shovel again. "You're doing a great job."

"Thanks," she mumbled as they both got back to work. Daphne tried extra hard now not to stare at Tom, but she slipped once and found *he* had stopped and was staring at her. He quickly flashed her a grin, stuck his shovel in the snow again, and meandered towards her. "Are you sure you've never built a snow cave before, Daphne?"

Daphne nodded, suddenly feeling nervous Tom had come closer to her than usual.

He wasn't wearing his face mask, and Daphne couldn't figure out why he was grinning. "Looks like you've done it several times," he said softly. He was staring at her eyes again.

Daphne just shook her head. *Why can't I think of anything to say?*

Tom clapped his gloved hands together. "Well, let me help you finish it now that I'm done shoveling."

"You shovel really fast," Daphne noted.

"Yeah?" Tom said, his eyes brilliant. "I suppose I should add it to my résumé. I might get far in life with such a talent."

Daphne smiled under her woolen face mask.

Tom frowned. "I can't see your smile with that thing on your face."

Daphne didn't know what to think of that, but she felt herself blush underneath the wool nonetheless.

"Come on. Let me show you how to make the door," Tom said, grabbing her hand.

Daphne didn't know how long it took them to finish the cave because the time passed quickly. By the end of his instruction, Daphne felt she really could survive in the woods in the middle of winter now if she needed to.

"Look at that!" Tom exclaimed when they had finished pouring water on the top. "Our very own bear cave."

"I like it. Let's go inside."

"Ladies first," Tom said, gesturing with his arm for Daphne to proceed.

Daphne ducked under the narrow doorway and stepped inside the tiny dome. Tom followed and promptly stuck a stick into the snow wall and hung up their lantern. The small space immediately illuminated. Then Tom dragged the shovel inside as well as his hunting rifle and closed up the cave with the ice block.

"I was only a Bear when I lived in one of these things for three weeks," Tom declared, glancing around at the walls.

"A Bear?" Daphne repeated, confused.

Tom grinned. "It's a rank in Cub Scouts."

"Oh, okay." Daphne realized that somehow they were both sitting on the cold ground leaning into each other as they talked.

"I was convinced I could make a snow cave on my own. When I had finished, I was so proud of myself I ran out into the field to tell the other scouts. However, before I could show anyone, my leader came to me and claimed I had built it so well a bear had come inside to live. The bear was so tall he broke the roof.

"Devastated, I ran back to my cave to see that the roof had totally collapsed," Tom paused to chuckle at this, "and then I asked my leader, 'Where's the bear?' He said he was buried under the snow. That night I couldn't sleep because I was terrified the bear would come after me." Tom let out another chuckle.

"Was it really a bear?" Daphne wondered.

Tom stared at Daphne in bewilderment. "What?"

"Was it—" Daphne stopped herself. "Bears hibernate in the winter," she pointed out unnecessarily.

Tom nodded before they both burst into laughter.

"Oh, Daphne," Tom sighed. "That was classic . . . never a dull moment with you." He got a bit more serious as he looked at her again. "Why do you still have on that daft face mask? I want to see your smile." He reached with one hand to remove it, but Daphne slapped it away. Tom looked slightly hurt by this, but mostly confused.

"I will do it," she said mildly, hoping to break the new tension. She slipped the wool off her face quickly. She saw Tom's eyes follow the length of her hair as she shook it out.

Tom spoke softly now. "I never want to invade your personal space, Daphne, but. . .sometimes you're confusing."

"That was my fault, Tom. I'm sorry."

Tom nodded once and looked at the ground.

Daphne took that moment to peer into his handsome face. He was perfect, and the poor man was stuck here with her. The thought of the unfair balance stabbed her with sudden sadness and a deep sense of unwanted exposure. She very nearly put her face mask right back on.

Tom looked up at her then, about to say something, but stopped short. "What's wrong?" he asked, looking concerned.

Daphne shook her head. "Nothing. I'm fine," she said, forcing a smile.

He didn't look convinced but let it go and resumed telling story after story of his scouting days. Daphne found herself resting her chin on her knees as she listened. She was entirely oblivious to the time. She could have been there minutes or hours; it all felt the same. Daphne laughed heartily as Tom told her of some of the pranks the scouts played on each other, and she grimaced in disgust as he shared stories of eating bugs or slipping in horse manure.

"I wonder how long we have been here," he said, looking around at the snow cave. "It's probably time to head back," he said, standing up. "I'll make you some hot cocoa at the cabin. What do you say?" he asked, stretching out a confident hand to Daphne. She grasped it firmly and allowed him to help her to her feet. Afterward, he promptly let go and then bent over to retrieve their face masks. "I'll let you put this on," he said, handing one to Daphne.

"Thank you," she replied, shyly.

Tom cleared his throat and looked away for a moment. Daphne had the feeling he wanted to say something, but he never did. Instead, he casually put his arm around her and led her out of the cave. A trembling sensation leaped up and down her spine.

They had been on their trek no more than five minutes when suddenly Daphne's right leg punched through the snow, lodging it into a deep hole while the other leg was still on top of the snow a couple feet above. She let out a surprised yelp and then laughed at the ridiculous sight. "I'm almost doing the splits!" she cried.

Tom chuckled. "It's a good thing you're flexible. Here, let me help you out of that." Tom gently put his arms around Daphne's waist to lift her out, but the snow under her leg collapsed even deeper.

"Oh!" Daphne cried.

Tom laughed out loud. "Now your splits are undeniable." The snow was now up to Daphne's mid-torso: her left leg was poking out the top just an inch above the ground. Tom grabbed her by the armpits this time and pulled upward. He made a little progress, but not much. "Wow, Daphne, you're really in there," Tom noted. Daphne tried to grasp the ground with her foot, but the snow was so tight around her she couldn't bend her leg enough. Tom yanked and yanked on her armpits, but then he fell into a hole. The two of them laughed at this. Fortunately, Tom was not in so deep he couldn't get out. He tried again to help Daphne. Daphne, however, found herself pushing against the snow floor with her stuck foot. This move only forced her to go even deeper.

Tom let out a reluctant laugh. "I can't believe how stuck you are. I think I'm going to have to go back to the cave and get the shovel."

Daphne let out a sigh. "This is so embarrassing."

Tom grinned. "It's quite the sight," he said, trying to suppress his laughter. "I'll be right back." Off he went, plodding through the snow. He turned around and pointed a teasing finger at her. "Don't move from that spot!" he commanded.

"Ha, ha!" Daphne called back.

Daphne glanced around at the frozen ground and then up at the gigantic pines above her. It sure was a good thing only the birds could see her like this. At that moment, she heard a rustling nearby. She peered harder into the trees and saw there was some sort of animal in her proximity. From this distance, it looked like an enormous weasel. *What is that?* The creature obliged by turning its head and padding its way toward her. Daphne froze in place, and her heart seemed to stop. This creature had a long nose pointing out of his oval face and a round, beefy body with long, pointy fur. Its hairy tail wobbled behind. Its legs were short and attached to big feet with long, thick claws. A wolverine. Daphne forced herself not to scream. She knew these animals lived in this part of the mountain all year round, though Tom had never mentioned it himself. Daphne also knew this creature would have no idea what she was and would have no problem tearing her up completely.

Frantically, she searched the dim, open landscape for any sign of Tom. He was nowhere in sight. "Tom!" she shrieked.

Daphne immediately regretted this, as she undoubtedly had the creature's undivided attention now. It was cautious at first, slowing its steps. Its eyes fixed on Daphne, and Daphne in turn fixed her gaze on it. The wolverine's steps became deliberate, and they were heading right toward her.

"Tom!" Daphne shrieked again, involuntarily. She groped at the snowy ground with her gloved hands and tried to push herself up, to no avail. The wolverine was getting closer. Daphne thrashed and kicked her leg into the air, desperately trying to grip the ground. When she did manage to get a firm plant with her hands, she pushed with all her might in an effort to free herself, but it was no use. This miniature, personal snow trap would not let her budge.

The wolverine was right next to her face now. She could see its ugly black nose had long hairs sticking out of it. Daphne forced herself to be still, but her breathing was still ragged. The furry animal cocked its head and began to sniff Daphne's face. Its nose felt like a little hacky sack being rubbed over her. Daphne was shaking ever so slightly before she felt the creature's breath seep through her face mask.

Daphne's involuntary shrieks bubbled out of her again. However, this time it caused the wolverine to bare its teeth and growl at her. Now Daphne's instinct was to sink even lower. The wolverine had already taken a swipe at her. She could tell she was deeply scratched through her face mask. The nasty animal circled around her, and this time she was able to kick it with her top leg. The wolverine yelped and then growled again and came after her once more with teeth and claws. Daphne covered her face with her arms, but the devilish beast ripped through her coat at her shoulder.

Quite suddenly, a gunshot fired into the air. Daphne and the wolverine screamed, but the animal had fallen to the ground. Daphne stared at it, horrified, as it lay there bleeding and whimpering. Another shot fired, and Daphne shrieked again. She covered her ears and squeezed her eyes shut. When she dared open them again, she saw Tom's face right in front of hers. "Daphne," he panted, grabbing her by the shoulders, "are you okay?"

Daphne nodded frantically. Tom kneeled beside her and put her face in his hands and kissed the top of her head. He gently rested his head against hers. *"Good night*, that was close." Tom let out a shaky sigh, and they both breathed heavily next to each other. For a long moment, they stayed quiet, just breathing, until Tom finally said, "Let's get you out of this hole."

Daphne waited patiently as Tom carefully dug and heaved the snow out from around her. When he finished, Daphne pulled herself up to level ground and rubbed the very sore muscles in her leg. "That position sure does hurt after a while," she said casually.

Tom pulled her up to her feet and hugged her tightly. Daphne hugged him back, and she noticed for the first time how wet her face was under her mask. She didn't know if it was tears or blood, but she decided now she could allow herself to cry softly. Tom caressed her back slowly up and down. Of course, she couldn't feel his hand as his thick glove rubbed against her thick coat, but still she had never felt so good.

Daphne wasn't sure why Tom kept kissing the top of her head or why he kept saying he was sorry over and over, as if somehow it were his fault she had gotten stuck in the snow and a freakish nightmare shaped as a wolverine had come to eat her alive. She wanted to say something about it, but she was too exhausted.

Tom pulled out of their embrace just enough to look her in the eyes. "I saw it going after you. Did it hurt you?" he asked. He placed a hand on her shoulder where her coat was all but gone. He touched it so softly Daphne didn't feel it at all. She rolled her shoulder back to assess any injury.

"I think my shoulder is fine, but it did scratch my face."

Tom looked instantly distressed. "Let me see."

"I just want to go back to the cabin now," Daphne hedged.

Tom nodded, picked up his rifle and shovel in one hand, and put his other arm around her.

"How did you know to bring your rifle?" Daphne asked.

"I always have some kind of gun with me, Daphne," Tom told her, "and thank the Lord for it, too."

Daphne nodded at that while Tom gently coaxed her head to rest against him. She wondered why Tom was being so affectionate. Her tired mind came up with no answers.

Chapter 11

Acne Girl

January 21, 2016
Dear Journal,

    I'm in Tom's woodshop right now. I like watching him work. After the traumatic wolverine experience, we decided to stay indoors for the next couple of days. Tom still goes on his daily hunts, of course. However, he has started going on early hunts and making it back in time for breakfast, so now I rarely have a moment away from him. Not that I mind. He is absolutely perfect. It literally hurts when I think of how much I like him. It seems the more I try not to have feelings for him, the more my heart betrays me. I tried to avoid him almost entirely after the wolverine incident. My face was already repulsive enough without the deep scratch that stretched the length of it. Fortunately, it is almost healed now. He has always found a reason for us to be together, though. He has never looked at me with disgust. I haven't allowed him to be affectionate with me since the accident. I know he doesn't mean it the way I want him to.

    "Journal writing again?" Tom asked.

Daphne looked up from her notebook. "Um, yes. What are you making there?"

"It's a desk," replied Tom.

"May I see it?" asked Daphne as she uncrossed her legs and walked towards the table where Tom was working.

Tom took a step back, allowing Daphne to take a closer look.

Daphne looked at the thick but smooth pine board. "The edges are perfectly round. How do you do that?" she asked Tom, turning around to face him.

Tom shrugged, but his eyes glowed with appreciation.

"This is an incredibly marketable skill you have, Tom. Have you ever considered being a carpenter?" Daphne inquired.

"What? I'm not worthwhile as a hunter?" Tom asked, as he wiped the sawdust from his hands.

"No, that's not what I meant at all," Daphne countered, feeling her cheeks get hot. "I only meant—"

"I'm kidding, Daphne," Tom said with a half-smile. He looked down at his hands. "I have thought about it. I just took this hunting job to get back on my feet again."

Daphne sensed she had hit a sore spot with him, but she didn't know what and didn't dare ask. "Well, you have to be really smart to be an expert hunter from what I hear. My uncle tried to explain to me once about the strategies... " Daphne would have continued, but she noticed Tom was smirking at her. "What?"

Tom chuckled. "You're trying to make me feel better. I'm not smart the way you are, anyhow," he said with a wink.

Daphne felt herself blushing. *Oh, my lands. How does he do that?*

Tom fought back a smile. "You're an art major, I assume?" he asked, throwing a towel over his shoulder.

"No, sports science," Daphne replied.

"Really?" Tom asked, surprised. "What made you choose that over art?"

"Well, athletics really changed me; I'd love to help others go through the same process."

"How did it change you?" Tom asked, giving her a speculative look.

"Well, it gave me some confidence once I discovered I have a knack for persistence," Daphne explained.

"Ah, I see," said Tom, nodding. He got a cunning look on his face. "Did it give you strength?"

"Of course," said Daphne, looking back at him curiously.

"How about an arm wrestle, then?" Tom challenged.

Daphne laughed. "Will that build some confidence in you? To beat a girl in an arm wrestle?"

Tom shrugged. "I just want to see what you're made of," he answered.

Daphne thought for a moment. "How about a leg wrestle?" she countered.

Tom looked at her suspiciously. "Done. Let's do it—but downstairs where carpet is under us."

Daphne was nervous and excited all at once for this little match.

Once they reached the front sitting room, Tom turned around to face her with a brilliant smile. "You sure you can beat me, coach?" he asked with a sly twinkle in his eye.

"Bring it on, cowboy!" Daphne exclaimed with a grin.

Tom lay down on the carpet on his back. "Does my accent bother you?" he asked.

"Of course not," said Daphne. "Actually, I...kind of like it."

Tom curved one side of his mouth up. "Good. Some people don't."

"Like who?" Daphne wondered, sitting down next to him.

Tom shrugged his shoulders against the floor. "Tanya."

"Your ex-fiancée didn't like your accent?" Daphne asked, dismayed.

"Never mind," Tom dismissed. "Let's get this match rolling."

Daphne scooted herself over so her hip was next to Tom's, her feet next to his head. Both of them lifted their inside legs straight up into the air so their ankles crossed. "Okay, on the count of three," said Daphne. "One, two,…three!" Immediately, Tom lost the latch with Daphne's ankle and went somersaulting backwards over his head.

"No way!" Tom exclaimed.

Daphne laughed out loud and clapped her hands.

"We're doing that again," said Tom, crawling back to his place.

"Whatever you say," agreed Daphne, still laughing.

They hooked ankles again. "I'm counting this time," said Tom. Almost on the moment he said three, Daphne had him flipping back on his head again.

Now Daphne was laughing even harder with her shoulders shaking on the carpet floor. She tried to stop once she saw Tom's face was almost as red as his hair, but her chuckles still escaped her.

Tom crawled over to her again so he was sitting close to her face. He had one knee up with his elbow resting on it. "How do you do that? No way those skinny legs of yours can be stronger than mine."

Daphne laughed again. "It's all about thrust and timing," she explained.

Tom sighed, still looking embarrassed. "One more time," he said, raising a finger.

"Okay," Daphne agreed.

This time Tom pushed at just the right instant, and Daphne's leg bent backwards until her ankle was almost on the floor behind her head.

She saw Tom lift his head. "Did I win?" he asked.

"Nope," Daphne called. "You have to flip me."

"But how do I..." Tom's eyes swelled in dismay. "Good *night*, you're flexible!"

Daphne smiled. "That's why you won't flip me," she explained.

Tom frowned and lifted his leg off Daphne's, and they both sat up.

"Are you a gymnast, too?" Tom wondered, his eyes wide.

Daphne shrugged, trying not to look smug. "When I was seven," she said. "What about you? Do you like sports?"

"And now you're saying hunting isn't a sport?"

"No, I—"

"Daphne, I'm kidding," Tom laughed, as he placed a hand on her leg, smiling hugely. Daphne had no choice but to blush like a tomato.

"I played on the hockey team for Brocksville, actually," Tom announced.

"You were on the university team?" Daphne exclaimed, suddenly excited. "Why haven't you told me that before?"

Tom shrugged.

"What year did you graduate?"

Tom grimaced, looking ashamed. "I didn't."

Daphne stared at him in silence.

"I lost my scholarship my junior year, and I quit," he explained sullenly.

"You quit the team, or you quit school?"

"Both."

"Wh-why?" Daphne asked hesitantly.

Tom shrugged again. "Not my thing, I guess."

Daphne raised her eyebrows as if to question him. "Tom, when we played the dice game, you created formulas to figure out every possible scenario, and you did it for fun. How can you say school isn't your thing?"

Tom smiled at that. "Math is the only thing I can do."

Daphne laughed once. "That's the only thing I *can't* do," she confessed.

"Ah-hah! I knew you had a weakness somewhere," said Tom with half a smile and a teasing glint in his eye. "I'm happy to know it." He was resting his elbow on his knee again.

Daphne scooted over to him and crossed her legs. "Are you happy with that decision, Tom?" she asked. "Did you come here to just...get away from all the people?"

Tom laughed once without humor. "No, I actually hate being alone out here," he confided.

"Well, you're not alone now," Daphne noted.

"I know," said Tom with a slowly fading smile. Chills ran down Daphne's spine at Tom's gentle gaze. "I don't know what I would do without you, Daphne."

Daphne just stared back at him. It was times like this she dared to hope Tom had feelings for her. It was the same way she had felt when he had coaxed her to snuggle up to his chest on the couch.

Daphne frowned and shook her head and looked down at the ground. She was sure he cared about her, but not the way she wanted. It was impossible.

"Why are you shaking your head?" Tom asked her.

"Oh, it's nothing." Daphne dismissed the question, waving his concern away.

Tom put one finger under her chin to lift her gaze to his.

"It's not *nothing*. What is it?"

Daphne forced a smile. "Really, Tom."

Tom reached for her hand and put it in his. "Why won't you tell me?"

Slowly, Daphne pulled her hand away and tucked it safely into her lap. She was tired of him playing with her. Maybe he didn't realize what he was doing, but it still wasn't nice.

Tom grimaced and looked away. "Daphne, are you…" he took a deep breath.

"Am I what?" Daphne prodded.

He turned to look at her again. "Are you not happy here with me?"

Daphne raised her eyebrows, surprised at his question. "I,…well, of course, I am, but…"

"But what?"

"I love your company, Tom," she told him, "but the longer I stay here, the more I feel indebted to you."

Tom sighed heavily. "Daphne, how many times do I have to tell you that you're not indebted to me? At all! I want you here, Daphne. I want you here with me."

Daphne felt her cheeks get red as her heart started to sing and ignite hope within her. Almost immediately she felt angry. *No handsome man would want an acne girl. Why is he doing this to me? So a poor, ugly girl like me will fall for his charm? Does he gain some hidden pride in this?*

"What exactly do you mean by that, Tom?" Daphne asked, her voice getting sterner. "If you're so lonely, then anybody would do, right?"

Tom was a little taken aback by her sudden sharpness. "Well, sure, that's how I felt at first, but now that I know you, I…I want it to be you." Tom swallowed hard, looking uncomfortable.

Daphne sighed heavily. Her heart was racing with two very strong, opposite emotions: hope in the truth of his words and anger at his deviousness. She felt his eyes on her as she battled inside herself.

"Daphne, will you please tell me what's wrong?" Tom asked her, shifting uncomfortably in place. " Usually, you're so cheerful and easy going. Did I…say something wrong?"

Daphne lifted her head sharply to look at him. "Yes, you're lying to me."

"What do you mean?" Tom asked, looking shocked. "I have never lied to you."

"You just did," Daphne protested, trying to keep her voice calm. She could feel angry tears threatening to spill over. She blinked rapidly, trying to push them back, but one escaped.

Tom reached up to wipe it away, but Daphne moved her face away, dodging his hand.

"What do you think I lied about?" he asked. "Let's set it straight."

"Every time you put your arm around me or say you want to be with me, you're lying. You know it's sending me the wrong message, but you're doing it anyway. It's so *mean*," Daphne said, but the truth of her words cut her soul.

Daphne didn't look up to meet Tom's eyes, but she could hear in his voice he sounded surprised. Why does he have to be such a good actor?

"Daphne, I might make a mistake like that once, but do you think I would do it over and over again if it didn't mean anything to me?"

"I guess," Daphne sniffed. "Because that is what you have done."

Tom sighed heavily. "I don't believe this. You think I've been playing you? Do you really think I'm that kind of a person?"

Daphne shrugged. "If the shoe fits."

Tom exhaled sharply and stood up, turning away from her with his hands on his hips. "I'm glad to know you think so much of me," he said bitterly.

Daphne stood, too. "Don't make yourself into a martyr, Tom." She rubbed her forehead. "I'm going to bed," she huffed, turning around and heading down the hallway.

"Come on, Daphne!" Tom called to her. "What's the real reason for this?"

Daphne spun around to see Tom standing in the same spot, looking right at her. The pained look on his face sent a pained feeling through her chest. "Why won't you believe me?" he asked, his tone soft.

Daphne felt like crying again, so she bit her lip to stop herself. Tom began walking slowly towards her. Daphne forced her tone to stay steady. "Because guys like girls they are attracted to, Tom. Everyone knows that."

Tom pulled his eyebrows together in confusion. "So?" He lifted his head as if a new thought had just occurred to him. "You think that's not the case with me? Why not, Daphne?" He was still inching towards her.

Daphne sighed heavily. "Are you really going to make me say the words, Tom? I'm not pretty! That's why!" She forced herself to look him in the eye.

He stopped in place and folded his arms across his chest. "Says who?"

Daphne exhaled angrily and tossed her head back to look at the ceiling. "Says everyone, Tom!"

Tom kept his stance but leaned against the wall beside him. "Really? Who said that to you, Daphne?"

Daphne felt completely frazzled and exposed, and more tears kept spilling over, despite all her efforts to keep them in. "I...I don't know. Nobody has really said those exact words, but I...I can just tell, okay?"

Tom didn't take his eyes off her, and it unnerved Daphne to the very core. "You told me two guys have kissed you. Right, Daphne?" Tom asked.

Daphne threw her hands up in the air. "What does that have to do with anything?" she asked, exasperated.

"Were they attracted to you?" Tom asked.

Daphne hesitated a moment.

"You knew they were, right?" Tom pressed.

"Believe it or not, Tom, I might have been rather pretty at one point, but pretending to be attracted to me *now* is so ridiculous and insulting!" Daphne shouted.

Tom shifted in his place a minute, unruffled by Daphne's reaction. "You used to be prettier?" he asked, still staring at her.

Daphne glared at him. "I can't believe you are still making me talk about the most mortifying thing in my life!" she exclaimed, her voice rising with every word. "Yes! I haven't always been a pizza face!"

Tom's head jolted back a bit as his eyes widened, and his whole expression softened. "It's not as bad as you probably think, Daphne," he said gently. "Besides, I like your rosy cheeks."

Daphne was crying openly now. "Ugh! Will you please stop pretending to like me?" She sobbed. "It makes everything so much worse."

Tom gazed at her another moment and then enclosed the space between them with one big step. He wrapped his arms around her, but she swiftly escaped his embrace. "Please stop, Tom," she cried.

Tom put his hands on her shoulders and ducked down a bit to look right into her eyes, but Daphne couldn't bear to look back at him. She struggled to free herself, but Tom held her fast. "I'm not pretending, Daphne," Tom promised. "I couldn't do that."

Daphne continued to cry, but she didn't pull away.

"You're a beautiful person, Daphne," whispered Tom.

Now she could pull away. "Stop it, Tom! Just stop it!" After a forceful release, she ran down the hallway to her bedroom and locked the door behind her.

Chapter *12*

First Impressions

Daphne lay awake in bed, staring at the ceiling. It was morning, and she wanted to get up and make Tom breakfast as a way of saying sorry for her bad behavior last night. She knew it would be unbearably awkward today. She couldn't stop thinking about all the things he had said. None of it made any sense.

She climbed out of bed, making it neatly right away. She stepped into her fuzzy, blue slippers Tom had bought her and made her way to the kitchen. She wanted to make Tom's favorite blueberry pancakes. She stopped short just outside her door when she ran right into the man.

"Excuse me," he said, taking a step back. "Were you headed to the shower?"

"Yes," said Daphne, deciding right then that was really what she wanted to do. "Where were you headed?"

Tom rubbed his neck. "Oh, I was just coming to see if you were awake," he said.

"Oh."

They both just stood there, staring in silence.

"Well, I guess I'll get going then," said Daphne.

"Yeah," said Tom.

Daphne quickly scampered to the bathroom while Tom slowly sauntered behind her.

"Daphne?" Tom called, just as she crossed the threshold.

Daphne stopped and twisted around to look back at Tom.

"I'm sorry if I was insensitive last night."

Daphne gazed back at his solemn expression. "I'm the one who needs to apologize," she confessed. "I shouldn't have yelled at you like that."

Tom gazed at her with another one of his pained looks. "Don't worry about it."

She tried to make out what that look meant, but she had no clue. She nodded and shut the door behind her.

She loved the hot water here. It didn't run cold after five minutes like the water in her dorm. As Daphne was drying off, she was surprised to hear several voices in the front room. They had visitors?

With sudden alarm, Daphne realized she had forgotten to bring her clothes into the bathroom with her. She rubbed her hair as dry as she could and wrapped her towel around her and peeked outside the door and down the hall. She saw a young man talking to Tom. They were both facing the movie room and not looking in her direction. She listened to the other voices in the room but wasn't sure how many of them there were. Six, seven, maybe?

Daphne contemplated which scenario would be more embarrassing: call Tom to have him bring her clothes or to be caught walking out in a towel. At least with the latter option, she had a chance of no one knowing. She decided to brave it and go for it. As quickly and as quietly as possible, Daphne tiptoed down the hallway towards her bedroom. She wanted to peek over her shoulder to see if anyone were watching her from behind, but she didn't want it to slow her down. She reached her bedroom within just a few seconds and swiftly closed the door behind her with her foot. She paused and listened intently to the voices down the hall.

"Um, dude, Tom, is it?" said a male voice.

"Yeah," said Tom.

"I just saw a girl walk down the hall in a towel."

Daphne cringed and felt her face burn. *Why am I always so unlucky?*

"Oh, uh, really?" Tom stammered.

"Is that your girlfriend?" asked the same man.

"Um, I…I don't…no."

"You don't know? Is there more than one girl here?"

"Hold it!" cried another voice. "No secrets now. What's this about girls being here?"

"What?" hollered another. "There's girls here? Where are they, Tom? Bring them out here!"

Daphne was beginning to think this group was all guys. Her heart began to race unevenly. *Why do I always have to be stuck in the most awkward and embarrassing situations?*

"One girl," Tom clarified.

"One's better than none. Where is she?" asked a new voice.

"Is she your girl or not, Tom?" inquired another.

Again, Tom was stammering. "I…um…"

Daphne heard a smacking sound, like someone had just slapped someone on the shoulder. "Come on! Don't try to hide it! Of course she's your girl. Why else would she be here with you?"

"It's not exactly like that," Tom countered.

"Sure it's not," chuckled the first man.

"What's her name?" asked another. "Is she hot?"

"She is," said the first man. "I just saw her walk out in a towel."

"What?" cried about three voices in succession as some loud footsteps stumbled around the room.

"What're you doing?" asked Tom, a bit exasperated. "She's already in her room. Go sit back down."

Daphne was still standing next to the closed door. Her feet seemed to be frozen to that spot.

"Well, go get her!" exclaimed a stranger.

"No," said Tom, defiant. "She'll come out when she wants. That might never happen since she has most likely heard our entire conversation."

"Ah, come on. We haven't said anything."

"Well, you better shut up before you do," Tom warned.

"There you go, man. She's definitely his girl. He is obviously protective of her."

"Aw, snap!" cried a voice Daphne hadn't heard yet. "I get to see girls maybe three times a year, and every time they're always taken."

"You see girls more than that," countered another.

"She's not really mine," offered Tom.

"What do you mean?" asked the first man.

"Well, I...I mean, we haven't really...drat! Y'all better not say anything when she comes out!" Tom exclaimed in a hushed voice.

"Aw, isn't that cute?" said one guy as if he were coddling a baby. "He's still nervous about her."

"Shut up, man!" cried Tom in softer tones. "She's going to hear you!"

"Dude, what's her name?"

"I'm not telling y'all anything," Tom protested.

"We're going to find out sometime anyway, man. Come on. What's her name?"

Tom sighed heavily. "Daphne."

"Hey, Daphne!" the man shouted loudly. "Come out here so we can meet you!"

Daphne felt her breath catch. Now there was no way she could pretend she didn't know anyone was here.

"Seriously?" Tom said, exasperated.

Daphne knew she wanted to eavesdrop no longer. She locked the door and walked to her dresser to find some clothes.

***

Tom was completely mortified by all of this. No way Daphne hadn't heard the loud mouth over there. She probably would never come out now. Tom was actually fine with that. He didn't know what to say to her anyway, let alone with a bunch of strange guys assuming things. He didn't care if they made fun of him, but he didn't want them to make fun of Daphne.

"Okay, come here all of you, or there's no way I'm feeding you," declared Tom, as he crouched down to his knees on the middle of the rug in front of the TV.

"Hey, no breaking promises! You told us there was bacon!"

"Like I said, not unless y'all come here," Tom insisted.

Some of the guys came and knelt next to Tom. "What're we doing, having a group hug?"

"Come on, guys," said one man...Doug, he remembered. He was the largest of the group and seemed to be their leader somehow. "Tom let us in here to give us a break from the wind. Come listen to him."

Reluctantly, the rest of them came to join the others on the carpeted floor. "Why are we doing this?" another asked.

"So Daphne doesn't hear," Tom explained.

"Dude, you really are into her, aren't you?" asked another guy.

"Shut up, Mark," said Doug. "Just let him talk. I'm starving."

Finally, all eyes were on Tom. He took a deep breath. "Daphne is not my girlfriend. I found her lost in the mountains about three weeks ago, and I'm letting her stay here until the weather clears up enough for me to take her back to the city."

"That's a convenient arrangement," smiled Mark, showing his yellow, crooked teeth.

"I'm telling you it's not like that. Daphne's a totally innocent girl, and—"

"How do you know she's innocent?" another asked with a low cackle. Someone else punched him in the shoulder. "Knock it off, dweeb."

Tom gave the wretched one a glare and then did his best to glower at all of them. "If any of you dares say anything inappropriate to her, or even give her a dirty look, I swear I will kick you back into that negative-thirty wind without a shirt," he threatened darkly.

Doug laughed lightly and patted Tom on the shoulder. "Easy there, Tom. We might look like rough mountain men, but—"

"No, actually, you don't."

Doug shook his head and laughed again. "I promise we'll be respectful, or I'll kick us all out myself."

Tom sighed. "All right, then."

Another tall man plopped backwards on the floor. "Can we eat now?"

"Aren't you greedy?" Tom noted. "You know if you guys had found a couple in here and it was the woman feeding you, you would be all smiles and thanks."

The tall man sat up. "And now you know we'll treat the girl that way, so can we please eat?"

Tom sighed and stood up. "Y'all are doing the dishes," he added as he walked over to the kitchen.

"We appreciate it, Tom," called Doug from behind him.

Tom waved his hand at him. "It's cool."

All the guys hovered over the breakfast bar like vultures ready to eat their dead as Tom fried up more eggs and bacon than he'd had in months.

Daphne still hadn't come out of her bedroom. After discovering what was "most mortifying" to her, he figured she probably would stay in her room until the guys left. Maybe it was for the best. He didn't want her to be embarrassed in front of this group.

As Tom tossed the sizzling bacon up and down, he couldn't help but wish the most mortifying thing in *his* life were something as trivial as a red face. He felt a little guilty thinking that since he didn't know what it was like. At least she didn't have huge mistakes in her past, like he did, that would follow her around and taint her life forever. Daphne was totally and completely a good person and could live free and clear from all that shame. Even if Daphne wanted him, and she didn't, he would never deserve her with all of her sweet goodness.

When Tom set out the plates and forks, all the guys wrangled for one as if their life depended on being the first one to stuff his face.

"Hold it!" Tom exclaimed. "We say grace in this cabin."

A few forks stopped shoveling, and others paid no heed. Tom promptly moved their plates away from them. "What the—!" exclaimed the blond guy, his mouth already full to the brim.

"He wants to say a prayer, Seth," muttered the tall guy next to him.

Seth gave him an irritated look, but nonetheless he set his fork down and folded his hands together. Once Tom saw everyone had stopped eating, he said a prayer to thank God for their blessings. The second he finished, the crowd clamored loudly for their plates again.

After the vultures had grabbed their food and were silently eating, Tom dished up some food for Daphne and set it aside.

He knew if he didn't do it now, the boys would clear everything out and she would go without breakfast. He dished up his own plate and leaned against the counter and started eating.

After a few minutes, Tom knew people were getting full because the loud chattering and bantering started up again. Tom was content to eat slowly and let them go at it.

Suddenly, a hush ran through the group. Tom looked up from his plate. Seth, who was sitting at the far end of the bar, was staring down the hallway and, without moving his head, whispered frantically to his friend beside him. "Dude, dude, dude!"

Tom translated that as: *I'm so shocked; I'm at a loss for words.* Then he saw what they were all staring at. Daphne. The sight of her shocked him so much he dropped his plate right onto the floor, scattering eggs and broken Corelle all over. Everyone turned to the sound of the sudden clatter.

"Oh, let me help you with that," offered Daphne, rushing over to him.

"N—no, I got it," stuttered Tom, picking up the Corelle with his fingers.

"Tom, you're going to cut yourself. Let me get a broom," Daphne offered.

"No, I'll get it, Daphne," Tom insisted.

"Hey, you must be Daphne."

Tom looked up to see Doug leaning over the bar with a childish grin on his face.

"Yes, that's right," she said, smiling back at him.

"Why don't you get something to eat? We've saved a spot for you over here by the fire," said Doug.

"Yeah, Daphne. You go ahead," Tom said. "I'll get this."

"Are you sure?" she questioned.

"Yeah, yeah. I made a plate for you. It's right over there." Tom motioned with his head to the counter behind her.

"Oh, thank you," she said, grabbing the plate and walking around the bar to where Doug and some others were sitting. Tom took the opportunity to look at Daphne now that she wasn't aware of his eyes. She was still standing and shaking hands with all the men in the circle. He almost didn't recognize her. She was wearing a dark green dress Tom was certain she had never worn before. It was smooth and shiny and fit around her slender body like a glove with its long sleeves and long skirt that went to the floor. Certainly not her normal breakfast attire, but he didn't mind.

Right now she was standing so Tom could see her profile as she was smiling and talking to Doug. Her long, smooth, brunette hair draped down her back, and some of it also fell down the front. It was so long it almost reached her waist. Daphne usually tied her hair up on top of her head. He didn't mind that look, but this was a pleasant change. From here, her skin looked as creamy and clear as a baby's. Her cheeks glowed with a touch of pink. Was she wearing makeup? He guessed that was the case. She turned so she was facing him. She was shaking hands with someone else now. Tom noticed her eyes popping out like jewels; the green in her dress brought out the green in her eyes. She was wearing black eyelash stuff. Her lips were a darker pink now. With sudden alarm, Tom realized how much he wanted to kiss that dark pink mouth.

"Dude, Tom!" exclaimed one guy at the bar. Reluctantly, Tom peeled his eyes off Daphne to look at the much less pleasant sight in front of him. It was Mark with the crooked teeth. "You've been staring at her for a solid five minutes. Get a grip."

Tom felt his face flush, and he bent down again to clean up his mess.

The group got more and more casual as the morning wore on. Daphne was never without a suitor by her side. The boys were clamoring for her attention now, just as they had been clamoring for bacon at breakfast. Daphne was all smiles and laughs and seemed to be enjoying every minute of it. All Tom could do was sit at the bar and sip his cider in silence.

The guys were certainly flirting, but at least they were behaving themselves as they had promised. Tom realized they were probably doing it so they could be in Daphne's company, rather than to avoid his threat, but he was still happy they were being nice. Of course, the way Daphne looked right now, she could probably get any guy to hang himself by his fingernails if she wanted him to.

Tom blew out a gush of air. *This is just great. Tanya is with Brad Pitt, and now Daphne is into this Doug guy. What does she see in the balding man anyway?* Tom glanced over at them again. Doug was smiling and talking with his hands, using huge gestures, while Daphne had her head thrown back, laughing a full, hearty laugh. Tom loved that sound. Doug must be funny. Maybe that's why she liked him.

When Daphne burst into laughter one more time, Tom couldn't take it anymore. He stood up from his seat.

"Hey, y'all!" Tom shouted.

The noise of the crowd lowered, and every head turned his way. "I promised you all food, and you promised me clean dishes. So go at it."

All the guys moaned in unison, but Daphne smiled. "Come on, boys. Let's go do some dishes."

"No, Daphne. You help all the time. The guys get to do it," Tom protested.

"Aw, Tom, you're just jealous you're not getting time with your girl, so you're going to force us to do the clean-up," said Seth.

"Yep. So, get going," Tom commanded. Daphne bit her lip and blushed deeply.

Doug slapped his legs. "Well, you heard the host," he said, standing up. "Get up, you bums."

"I'll let you guys do it," said Seth with a fake yawn as he put his legs up on the ottoman. "Won't be room for me in there."

"Get up, Seth," demanded Doug, grabbing him by the shoulder and pulling him along with him as he walked.

Seth stumbled to his feet, yanking himself free from Doug's hold. Doug ignored his glare and followed him into the kitchen.

Once all six guys crowded into the kitchen, Tom walked over, his cider still in hand, and sat on the chair next to Daphne. She looked a little uncomfortable but smiled kindly at him.

Tom leaned forward so his elbows rested on his knees. His head turned in Daphne's direction. "Looks like you might be adding six more men to that kissing list of yours before the day is over," Tom teased with a forced smile.

Daphne blushed and looked away.

Tom took another sip of his cider. "You look different this morning, Daphne," he noted.

Daphne glanced back at him. "You don't like the look?" she questioned, raising her eyebrows.

Tom shook his head. "That's not what I said." *She has no clue, does she?* "What made you decide to get all dressed up?"

Daphne shrugged. "It's nice to make a good first impression every once in a while," she said, smoothing out her dress on her lap.

"Well, our P.O. Box is going to be stuffed with flowers and letters from now on, I'm sure," Tom said jokingly.

Daphne laughed lightly, shaking her head. The blush on her face made her look all the more beautiful. "You like to flatter me, Tom."

Tom took another sip of his cider. "So, which one do you like best?" he asked.

Daphne shrugged. "It doesn't matter. I won't see them after today anyway."

"A couple of them may do all they can to change that," Tom pointed out.

Daphne opened her mouth to speak, but Seth beat him to it. "Hey, Tom! Can we watch your TV?" he called out, walking towards them.

Tom looked up at his approach. "Uh, yeah, sure."

Seth held out his hand to Daphne. "Would you like to join us?" he asked.

Daphne smiled warmly. "Of course," she said, taking his hand. Seth gently helped her to her feet.

Tom stood up, too, and stuffed his hands into his pockets, clenching his teeth as he watched the two of them walk hand-in-hand to the couches in the movie room.

Chapter 13

Slap in the Face

Daphne was surprised it was already nighttime when Doug announced they needed to go to bed. The group had to get an early start the next morning.

The day had been so light and fun while the lot of them played board games and watched football and snacked on popcorn. Her stomach still hurt from laughing so hard during a game of charades when Doug pretended to be a silent, bleating goat.

"What time do you figure we have to leave, Doug?" asked Mark.

"About 4 am," replied Doug.

The group groaned loudly in unison.

"We spent the whole day here. How else do you think we'll reach Witchita before sunset tomorrow?"

"How many miles do you have to cross before you head back to town?" Daphne inquired.

Doug was sitting in the large recliner, taking off his shoes. "Just enough to get the right number of animal heads," he said, looking up at her.

Daphne grimaced at the thought of that but tried to smile. Doug grinned back. "When do you head back to school?" he asked.

"I'm not sure," she said, glancing at Tom.

"The roads will probably clear up enough in about a week," Tom offered.

"Well, that sounds like the same time frame when we'll be on the road to head back to the big city. I'd be happy to stop by again and take you," Doug offered, looking up at her expectantly.

Daphne saw Tom cringe and look out the window. Daphne didn't quite know what to do. She didn't think it likely Doug would be able to keep that promise, considering they might have setbacks finding elk. "Are you sure that won't be terribly out of your way, Doug?" Daphne asked.

"Not at all," Doug replied. "The diversion would be small. Well worth it," he added with a smile.

Daphne's heart was racing for some unknown reason. Why was this such a hard decision? Perhaps it was because every person in the room was waiting for her to choose between Doug and Tom.

Daphne turned to Tom again. "Do you have a reason to go to town other than taking me there?" Daphne inquired.

Tom looked a little flustered. "Well, yes," he said. "I have to go to the post office to...well, you know why," he said.

Did she? Oh, right. He needed to mail a check to his family. Daphne deliberated another moment. She glanced back at Tom again. The look on his face made up her mind.

She turned back to Doug. "I've been planning on going back with Tom all along, so I think I'll stick to that plan."

Doug's face fell at her words. "All right then," he said, trying to smile. "We'll miss your company, though."

Daphne smiled back shyly, and Doug turned his attention to taking off his other shoe. Daphne noticed the guys were beginning to roll out their sleeping bags on the floor. "Oh, there are lots of beds in my room," Daphne announced. "I can sleep out here for one night."

"Really?" exclaimed Mark. "I get to sleep in a bed?"

"No way!" called out Doug. "We are not kicking a lady out of her bed. Plenty of space for us on the couches and floor."

"Oh, no, really, Doug. I don't mind," Daphne protested.

"Let him be a gentleman, Daphne, and sleep in your own bed," Tom blurted out.

Daphne looked over to meet Tom's gaze. A fire burned in his eyes Daphne couldn't explain. What was he upset about?

"Okay, well, it was nice to meet you guys," said Daphne warmly. "Have a safe journey tomorrow."

The group waved and mumbled "Goodnight" and "Nice to meet you." With that, Daphne started to make her way down the hallway to her bedroom.

"Hey, wait a minute, Daphne!"

Daphne turned around to see Seth reaching his arms out to her. "You can't say goodbye without a hug!"

Daphne grinned and met him halfway before he embraced her in a huge bear hug. "I'll miss you, you pretty little thing," he said. Daphne pulled out of his hug and smiled up at him. "I'll miss you, too, Seth."

Doug stood up behind them. "Me, too, Daphne?" Before she knew it, she had given all six of the large men a goodbye hug. Some of them even kissed her hand as if she were a princess.

"All right now, goodnight, you guys," she said pleasantly with a wave.

When she passed Tom in the kitchen, she noticed something was still undoubtedly upsetting him. She paused a moment to give him a questioning look. He tried to smile, but it turned into more of a grimace.

"What's wrong?" she mouthed.

Tom just shook his head. She stepped closer to him so he could hear her whisper. "Do you want to talk about it?"

Tom swallowed. "You might not want to hear it, Daphne," he said a bit sourly.

Daphne furrowed her brow in confusion. "Should I have taken Doug up on his offer to take me to town?" she asked.

A look of surprise crossed Tom's face. "No. I'm glad you didn't."

Daphne was surely confused now. Did he get into a scuffle with one of the guys? "Well, I'm here if you want to talk," she declared. "Just don't go pretending you like me again." She meant it as a joke, but Tom didn't think it was funny as she saw his eyes bulge in dismay.

"I'm sorry," muttered Daphne. "I won't bring that up again."

He laughed once without humor. "You know, Daphne, even with your big eyes, you sure are blind." A thick curtness colored his tone.

"What does that mean?" Daphne asked, feeling a little defensive.

Tom shook his head again, pursing his lips tightly together. "I don't want to explain it right now."

It was no use. She wasn't going to be any help to him at the moment. "Goodnight, Tom," she said, leaving them both confused.

Daphne had just changed into her pink nightgown that, once again, came from Tom, when she heard a knock at the door. "Who is it?" Daphne called.

"It's me," came Tom's muffled voice through the door. "May I come in?"

Daphne walked to the door and unlocked it. She cracked it open just enough to make sure it was only Tom. A nightgown wasn't exactly the attire she wanted the others to see her in.

Tom was alone, so she opened the door and motioned for him to come in. She closed the door behind him and then walked back and plopped herself on her rosy bed. Tom stayed a good distance away. She realized the few times Tom had been in her room, he had always done this. It was very gentlemanly of him, and she appreciated it. She felt safe with him.

"Do you think I'm chopped liver?" he asked abruptly.

"What? No, Tom, why—"

"Because that's how you treated me today."

Daphne was completely shocked at this sudden accusation. She moved to hang her legs over the edge of the bed. "I don't understand, Tom. How did I do that?"

Tom's jaw was tight and his cheeks ruddy. "I've done a lot for you, Daphne, and I don't expect payment like you keep suggesting, but I would like to be treated with some regard."

Daphne just stared at Tom, utterly dumbfounded. *What have I done?*

Tom grew more flustered by her silence. He walked briskly to the other side of the room, grabbed the wooden chair from the writing desk and carried it over to Daphne's bed. He sat it down a few feet away from her, and he sat down hard. He leaned his elbows onto his knees, as he often did and looked directly into Daphne's eyes. The intensity of his stare caused Daphne to shrink back in her skin a bit.

"I've given you a place to live for a month now, and those guys out there," he pointed one long arm towards the door, "come waltzing in here for one day, and because of their good looks and good jokes, you give them more attention than you have ever given me, and they haven't done a single thing for you! And I...I try to do so much for you, Daphne!" His anger had lost much of its steam by the time he had finished his statement.

Daphne went through the day in her mind, still not knowing how she could have done things differently.

"Tom, I tried to include you in all the games, but you wouldn't join us."

"That's because you were laughing your head off at baldy out there, and I couldn't stand it!" Tom exclaimed.

"Well, what did you want me to do? Leave our guests to themselves while I cuddled with you in the corner? You know that doesn't mean anything to you anyway!" Now Daphne was feeling a simmering anger too.

Tom's face hardened as he pointed a finger at her. "Don't you dare say that to me again," his said, his voice low. "You don't get to decide what means something to me and what doesn't. Because, frankly, my dear, you don't have a clue."

"Oh, don't I?" Daphne shot back.

"No, Daphne. You don't," he said, his voice hard. "If you did have a clue, then you would know every one of those moments meant everything to me. If you had a clue, then you would realize you are the only person I want to be with. If you had a clue, then you might understand why I am so wretchedly jealous of those stupid guys out there you flirted your heart out with today!" By the time Tom finished with his rampage, he was so exasperated and red in the face he had to take a few deep breaths.

"I've been a lot of things in my life, Daphne, but I have never been fake. The only reason you don't believe me is because you're too insecure about yourself."

Tom's comment felt like a slap in the face. Daphne sensed her heart race even faster with adrenaline, but she couldn't move her mouth to cut in.

Tom continued his charge against her in the same curt tone. "You're so worked up about one little thing that's wrong in your life you refuse to see all the other good things and accept someone who truly cares about you." He was losing steam again as he took another deep breath. "Like I do," he said, his tone uneven.

Daphne had absolutely no words for this. This was unbelievable.

Tom sighed heavily again, sounding frustrated. "I didn't mean to come in here and lose my temper. I'm sorry," he murmured, trying to bring his breathing back to normal. He looked Daphne in the eye again. "I'll leave you alone tonight, but please tell me whether or not you want me sooner rather than later, okay? I can't bear this much longer."

Daphne stared at Tom, completely speechless.

Tom swallowed hard and rubbed his hands together slowly, not meeting Daphne's eyes. "I know you deserve someone better than me, but...just tell me how you feel soon, please."

Daphne's heart was beating so furiously inside her chest she was sure it would burst at any moment. Tom looked up at her again. "Can you give me a nod or something?" he asked.

Daphne nodded.

Tom ran a hand through his hair, and Daphne found herself following the motion with her eyes. Tom rested his gaze on her face again. He shifted as if he were going to get up but then stopped again to stare at Daphne a little longer. "You really did look gorgeous today, Daphne," he said softly.

Daphne felt her cheeks burn as Tom got up from his chair and returned it to its proper place at the writing desk. She couldn't look at him as he left the room without another word.

Chapter 14

Rude Awakening

Daphne was sitting on her bed reading a fantasy book, trying to keep her mind off Tom. It was too much for her thoughts to handle at the moment. All was quiet in the front room, so Daphne figured everyone must be close to sleep. She slipped on her slippers and tiptoed to the bathroom, bringing her facial cleanser—that Tom had bought, of course—along with her. She washed and rinsed her face twice so when she dried it, she wouldn't leave behind a residue of makeup. As she opened up the door, she was surprised to see a figure standing just outside. It was Mark, the guest with the crooked teeth. He blinked in the light of the bathroom for a second before he saw Daphne.

"Hey…whoa!" he exclaimed. "You look like a different person."

"Excuse me, Mark," Daphne said, feigning indifference to his statement.

"It's a good thing you wear makeup in the day, Daphne," he snickered.

Daphne scooted around him and out the threshold.

"Hey, Daphne," greeted another voice. It was Seth this time.

"Look at this!" cried Mark as he flipped on the hallway light. Daphne blinked in the brightness. Then she saw the look on Seth's face. He looked surprised and a little appalled.

"Your beauty queen has a face full of zits!" Mark taunted.

Seth looked a little embarrassed at Mark's comment. "So what, Mark? Get out of my way so I can pee."

Daphne was too mortified to say anything, so she spun around and scurried back into her bedroom, closing the door behind her. Instantly, she found she was out of breath.

She heard Tom's bedroom door open, but she was too frazzled to concentrate on what he was saying. He sounded angry.

Daphne walked slowly to her bed as Mark's loud, menacing voice pierced her ears. "Ah, give me a break! I just find it funny everybody was all over her today when really she..."

"Shut your face!" Tom shouted. "Just shut up!"

It was Doug's voice she heard next. "What's going on? Doesn't anybody want to sleep tonight?"

Three, maybe four of them were all talking at once. Daphne couldn't make out what anybody was saying, nor did she want to anymore.

She lay down on top of her bed and tried to breathe without letting the tears come. That effort didn't last. Before long, she was shaking with sobs as the yelling in the hallway continued.

"You can't kick us all out because of one idiot!" Seth shouted.

"Oh, yes, I can!" Tom hollered back. "I don't owe you anything!"

"That's not what you said," Doug argued authoritatively. "You never said it would be all of us."

A slight pause occurred in the dispute, and then Tom spoke. "Fine. Everybody BUT Mark can stay. He's the one who broke his promise."

Mark screamed a stream of profanities so loud Daphne had to cover her ears. Everybody was talking all at once again. Daphne promptly stood up and marched her way to the door and opened it abruptly. All heads turned sharply in her direction. Daphne was surprised to see all the men crowded into the hallway. She forced herself to speak in a composed manner. "Don't make him leave, Tom. He might die out there alone."

"That's fine with me," growled Tom, his face enraged. Mark then took one giant swing at Tom, but Tom pushed him over to the side before Mark's fist reached his face. Mark scrambled to his feet to lunge at Tom again, but Doug was behind him and held him fast.

"Get a hold of yourself, man!" Doug spit sternly, "or your job is going to be at risk, too." He glanced up at Daphne as Mark futilely tried to squirm free. He looked surprised and abhorred, just like Seth had. When he saw Daphne staring back at him, he quickly smoothed out his expression. Resentment seized her. *How dare he flirt with me all day today and then give me a look like that?*

Daphne turned her gaze back to Tom. "Tom, please don't kick anyone out."

Tom had his hands on his hips and was breathing heavily. He glanced back at her with so many emotions on his face Daphne couldn't pinpoint a single one of them. "Fine," he finally said. "If that's what you want."

Daphne nodded and shut the door again.

"Ah, isn't that sweet?" Daphne heard Mark say. "He'll do anything for his girl."

"Shut up before I change my mind!" Tom yelled at him.

Daphne closed her eyes and inhaled deeply. She hated, simply hated, that Tom was being mocked because of her. She walked to her bed, completely incapable of stopping the coming sobs. She was grateful, at least, she didn't make a sound.

The boys took an eternity to quiet down, but eventually they did. Now the cabin was completely silent besides the spontaneous popping and crackling of the subtle fire in Daphne's bedroom. She rolled onto her side so she could glance up and out of the window to see the shining moon streaming through the sky and down to her pillow. She had to get out of here. She couldn't bear it another minute.

Her bedroom door clicked open behind her and then closed again. She wanted to roll over to see who was invading her privacy, but she found she couldn't move. Now someone was climbing onto the bed, scooting his body next to hers, and wrapping his arms around her. She didn't see his face, but she knew it was Tom. This only caused her to cry more. Tom said nothing as he kissed her hair over and over again and gently stroked her shoulder all the way down to her fingertips and then up again. He did this over and over as Daphne continued to weep silently. He didn't speak, and she didn't want him to. She was just glad he had come.

Chapter 15

Blue in the Face

Daphne awoke in the morning feeling like she had just been buried in wet cement. She jumped in place when she saw Tom lying sound asleep next to her. They were both still on top of her comforter, and Tom was still in his t-shirt and jeans from the day before. Daphne glanced over his bulging biceps under his short sleeves as she recalled how last night Tom was able to push a plunging Mark, who was bigger than he, over to the side with seemingly little effort. Slowly, Daphne sat up and got to her feet, trying not to move the bed too much so as not to wake Tom. She put on the fuzzy slippers she was growing to love and shuffled her way out the door and to the kitchen. She flicked on a dim lamp at first to see if the men had left. They had. The only lingering sign they had been here were the indents their sleeping bodies had made in the long carpet. She sighed with relief. Quickly, Daphne mixed up some flour and butter and frozen blueberries, poured them into some muffin holders, and put them into the oven to bake while she took a quick shower. When she got out, she could already smell the fresh muffins. Moving as fast as she could, she slipped on a sparkly blue sweater and black jeans.

Daphne got to the kitchen just in time to get to the muffins before the timer went off. She pulled them out of the oven and set them on top of the stove. She admired the lovely golden tint on each of them. "Perfect," she said out loud. She scurried back to the bathroom to put on her makeup. After last night, it was just too humiliating to go without it...even if she were around Tom.

She didn't want to risk waking Tom up with a hair dryer, so she brushed her hair straight and let it hang to dry on its own.

When she came back into the kitchen, she was surprised to see Tom standing by the stove, frying some eggs. He glanced up at her and smiled. "Good morning."

"Good morning," she returned, putting her hands in her back pockets. "I didn't hear you get up. I wanted to make you breakfast."

"You did," said Tom. "Those muffins look amazing. I loved waking up to the smell of them. It reminded me of home," he said, flipping an egg.

"Is that a good thing?"

Tom glanced up at her and smiled. "Absolutely."

Daphne stared at Tom as she thought of his angry words last night. Everything he had said was true, but it still cut her to the quick.

Tom glanced up at her once. He placed the spatula in the pan and turned to face her. "What's wrong?" he asked softly.

Daphne wanted to speak, but her emotions were coming to the surface again. She took a deep breath to keep her tears from spilling. Tom walked slowly and stopped right in front of her. Although he didn't touch her, Daphne found she wanted him to.

"Daphne," he said softly, meeting her eyes.

"You've done so much for me, Tom, and I don't know what else to do to show you I'm grateful."

Tom continued his gentle stare. "How about a hug?" he whispered.

Daphne wrapped her arms around him, and Tom embraced her tightly, but tenderly. "Daphne, I was wrong to accuse you last night. You've always been grateful, which is one reason I...I love you."

Daphne froze at his words.

Tom began slowly to caress her back. "Please, believe me, Daphne. I love you so much." He was whispering now.

Daphne squeezed him more tightly but was at a loss for words.

"The only reason I said you weren't treating me well is because I was so jealous of those daft guys who flirt better than I do."

"You don't have to be jealous, Tom. I don't want any of them. I want you. Only you."

Tom pulled out of the embrace just enough to look Daphne in the eye. "You do? Do you really, Daphne?" he asked with a pleading, yet hopeful expression.

Daphne nodded as a tear streamed down her face. "I have for a long time," she whispered. Tom's eyes swelled and without another moment's delay, Daphne's face was in his hands with Tom's lips pressed against hers. They were soft and warm and hungry and tender and inviting. After a short, passionate moment, he stopped and rested his head against hers. "Thank you for believing me, Daphne," he breathed.

***

Daphne and Tom were sitting on the sofa. Tom had one arm around Daphne, and his other hand was playing with her fingers. Completely delighted with this, Daphne snuggled into his shoulder.

Tom hugged her closely to him. "That was a terrible movie," he announced. "We should celebrate now that it's over," he murmured and leaned in to kiss her on the lips.

Daphne kissed him back for a moment. "I can't believe I'll be going back to real life in a week. I feel like I've known you forever," she murmured.

Tom gazed at her in a way that was beginning to feel familiar. "I agree," he said as he resumed playing with her fingers.

"I can't wait to get back to the city so I can start taking my antibiotics again," Daphne declared.

"Antibiotics for what?"

"For my rosacea."

"Ah," said Tom. "Will that make your rosy cheeks go away?"

"Somewhat."

"That's a shame," Tom said, staring at her with probing eyes and a slight grin.

Daphne blushed all the more and looked down at their hands. "Would you be able to spare an extra day to come visit my dorm room when you take me to the city?" she wondered, looking back up at him.

Tom raised his eyebrows. "Of course. Will you be able to spare a day and meet my family?"

Daphne's heart skipped a beat. "Yes, I can, but your entire little town will hear about it, I'm sure."

One side of Tom's mouth curved up a bit. "No doubt about that."

"I'll wear makeup in public so you won't have to be ashamed of me."

Tom threw his head back to look at the ceiling. "Oh, Daphne! If only I could tell you how striking you are."

Daphne was glad Tom was looking at the ceiling at that moment as she could feel her blush was worse than ever.

"And besides," he declared, looking back at her, "I loved you before I ever saw you with makeup or a fancy dress on."

"So you won't be ashamed of me?" Daphne asked hopefully.

Tom frowned with deep disappointment on his face. Almost immediately another thought occurred to him, and he grimaced hard and turned his head to look away.

Daphne's heart sank, and she slid her hand out of Tom's and stared blankly at the rolling credits of the movie.

"Hey! I need that back," Tom complained as he quickly grabbed her hand and put it back in his.

"You *will* be ashamed," Daphne accused. "I can see it on your face."

Tom looked surprised and confused for a moment but soon understood. He shook his head swiftly. "No, not at all, Daphne. That's not what I was thinking of."

"What else could it be?" she challenged.

Tom sighed heavily, suddenly looking very uncomfortable.

Daphne was uncomfortable, too, so she grabbed a handful of leftover popcorn sitting on the coffee table in front of them. She chewed and watched Tom as she patiently waited for an answer.

Tom sighed hesitantly. "You might be ashamed of *me*, Daphne—eventually."

Daphne rolled her eyes. "That's the most ridiculous thing I have ever heard," she argued, grabbing another handful of popcorn and tossing it into her mouth.

Tom replied firmly. "Don't roll your eyes at me. And no it isn't. I haven't told you a lot. I'm not as good a person as you think I am."

Daphne couldn't help but roll her eyes again. "And what have you done that's so awful, Tom Multon?" she pressed, stuffing her mouth once more.

Tom glanced up at her with uncertainty in his eyes. He let out a big, slow gush of air as if to calm himself. "I guess I do need to tell you before we get married."

Abruptly, Daphne gasped, causing the popcorn she was chewing to block her airflow completely. She tried to cough and breathe at the same time, but neither was working. Tom was slapping her on the back, but the force of it seemed only to make it worse. The room around her was getting blurry, and the air that should have been escaping her throat exploded inside her head. She stood up and pressed her palms to her temples, expecting to blackout any moment.

She felt an incredible force under her sternum—like someone was punching her from the inside out. The lodged kernels ripped their way through her throat and mouth, flying across the room and landing all over the floor. Now Daphne stood in place, coughing and hacking for a good minute or two. Tom was back to slapping her on the back. He was saying something too, but Daphne couldn't understand what it was. Finally, Daphne stopped coughing and could focus on breathing. Tom helped her sit back down on the sofa, and he sat down next to her. He had his hand on her upper back, trying to look her in the eye. "Are you okay now?" he asked.

Daphne nodded, still breathing heavily.

Tom rubbed his hand smoothly back and forth over her shoulders. "Good *night*, that scared me to death!" he cried in hushed tones.

Daphne put her elbows on her knees and her head in her hands. "I thought I was going to keel over right there and then."

"Me, too," Tom breathed, still rubbing her back.

As Daphne leaned over farther, she felt a piercing pain in her side. "Ah!" she exclaimed abruptly, jolting back and grabbing her side.

Tom glanced down to where Daphne's hand was. "Are you all right? Did I hurt you?"

Daphne cringed as she rubbed her sore spot. "Yes, but it's better than being dead, so thank you," she muttered.

Tom exhaled deeply. "I'm so sorry."

Daphne tilted her head slightly, giving Tom a disapproving look. "Don't apologize. Thank you," she said solemnly.

Tom gazed back at her and nodded slightly.

"I guess I won't mention marriage again while you're eating," Tom decided.

Daphne turned her head sharply, and the two just stared at each other with unfathomable, questioning looks.

Chapter 16

Familiar Strangers

"We've got to get you to a doctor, Daphne," urged Tom. "I can't bear to see you like this anymore."

Daphne lay on her back on the couch with her head propped up on the couch's arm. "I'll be fine," she whimpered.

"You can hardly breathe. That's not fine," Tom countered, as he came to kneel beside her, taking her hand.

Daphne weakly squeezed his hand in return. "You said the roads would be clear on Friday. I can make it until then."

"I said it would be safest to go then, but we could probably leave today and be okay. You're not going to get better here, and I can't do anything to help you."

Daphne took a shallow breath. "I had the time of my life on that snowmobile of yours, now the thought of getting on one makes me hurt even more."

Tom sighed and bowed his head into her hands. "I can't believe I did this to you," he groaned. "I cannot tell you how sorry I am."

"Would you stop apologizing for saving my life," Daphne chastised weakly.

Tom lifted his head. "I wish I could have done it without hurting you."

"Well, living hurts sometimes," Daphne claimed matter-of-factly.

"You got that right," Tom muttered, standing up. "I'm going to go pack our things."

"I'm sorry I can't help you."

Tom rubbed a finger underneath her chin. "I know, sweetheart."

Daphne half-smiled. It was awful being an invalid and having to watch Tom lug everything out of the cabin alone. She sat up enough so she could peer out at him through the glass window and watch him carefully pack the large trunk of the snowmobile. She was beyond disappointed their last couple of days together had to be spent with her moving around as if she were ninety years old. Poor Tom had to do everything for her. He did it willingly and without a single sign of annoyance or impatience. Daphne admitted to herself he would be a very good companion. Tom would certainly be easy to love. Love. If Daphne had any idea what that was, she thought it might be something similar to Tom. No matter what he said he was or how he used to be, Daphne was absolutely positive Tom had turned out to be the most unselfish person she would ever meet.

The next hour was a blur, but soon enough Daphne was sitting on a snowmobile, absolutely dreading the physical pain that was sure to come from this ride.

"You sit in the front," Tom insisted as he scooted in behind her. "You will get bounced around less up there."

Daphne nodded. Tom had long arms, so it was no problem for him to reach the throttle from behind her. "Just let me know if I need to slow down, okay? No hurry."

"Okay," agreed Daphne as Tom revved the engine.

This ride was certainly the smoothest ride she had been on with Tom. She was very aware of his effort to avoid jumps and bumps and sharp turns. It still didn't stop Daphne from being completely without breath, though, as the constant vibration of the snowmobile jolted her sore and broken body. Her tears froze to her cheeks underneath her face mask as they moved farther and farther out of the mountains.

Even though Tom only stopped twice to give Daphne a break from the ride, it still took a good four hours to arrive at a main highway. Fortunately, the nearest hospital was only two miles south, and Tom promptly took the shortest route.

"How are you?" Tom asked when he leaped off his parked snowmobile.

Daphne just moaned softly. Tom kissed her nose through her face mask and gently gave her a loose hug. "You made it. We're here."

Daphne nodded in agreement as Tom gently helped her stand up. "Would it hurt less if I carried you?" he asked.

Daphne shook her head emphatically.

As they entered the building, Tom didn't hesitate to ask for a wheelchair. Before long, he was pushing her behind a nurse. The hospital was pretty ordinary looking except for the thick, narrow, red carpet that ran down the middle of the hallway. Daphne's vision went blurry as she watched it roll beneath her, so she leaned her head back and closed her eyes.

"Hey, Tom!" someone called.

Daphne opened her eyes to see who had spoken, but the person was behind her. Tom stopped pushing her chair.

"Oh, hey, Mike. How are you? Long time, no see."

"Yeah, I'll say," Mike agreed. "Hey, sorry to hear about your dad. I'm sorry I didn't make it to the funeral."

"Oh, uh, it's okay, man. It's fine."

"So, you have an injured friend?" Mike questioned as he walked around to the front of Daphne's chair. He was kind of a big man, tall and a little bit wide. Even though Daphne had put makeup on this morning, she was glad she still had her face mask on. Certainly the snow and wind would have washed it all off by now.

"This is Daphne," Tom introduced her.

Daphne gave a slight wave.

"Hi, Daphne," Mike said with a smile. "Are you okay?"

"I'm perfect," Daphne said sarcastically. "I just like to come to hospitals for fun."

Mike chuckled at that. "So, what—"

"Are you ready, sir?" the nurse asked impatiently.

"Oh, yes. I'm sorry." Tom began pushing the wheelchair again.

Mike started walking alongside Tom, and Daphne heard him whisper. "Is she your new girlfriend?"

Daphne felt Tom shrug behind her. Mike let out a low chuckle. "Good luck with that, man," he said, giving Tom a slug on the shoulder. "See ya 'round."

"See ya," said Tom.

***

Daphne and Tom sat in a cold, stale clinic room, waiting to see the results of Daphne's X-rays. She was sitting on the paper spread across the hospital bed, dangling her feet over the edge. How glad she was to have some feeling finally back in her toes and nose.

"I'm beginning to feel a little less numb," Tom announced. He was sitting on a chair at the foot of the hospital bed, looking up at her.

Daphne grinned. "That's exactly what I was thinking."

Tom smiled slowly. "Did your ribs ever get numb out in the cold?"

Daphne shook her head. "Nope. They, apparently, are too stubborn for that."

Tom gazed up at her sympathetically. "I'm so sorry."

Daphne gave him a tired look. "What can I do to get you to quit saying that?"

Tom sighed. "I don't know. I don't think I'll feel better until you do."

Suddenly, their conversation was interrupted by a knock on the door. "Tom, are you in there?"

"Is that you, Mike?" Tom called.

The door latch clicked open, and Daphne turned her head the opposite way and stared at a poster that explained symptoms of the flu. She didn't feel good enough to make friendly conversation.

"What are you doing here?" Tom inquired.

"I was just wondering if you and Daphne wanted to meet up with us after you are done here," said Mike.

"Us?" Tom wondered.

"Me and—"

"Excuse me, sir. This is not your room," said a man. Daphne recognized it as Dr. Gray who had spoken with them when they first came in.

"Oh, I...okay," said Mike. Daphne heard footsteps retreating down the hall. The doctor stepped in and closed the door.

"Is that pain medication working yet?" asked Dr. Gray.

Daphne turned to look at him. "Not yet."

"It won't be much longer. Well," the doctor said, holding up some X-rays to the wall so the light hit them just right, "as you can see right here and here, you have two broken ribs."

Tom exhaled sharply and shook his head. Daphne, however, was not surprised. Her body had been telling her this ever since the moment she spit out that dreadful piece of popcorn.

"It looks like one break happened more recently than the other."

Tom and Daphne looked at each other, confused.

"What kind of activity have you done since your Heimlich episode?" asked Dr. Gray.

"Nothing but ride a snowmobile," answered Daphne.

The doctor lifted his head as if discovering something new. "You probably broke the second one on the ride."

"I tried to drive slowly and carefully," Tom said, baffled.

"I'm sure you did," said the doctor, "but after one broken rib, it's easy to break another if you do more than, well, nothing."

Tom was getting paler by the moment. "There was no other way to get her here," he said softly.

Dr. Gray placed his hand on Tom's shoulder for a brief moment. "You did the right thing." He turned to face Daphne. "I am going to send you home with a spirometer. It measures your lung capacity so you can see the improvement as your ribs heal. It's important to take your medicine every four hours; otherwise, it might be too painful to practice your deep breathing."

Daphne nodded. "Thank you, doctor."

"If you can get someone to drive you somewhere, rather than ride on a snowmobile, I would strongly recommend it," the doctor said.

Tom pursed his lips and nodded.

***

Tom was once again pushing Daphne in the wheelchair down the hall. "I'll get a hotel room for you tonight. Maybe I can find Mike to see if we can catch a ride with him."

"I don't want to put anybody out, Tom," Daphne said, "including you."

Tom sighed. "You can't break another rib, Daphne."

Daphne sighed, too. "Hey, that breath didn't hurt," she said, excitedly.

"That's good, but you still need to take it easy," said Tom, spinning her chair around slowly so it was facing him. He knelt down in front of her. "Is it okay if we meet up with Mike?"

"Do you think he is waiting for us?" Daphne questioned.

Tom nodded. "Knowing Mike, probably. Let's go look in the waiting room."

"I'm a mess, Tom."

"Nobody will care, Daphne. They understand you've been in the hospital."

"I know. I just don't want to embarrass you in front of your friends."

"I don't..." And then, he stopped himself. *Think of what she needs*, Pa would tell him. "How about I go get your bag, and then I'll look for Mike while you clean up a bit?"

"Is that okay?" Daphne asked, raising her eyebrows.

"Of course," Tom said. "If that's what you want."

Daphne nodded. "I would really appreciate it."

Tom smiled. "Be right back."

After Tom had retrieved Daphne's bag from the snowmobile and picked up Daphne's prescriptions, he made his way to the waiting room.

Yep, there was Mike, just as he had expected. Once Mike got something into his head, he never stopped.

"Hey, Mike," greeted Tom, sitting on the large sofa-like chair across from him.

"Oh, hey, man! I'm glad you came looking for us. We were just about to leave. This is Brad," he said, pointing to his friend sitting on the couch next to him.

"Hey, what's up?" muttered Brad.

"Hey," Tom said with a brief wave. Looking at Mike and Brad side by side, Brad looked like a toothpick. Tom might even classify him as a surfer boy with his shaggy blond hair barely out of his eyes.

"Where's your girl?" asked Mike.

"She's changing," Tom responded. "Look I—"

"Oh, so you do admit she's your girl now?" Mike asked with a grin.

Tom shook his head. "She's...uh...I don't know."

Mike and Brad both laughed together.

"He's still nervous about her. This will be fun to see," laughed Brad.

Tom sighed and leaned back in his chair, thrumming his fingers on either side of the armrests.

"Is she different than Tanya?" asked Mike.

"Yes," Tom said without hesitation.

"How so?" Mike cocked his head to the side, looking curious.

"Well, she's nice, and she has a brain," answered Tom matter-of-factly.

Mike and Brad both laughed out loud again.

"What's her name?"

"Daphne."

"Oh, really?" said Brad, leaning back and putting his ankle up on his knee. "I dated a Daphne once. What's her last name?"

"Zollinger," Tom answered.

Brad's face froze in a look of surprise. "No way! That's her!"

Mike let out a high cackle. "Sweet!" he exclaimed, rubbing his palms together quickly. "This will be awesome watching the two of you squirm over her."

Tom tilted his head back to look at the ceiling. "And just when I thought things wouldn't be awkward."

"Ah, don't worry about it, Tom," Brad said. "It was a long time ago."

"How long ago?" Tom wondered.

"Oh, we were sixteen, so five years ago maybe?" Brad said.

"Is she hot?" asked Mike. "I only saw her with all of her snow stuff on."

"Oh, yeah," said Brad. "She's—"

"Shut up," Tom said abruptly, trying to sound nonchalant. "I don't want to hear y'all talk about her."

The guys laughed again, and Brad clapped his hands together. "He's into her."

Tom cleared his throat and decided to change the subject. "I need a favor, Mike," he announced.

Mike let out another burned-out laugh. "Oh, yeah? Already?"

Tom smirked.

"I'm just kiddin'," Mike chuckled. "I'm sure I owe ya one, anyway. What's up?"

"Daphne and I need a ride to a Holiday Inn or something."

"Ooooohh!" Mike and Brad exclaimed together and laughed some more.

Tom rolled his eyes and his head all at once. He was so glad Daphne wasn't here for this. "Not for that reason, you idiots!"

"Then, what reason would it be?" asked Mike with a laugh in his voice.

"The doctor told her not to ride on a snowmobile, and that's all I have. We won't be sleeping in the same room."

"Seriously?" Mike asked.

"Daphne's a good girl," said Brad, moving just his eyes to look at Mike.

"Ah," said Mike. He turned to Tom. "Are you that good?" he asked, with a teasing look on his face and cocking his head to the side again.

"Shut up," Tom muttered again. "Now can you give us a ride or not?"

"I already said yes, man. Do you need a ride to Brocksville in the morning?"

Tom raised his eyebrows. "Yeah. Are y'all still going to be around?"

Mike and Brad looked at each other and nodded. Tom guessed that was all he wanted to know. "Well, awesome. Thank you," said Tom.

Mike nodded once. "Sure, man. It would be good to catch up more."

"Well, actually, on the way to Brocksville, it might just be Daphne," Tom clarified.

Mike furrowed his brow. "Why? Where are you going?"

"I need to get back to Little Pine."

"What for?" Mike asked, still confused.

"That's where I live. I have a job there," Tom explained.

"What's the job?" Mike asked.

"I'm a hunter," said Tom flatly.

"You get paid to do that?" Mike questioned, raising his eyebrows.

Tom nodded but didn't feel like giving any more of an explanation.

"Okay, well, that's pretty sweet. Right on."

Tom nodded. "Thanks. I'm going to look for Daphne now," he declared, standing up.

"I'm right here," said Daphne from behind him.

Tom turned around to see Daphne walking slowly towards them. "Hey!" he cried, walking around his chair to meet her half way. "Why are you walking? I was just about to go get your wheelchair."

"Oh, I think I'm okay but thank you," she said as Tom grabbed both her hands. She looked just a little pale, but she looked good. She was wearing that blue, sparkly sweater again with her hair bundled neatly on her head.

"Did Mike say it was okay to give us a ride?" she whispered.

"Yes," Tom whispered back. "Are you sure you're okay?"

She opened her mouth to speak, but Brad beat her to it.

"Hey, Daphne," he said in a low voice. He was now standing beside Tom.

Daphne turned to look at him in surprise. "Brad?" she exclaimed in surprise.

"That's me," Brad smiled, opening his arms wide.

Daphne's eyes opened even wider as Brad stepped in to give her a hug.

"Whoa!" cried Tom, pushing him back with one hand on Brad's chest.

Brad shot him a confused and annoyed look.

"She has two broken ribs," Tom explained.

"Oh!" Brad cried in surprise, looking at Tom and then Daphne. "Well, then, easy now," he said, taking a slow step towards Daphne and carefully wrapping his arms around her. Daphne returned the hug with the same weak gesture.

"It's great to see you again," Daphne said, pulling out of the hug.

"You, too, Daphne," Brad grinned, showing all his teeth. "You, too."

Now Mike stood up from his seat. "It's good to see you're feeling a little better now, Daphne," he said as he walked over to where they were all standing and reached out his hand. Daphne extended her own to give him a feeble handshake.

"I am, thank you."

"You look a lot different, though. Last time I saw you, you were like a little snowy puppy," Mike teased childishly.

Daphne smiled one of those glowing, brilliant smiles. *Oh, no. Do I really have to suffer through another flirting session?*

Why would she do that to me now? Before he could complain to himself much longer, Daphne had taken his hand in hers, which pleased him tremendously. He noticed the other two both took a step back and put on polite smiles.

"Tom, here, has told us all about you," Mike claimed.

"Oh, he has, has he?" said Daphne, eyeing Tom with suspicion.

Tom threw Mike a disparaging look but said nothing. Mike just grinned in return.

"How did you break your ribs, Daphne?" asked Brad.

Daphne continued to look right at Tom. "Um—"

"I did it," Tom confessed. He glanced at the other two to see their shocked faces. Daphne also looked a little surprised.

Brad was shaking his shaggy head. "Uh, why—?"

"Daphne was choking, so I gave her the Heimlich," Tom explained. "But...a little too hard, obviously."

"Ouch," Mike said, looking pained.

"Didn't all those sports toughen you up any, Daphne?" asked Brad with a teasing smile.

Daphne smiled back a little shyly. "Guess not."

"Well, let's get something to eat, shall we?" suggested Mike.

"Wait, I have to pick up my prescriptions," said Daphne.

"I already got them for you. I put them in your bag," Tom declared as he lifted it up on his shoulder.

Daphne hesitated slightly. "But I need two."

Tom smiled knowingly. "I got them both."

"Oh...thanks. I'll pay you back for them."

Tom smiled and shook his head. "It's on me, Daphne."

"Ah, see!" cried Brad, slapping Tom on the back. "Good old-fashioned chivalry. Now come on, love birds. Let's go eat."

***

Daphne was quiet through most of dinner. The guys were still talking about cars, which Daphne knew nothing about. She didn't mind since she was starving, and her glazed chicken was delicious. She almost felt normal again. The wrenching pain in her side had turned into a dull ache. She was finally warm and her stomach was slowly getting full.

Tom and Mike had started reminiscing quite loudly about some video game they used to play together in high school. Since Brad was temporarily left out of the conversation, he turned his attention to Daphne. He was sitting directly across from her, so it was easy to notice his boyish face.

"So, Daphne, how do you like being with Tom?" Brad asked, looking very interested in what her answer would be.

Daphne raised her eyebrows and finished chewing before she spoke. "I like it fine."

"Yeah? He seems like a good guy."

"Absolutely," Daphne agreed, wiping her mouth with a napkin.

"He's a little protective of you," Brad noted.

"How do you mean?" Daphne asked.

Brad shrugged. "Well, like when he stopped me before I gave you a bear hug, and just some other things he said before you came to the waiting room."

"Like what? What did he say?" Daphne inquired, a little too curious.

Brad shrugged again. "Just...protective things."

Daphne furrowed her brow. "Well, that was specific."

Brad grinned. "He seemed a little uncertain about your relationship, though. You're not playing him, are you?" he asked with a conniving look.

"Ha, ha," muttered Daphne, taking a sip of her ice water.

Brad folded his arms on the table and leaned over, closer to Daphne. "It sounds like you two need to have a little DTR."

Daphne rolled her eyes. "I hate that acronym," she said, taking another sip.

"Have you not had one yet?" Brad asked, raising his eyebrows.

"Had what?" asked Tom, suddenly joining in on the conversation.

"I was just wondering why you and Daphne here," Brad commented, gesturing towards her, "haven't had a DTR yet."

"What's a DTR?" asked Tom.

Brad gave Daphne a feigned, surprised look. "Seriously, Daphne?" he mocked, jabbing a finger at Tom with a wide grin.

"What is a DTR?" Tom repeated.

"Define the relationship," answered Mike, before taking another bite of his second burger.

Tom lifted his head slowly in acknowledgment, and then he gave Daphne a curious look. "Did you—?"

Daphne knew what he wanted to ask. He wanted to know if Daphne had told Brad about his comment.

"No," Daphne answered.

Tom glanced back and forth between Daphne and Brad as if their faces would tell him what they had been talking about.

"Look," Brad said, "I just asked her why you were so unsure about your relationship. She seemed to know. That's all." He shrugged and took another drink of his Coke.

Tom stared at Daphne, his face full of questions.

"Doesn't the girl always know what's going on and the guy never does?" asked Mike with his mouth full of something. "Isn't that how it always is?"

"Yeah, probably," Brad agreed, grinning. "At least that's how it was when Daphne and I were together," he said with a wink.

Daphne felt her cheeks burn as she scowled back at Brad.

After that, there wasn't much but small talk among the group until Tom asked for the check. "We can pay for our own, Tom," claimed Mike.

"Nah, consider it reimbursement for your gas and time," said Tom as he slapped some cash on the table.

Mike shrugged. "All right, then," he said. "Let's get you guys a room."

Daphne saw Tom give Mike an evil glare.

"I didn't mean that!" Mike cried, feigning innocence.

Tom said nothing else as he stood up and held Daphne's coat out to assist her. "Thank you," said Daphne. She really was grateful; it was still hard to move much.

Chapter *17*

Secrets

At the hotel's front desk, Tom paid for two adjoining rooms. Daphne moaned to herself as she realized she had lost track of all the things she owed Tom. She would definitely have to put this on the list.

As they were walking to the nearest elevator, Daphne realized something else and gasped with sudden alarm.

"What? What is it?" Tom cried, his eyes fluttering over her with worry. "Drat, you've probably been moving too much."

"You paid my hospital bill," Daphne accused in a fierce whisper.

"Of course I did. I'm the one who broke you. Are you sure you're okay?" he asked, looking down at where Daphne still held her side.

"Tom!" Daphne exclaimed as quietly as she could while they entered the elevator. "That was the one thing you didn't have to pay! They could have just sent me a bill! *Me*!"

"You don't have enough for that bill," Tom assumed.

"Of course, I don't, but that's not the point!"

Tom chuckled as he punched a number four button on the wall and kept his eyes straight ahead as the doors to the elevator closed.

"I told you from the very beginning, Tom, I would pay you back for everything when I could."

This time Tom turned his head in her direction. "And I told you I wouldn't take a penny of it."

Daphne exhaled sharply. "How much was the bill, Tom?"

Tom shrugged, moving his eyes back to the door. "It's a secret."

Daphne threw her head back and groaned, and then she suddenly gasped in pain. How was it possible every tiny movement she made hurt her ribs?

Tom looked down at her sharply. "Don't be upset about this. You'll hurt yourself."

Daphne attempted a deep breath and tried to calm down. He couldn't do this. It was too much. She wouldn't allow it.

The elevator doors opened. Daphne turned to face Tom and gave him her best pouty face. Tom's lips twitched as he motioned with his head for her to exit.

She stepped out of the elevator as Tom hefted one bag onto each shoulder and led her down the hall to room 413. He dropped the bags promptly onto the floor and slid his keycard in and out of the lock. He opened the door without stepping inside. "This is your room," he told her.

"Okay."

Tom leaned one shoulder against the wall. "I know it's getting late, but do you mind if I come in and talk to you for a minute?" he asked.

"Yes, we do have something to discuss," Daphne said pointedly.

"You're not paying me back, Daphne," Tom said seriously. "We don't need to discuss that."

"Okay. We won't discuss it, but I will pay you back. I won't be able to live with myself knowing I owe you everything in the world."

Tom didn't take his eyes off her as he pushed himself away from the wall. He continued to stare at her a moment until, finally, he reached to pick up her bag and carried it inside. Daphne followed closely behind. "Where do you want this?" he asked, turning around.

"How about on that table over there," Daphne suggested, pointing to the round, wooden table in the corner of the room. "That way I won't have to bend much."

"Then that's where it will go," he said, walking past the queen bed and placing her bag—his bag, really—on the table-top.

He turned around and began to walk towards the door. "I'll be back in a minute," he promised. Tom almost had the door closed when he opened it again to peek his head inside. "Do you need any extra time alone before I come back?" he wondered.

"Nope. Come over whenever you want."

Tom nodded and closed the door.

Daphne climbed onto her bed and lay on her back with her hands behind her head. She began practicing her breathing as the doctor instructed.

Tom wasn't gone five minutes before he was knocking at the door.

"Is that you, Tom?" called Daphne.

"Yeah, it's me," Tom said through the door.

"Come on in."

When Tom saw her on the bed, breathing slowly, he immediately looked concerned. "Are you all right?"

Daphne nodded. "Just practicing breathing," she told him.

Tom came and sat on the bed next to her and rubbed her leg gently. "Does it hurt?"

Daphne nodded again. "I think it's time to take my medicine."

"I'll get it," Tom said in a rush as he stood.

Daphne sat up and shifted so her legs were over the edge of the bed, not quite reaching the ground. She could hear Tom in the bathroom, turning on the sink. A moment later he came back with her pill and a plastic cup of water.

"Thanks," Daphne murmured, taking it from him and drinking every last drop. She set the cup on the nightstand next to the bed and turned to see Tom staring at her again. Somehow this time it was different. He looked sad and full of...yearning?

"What does that look mean?" Daphne asked.

Tom looked away towards the window and the blinds fluttering in tune with the heater unit.

"Daphne, I..." he said softly.

Daphne patiently waited for him to finish, but he didn't.

"What is it, Tom?"

"You know what I want to ask," Tom said, turning to look at her again.

Daphne's cheeks burned. She *did* know, but what could she say? She couldn't say yes or no. Neither one felt right.

Tom seemed to grow more sad and anxious as the seconds ticked by. "Just tell me what you're thinking, Daphne."

"I really don't know," Daphne confessed. She tried to breathe deeply, but the sudden intense feeling in the room was making it difficult.

"Would it help if I told you about my plans?"

Daphne cocked her head to the side. "I'm certainly curious now."

Tom leaned into his comfortable pose with his elbows on his knees. "Well, my hunting contract ends in the spring, and I was planning on moving back to town afterward. I'll go back to college and get my business degree. Then I might be successful in starting my own carpentry shop." Tom smiled ever so slightly.

"Really?" Daphne asked, intrigued by this new idea of his.

"Absolutely. Maybe I can get a coaching job, too."

Daphne smiled at the picture he described: Tom working in his shop and coaching a hockey team here and there. A sudden adrenaline rush coursed through her veins. She started breathing deeply, and it wasn't by choice this time.

"You're going back to school *and* hockey? What's gotten into you, Tom Multon?" Daphne asked with a teasing grin.

Tom smiled shyly and ducked his head a little. "You make me want to be a better person, Daphne."

Daphne smiled brightly. "Thank you. That is probably the best compliment I have ever received."

Tom started slowly running his fingers through Daphne's hair. "It's the truth," he said softly. "That's why I want to marry you. I...I need you, Daphne." He met her eyes with a gentle gaze.

Daphne's heart began to pound all the more. That look grabbed her heart. She inhaled deeply to gather courage for her next question. "Tom, did you know that I...I've saved myself for marriage?"

Tom smiled sweetly and brushed a hair from her face. "Of course, I knew, Daphne. Why?"

"Well, I was wondering if you had."

Tom grabbed her other hand and squeezed them both tightly. "Yes, Daphne," he said seriously. "Tanya hated me for it, but...yes, I have."

"And there wasn't another girl either?" Daphne wondered.

Tom shook his head more vigorously. "Somehow my conviction to wait stuck with me."

Daphne sighed heavily with relief.

"Anything else you're wondering about?" Tom asked her.

Of course, there was, but how could she talk about it?

***

Tom stared at Daphne's face. Hope and desire ached within him so much it hurt. *Why does she still look worried? Does she really not love me? What else could it be?* Daphne's silence felt like somebody was slowly plunging a dagger into his heart. Ever since he had started to clean up his life, he had tried *so hard* to be a person his pa would be proud of. Obviously, it wasn't enough. It wasn't enough for Daphne.

"Please, tell me what you're thinking, Daphne," he pleaded desperately.

Daphne looked up at him for a brief moment and then down at their hands again. The flash of grief he saw in them was agonizing. He dreaded the words he knew she was going to say. *"I'm sorry, Tom. Can we just be friends?"* He hated, even abhorred, those last five words. They were the worst five words in the entire English language.

Daphne started to rub her thumb over his. "Tom, I know you are so unselfish and you always try to focus on what's important, and that's why you think we are a good match, but..."

Oh, no, please, no. Don't tell me this is happening to me. Not again. Not again. Please, not Daphne. He felt a tear fall on his wrist, but it wasn't his. He put a finger under Daphne's chin and tried to coax her to look up at him. She wouldn't budge. Her shoulders were shaking just a little bit. He placed his palms on either side of her face and moved her head upward. Her beautiful green eyes filled with tears. She wiped them away quickly before they could fall again.

"Daphne, I can't bear this any longer. I love you," he whispered fervently.

Daphne laughed once without humor and wiped her eyes again. Then she grabbed his hands from her face and held onto them and put them into her lap. She was looking down again. "Tom, I know you think highly of me, and I appreciate it, I do. You're more than wonderful. More than I could ever hope for."

Wonderful, like a friend? Oh, please, Daphne, spit it out.

"It's selfish to ask you this, I think," she claimed.

"There's something selfish in you? I would love to hear it, but you have to tell me before I go mad."

Daphne sighed and looked up at him. "Why did you want to marry Tanya, Tom?" she asked.

Totally caught off guard, Tom jerked his head back. He did not like where this was going. "It was a stupid idea, Daphne. I don't know, but she certainly didn't have anything like the qualities you do."

"She was pretty, though. Right?" she assumed.

Oh, not this again. "Daphne, I hope you are not implying what I think you are."

"Tom!" Daphne cried, suddenly upset. "I know I'm everything on that responsible list of yours, but don't you think you should be attracted to me, too?"

"Blast it, Daphne! I am!" Tom exclaimed, matching her tone. "Of all the things in the world to worry about, that is not one of them!" Did she really want him to explain all his thoughts on the matter? How could she not sense how much he wanted her?

Daphne was crying now. "I know I'm insecure about it like you said before, and I don't want you to have to deal with that either," she sobbed.

Tom relaxed a bit and softened his tone. "Daphne, look at me."

She shook her head.

Tom sighed. He put his hands on either side of her head. "Daphne. Please, look at me," he implored.

Daphne lifted her eyes to look at him. "Do you think *I* am not insecure about anything? Good *night*, I am insecure about nearly my entire adulthood."

Daphne sniffed but said nothing.

Tom continued to look right into her eyes. "I don't care if you're not perfect in every single little way possible. I love you. You, Daphne. I love you just the way you are."

Daphne's eyes began to fill with fresh tears. These were good tears; he liked those.

"And blast it all, you're beautiful," he said sternly. "I'm attracted to you in every way, so you better stop this thinking of yours and get used to the idea."

Daphne pursed her lips and wiped her tears again. "I want my rosacea to be gone permanently, not just come and go. I'm so tired of it."

Tom rubbed her hand firmly. "I bet you are. Just keep smiling. In the meantime, I love you anyway."

Daphne looked at him with such wonder. "I love you, too, Tom," she whispered.

Tom's heart leaped and accelerated. *Finally! Finally, she said it!* His face split into a bright smile. "Good," he said, leaning in to give her a kiss. She kissed him back longer than he had expected before she broke away again and rested her forehead against his.

"Will you marry me, Daphne?" he breathed.

"You never did tell me what you said I needed to know."

Tom groaned out loud. *Well, so much for Daphne wanting him.*

They both lifted their heads, and Tom brushed through Daphne's hair with his fingers. A deep aching of dread seized him, but she did deserve to know. He had to do this. He knew it would hurt Daphne; that thought sliced his soul.

"I'm an alcoholic, Daphne," he murmured, taking a deep breath.

Daphne's head shot up with a look of shock. "What? Are you joking?"

Tom clenched his jaw together and shook his head. "No joke."

"I've never seen you have a single drink," she pointed out.

"I *haven't* had a drink in two years. That still doesn't change the fact."

Daphne was still staring at him in horror. "Is that why you quit school?"

"That's why I got kicked out of school," he said simply.

Daphne raised her eyebrows in dismay. She hesitated a moment and then asked, "Did your dad—"

"No!" Tom cringed visibly. To have his pa mixed up with his behavior cut him to the very core. "You can't find better folks than my family."

"I'm sorry, I...I didn't mean to imply...I'm sorry," she mumbled, looking uncomfortable.

Tom shook his head and got up to sit in a chair so he was across from Daphne now. "It's not your fault. It's my fault. My family now has to bear the shame of it forever." Tom rubbed his hand over his chin and had to look away from Daphne's penetrating stare.

"How did you, I mean...why did you start?" Daphne asked him in almost a whisper.

Tom glanced up at her. She looked concerned.

Tom inhaled deeply. "I was coming home from class one day, upset about a grade I got on a paper I had written. I got an F. My professor, in her comments, basically told me I was pretty stupid."

"She did not."

"Not in those exact words, but she did tell me to go back to the eighth grade."

"Seriously?" asked Daphne, furrowing her brow.

Tom nodded. "Anyway, I was pretty miffed about it when I arrived at my hockey game. We were in the semi-finals. I played horribly that day. My worst game ever by far. The opposing team scored three goals all because of my defensive mistakes."

"We've all had bad games, Tom," Daphne said reassuringly.

"I know, but up to this point, I had never been more humiliated in my life. My fans were booing me as I skated off the rink."

"Seriously?" Daphne asked again, with the same puzzled expression.

"Yes, and my coach was so furious he ripped me a new one in front of everybody, and I…I *cried*," Tom spit out. He gestured with stiff, straight arms out in front of him as he continued. "They put a *picture* of me in the paper! *Crying!*" Tom put his head into his hands and moaned loudly. "It was so, beyond…anything I'd ever experienced." He lifted his head to look at Daphne again, whose face was solemn. "And to top it off," Tom continued in the same harried tone, "when I came home to my dorm room, I found my roommate making out with my girlfriend on the couch. She broke up with me."

Daphne cringed. "Sounds like a horrible day."

"Yeah," Tom said with sharp breathlessness. "So, anyway, I didn't want to go back to school. I didn't want to go back to hockey, and I didn't want to go back to my dorm. I went anywhere but those three places. Unfortunately, it was a place that involved booze." Tom rubbed the back of his neck. "Of course, once I started I couldn't stop. At first, I didn't care because I liked not feeling anything, but once my professors dropped me from their classes and my scholarship funds also dropped—then I cared."

Daphne rubbed two firm palms on either side of her head and blew out a gush of air. *This is a lot to take in.* "Where did you go? Back home?" Daphne managed to say calmly.

Tom shook his head. "I wish I had, but I was too proud, too ashamed. I moved in with a bunch of losers I met at a bar. *That* was my worst mistake."

"They were drunks, too?" Daphne assumed.

Tom nodded. "Every one of them. They ruined me."

Daphne filled her cheeks up with air and blew it out slowly. "How long did you stay with them?"

"Two years. Two *wasted* years," Tom muttered, shaking his head.

"How did you get out and get better?" Daphne wondered.

Tom's already broken heart broke in half at her question. "My pa dragged me out," he whispered. "Literally."

Daphne leaned forward and grabbed Tom's hand with hers, giving him the softest, kindest look he had ever seen. His heart beat rapidly as it courageously still hoped she would accept him.

Daphne looked down at their hands and slowly rubbed hers on top of his.

"Then what?" she whispered.

Tom shrugged. "Then my parents helped me through AA and suffered through all the small-town ridicule."

Daphne looked up into Tom's eyes. "What about Tanya? How does she fit into all of this?"

Tom laughed once without humor. "She was the one who was making out with my roommate that day."

Stunned, Daphne raised her eyebrows.

"Once I started getting better, she came back to me. I think it was mostly because she felt somewhat responsible for what I did." He shook his head. "Ridiculous, of course. I really don't think she ever liked me all that much to begin with. I was just anxious to marry her because she was the first semi-good thing that happened to me after all that, and I wanted to hold on to it."

Daphne nodded slowly, looking deep in thought. "So then why did you break off your engagement?" she asked.

Tom took a deep breath. "She broke it off," he replied. "Like I said, I don't think she ever really liked me."

Daphne nodded again as a slow smile curved on her face. "Well, I think you have won first place for the most interesting story I have heard all year," she said.

Tom smiled sadly and gazed at Daphne as she picked up their hands and kissed his.

"You don't hate me?" he asked.

Daphne shook her head. "I couldn't."

"I'm so sorry," he whispered.

"Why are you apologizing to me?" she asked.

"Because whomever I associate with now, no matter what the connection, I'll bring shame to."

"Nobody can blame me for being with someone who has already cleaned up his life," Daphne countered.

"You forgive me?"

"It's not very hard, Tom."

Tom shook his head. "You're amazing, Daphne," he murmured, staring at her beautiful eyes. "Will you still marry me?"

***

Daphne held her breath as she stared at Tom. She didn't want to lose him, but could she really *marry* an alcoholic? She did love him, and he had changed. Right? Tom was an exceptionally good person no doubt. What if he *did* relapse?

Tom stood up abruptly and began pacing back and forth while rubbing his neck. "I have *never* wanted to know someone's thoughts more than I do right now." He stopped short and dropped his hand to his side. "Is it the alcoholic thing, Daphne?" he asked. "Are you ashamed to be with me because of that?"

"Not ashamed, Tom. Just...worried," she confessed softly, avoiding his probing gaze.

Tom let out an anxious sigh. "Worried that I will drink again?"

Daphne nodded, still looking at the floor.

Tom ran a frazzled hand quickly through his hair and then rushed to sit in front of her again. Daphne looked up at his face. His expression had never looked so stressed.

"I swear to you, Daphne. I *swear* I will never have another drink again. I learned my lesson. I *promise* you," he spoke softly, but severely.

Daphne's heart wrenched inside her. She couldn't bear to see Tom like this. She grabbed his hand and put it in hers.

"Tom," she said soothingly, running her hand over his. "I can't imagine how you are feeling right now, but marriage is a huge decision! I can't make a decision in an instant."

Tom rubbed one palm over his forehead, which was beginning to perspire. "Okay, I can understand that."

"I think it would be best to put everything on hold."

Tom looked at her sharply. "What does that mean? *'Put everything on hold'*?"

"Let's pick things back up when we both get settled into real life."

"In Brocksville, you mean?" Tom asked.

Daphne nodded.

Tom cleared his throat. "Let me ask you something, Daphne. Are you saying you want to break up and then see if you want to date me when I get to Brocksville? Or are you saying you'll wait for me to come, and then we'll move things forward?"

Tom appeared overly anxious and distraught. "Daphne, tell me if you will be dating other people in Brocksville," he demanded.

Daphne hesitated. "You don't want me to?"

"Of course, I don't," he replied right away. "What do you want?"

"I...I don't know. If we aren't engaged, then—"

Tom clenched his jaw and looked away. Daphne wasn't trying to upset him. She was trying to do the smartest thing.

Tom inhaled deeply. "Daphne, you just told me you loved me. Is that not true?"

Daphne suddenly started to feel very nervous. "Of course I do, Tom. It would be impossible for me not to."

Tom stared at her with a thoughtful gaze. "Then you must not love me like I love you."

Daphne opened her mouth to speak, but Tom cut in.

"Because if you did, you would say without hesitation you would wait for me and I would be yours when I came back. Guaranteed."

"No, I—"

"It's not like I am joining the military and will be gone for four years or something, Daphne. It'll only be four months."

"A lot can happen in four months, Tom," Daphne noted.

Tom pursed his lips and hung his head low. "Then you don't love me the same way," he said, looking back up at her. His expression was a mixture of frustration and sadness.

Daphne wanted to say something to make him feel better. After all, he deserved it. He had been more than sensitive to her tonight and had given more to her than she could ever imagine. She also knew there was nothing to say. She knew she would feel guilty about hurting the man who had been so good to her. Even still, she couldn't say yes. It wasn't right. Not now.

Tom stood up and turned his back on her and scratched both hands through his hair.

He took a deep breath and spoke to the window. "All right. Well, maybe I'll see you around in the spring," he said.

He turned around to face her. "I'll call for someone to come help you with your bag in the morning. Don't hurt yourself by trying to carry it on your own. I'll have a cab waiting to take you back to the university."

"But..."

"Just," Tom interrupted, with his hand held out, "let me do that."

Daphne nodded. "Thank you, Tom. You're very generous."

He abruptly leaned over to kiss her forehead. "Goodbye, Daphne," he whispered.

"Goodbye," she replied, but he was already close to the door. She watched him step through the threshold before he suddenly pivoted to face her.

"Daphne?"

"Yes?"

"You really are beautiful," he murmured.

Before Daphne could respond, he left the room, closing the door tightly behind him.

Daphne lay back on the bed again, and she felt a sudden wave of sadness and emptiness wash through her.

What did I just do? Tom was gone. She would miss him. She would miss him more than anything.

Chapter *18*

Spit it Out

May 25, 2016
-Four months later-

"College," Ma nodded her head, smiling pleasantly. "I'm so happy you are doing this again, Tom."

Tom watched his stout mother stand in front of the kitchen sink, scrubbing a pan hard with the sound of steel wool scratching against metal. Even from his seat at the kitchen table, he could see her forearms drenched in soap and water all the way to the purple sleeves rolled up past her elbows.

"You think it's too late for me?" Tom asked.

"Oh, no, son. It's never too late. I'm proud of you. I really am." Ma turned her gaze toward Tom for a moment and smiled sweetly at him.

Tom returned a small smile. His mother was so good. He couldn't fathom how easily she had forgiven him for all the turmoil he had put her through. "I hope you know how grateful I am for all you have done for me, Ma."

Ma turned toward him again. "You're welcome, son. Now, I'd be grateful to you if you'd help me with these dishes."

Tom immediately got to his feet. "Oh, I'm sorry, Ma. I would have helped sooner if my feet weren't so tired from standing through that awful university orientation today."

Ma smiled at him again. "I know. That's why I let you rest as long as you did."

He and his ma washed and rinsed and dried the dishes in silence for a few minutes. He was happy to be at her side.

"Are you planning on seeing that girl once you move to Brocksville?" Ma inquired.

"Which girl is that?" Tom asked as he watched the circular motion of his towel.

"You know who I mean," Ma said as she twisted the plug in the sink to let the dirty water drain.

Tom sighed and dried the other side of his plate more slowly. "Yes, I'm planning on it, but I'm also not planning on anything coming of it," he said softly.

"You already sound discouraged," his mother said, drying her hands.

"Nah," Tom said as he started to unload the drying rack by placing some plates in the cupboard above him. He had only picked up three plates before he felt his mother's stare. He stopped and twisted to look at her. She was facing him now with one hand on her hip, her dark green apron streaked with dampness. She had that motherly look on her face…the look he remembered when he came into the house covered in mud from head to toe with a handful of worms.

"You like this one. Daphne," she declared.

It was pointless to deny it. Tom shrugged. "So?"

"And you think a lot about her," she pointed out. It almost sounded like an accusation. Now she was definitely being his mother as she somehow found it necessary to state the obvious.

Tom raised his eyebrows and shrugged again as he resumed emptying the drying rack.

"Son, look at me," Ma insisted.

Tom moaned softly and shifted to face his mother.

"Even with Tanya you didn't act this way," she professed.

Tom cringed. Did his mother really still think about that awful time?

"With Tanya, you were so convinced you loved her, you wouldn't listen to reason. You were infatuated, but not in love."

Tom pressed his lips firmly together and forced himself to set the towel down gently on the table. "That's not fair, Ma. I did love her, even though it didn't make sense. Now do we have to talk about Tanya? She's the last person I want to think about."

"That brings me to my next point. You never thought about Tanya the way you think about this girl, Daphne."

Tom wrinkled his brow. "How do you know what I think?" he asked.

His mother quickly started to wipe off the counter with a damp cloth as she spoke. "Well, it's because of what you say. When you talked about Tanya before, you would just tell us the fun things you did together or how thick her hair was. Things like that. When you talk about Daphne, you talk about deeper things, like her character, her values, her goals. It's easy to see how much more you truly admire Daphne."

This time Tom groaned loudly. He usually appreciated that he had a relationship with his family that allowed him to speak somewhat freely. However, at the moment, he wished he had never mentioned Daphne's name. He grabbed some glasses that were still a little wet inside and placed them a bit forcefully into the cupboard next to the plates.

His mother rinsed her washcloth in the sink and then turned to face Tom again in the exact same position as before—her hand on her hip, ready to force out a confession.

"You still haven't told me everything about this girl," she accused.

Tom tossed his head back and sighed as he shut the cupboard door. "Ma, how many adult sons do you know who give their mothers details about their love interests?"

"I don't care what other people do. You need to talk to me about this. Your broken heart from before seems to have ripped open again."

Tom cringed again as his mother's words described exactly how he felt. He closed his eyes for a long moment and turned so his back was leaning against the counter. He folded his arms and stared at his feet.

"You know you cannot hide this from me much longer," Ma continued. "I have given you time to digest whatever it is that's been bothering you this past month, but I can't take your moping much longer. Now tell me what happened," she demanded. "You two were obviously involved somehow."

Tom tilted his head back to stare at the ceiling. "No, not really, Ma."

Tom's mother must have thought Tom didn't see her hand on her hip because she lifted it and pinned it there again. "Didn't you tell her how you feel? A girl can't do anything if you don't tell her!"

Tom moved his head to give his mother a confused, exasperated look. His ma almost sounded mad. "I would talk about it if I wanted to, Ma."

Ma sighed an enormous sigh, as if trying to calm herself. She took the towel Tom had placed on the counter, folded it neatly, and tucked it over the self-made hanger next to the sink. Slowly she turned to face her son again.

"Thomas, you'll never understand how a mother worries about her son."

Tom cocked his head to one side, giving her a disapproving look. Now she was playing the sympathy card.

"Just tell me if you told her how you feel," she insisted.

Tom shook his head in frustration and stared at the ground again. He did want to talk to someone about this. Maybe his ma sensed that, but it was too humiliating to speak out loud.

"Does that little shake of the head mean you didn't?" his mother asked softly.

"I asked her to marry me, Ma," Tom announced abruptly, looking back up at his mother. "She said no."

Ma's eyes widened to twice their original size, looking completely surprised.

"She doesn't love me," Tom whispered bitterly.

Ma's face softened into complete sympathy and sadness. "Oh, son," she said as she stepped toward him and embraced him in the tightest motherly hug she could muster. Tom returned her embrace, desperately wishing his mother's love could fill the agonizing void inside him. He knew it couldn't.

Chapter 19

David

Daphne walked out of her college English class, a blue binder tucked under her arm. The broad hallway was filling up with pupils from all the rooms connected to the hall. She paused a moment to see which exit would have less traffic.

"How did you do on your term paper?" came a voice from behind her.

Daphne turned around to see one of her classmates.

"Oh, hi, David. Um, I did well, I guess. I got an A, so Professor Harper must have liked it."

"You got an A?" David scratched his head, his cheeks ruddy. "I wish I did. I never seem to remember what I read, so it's hard for me to write a paper about it."

"Well, the term paper isn't a huge chunk of your grade, so I'm sure you will do just fine in the class."

David smiled a little at that. Daphne liked the way David looked. He had deep blue eyes and sun-bleached hair, and his skin had a tan tone to it. He wasn't too tall or too short. There was really nothing not to like about him. She did feel a little strange when she would catch him staring at her. She didn't quite know why she felt creeped out because whenever he spoke to her he seemed perfectly nice.

David took a deep breath. "It feels good to have the semester over. That was my last final."

"Oh, really? Congratulations. I have one more after this," said Daphne.

"When?"

"In a few minutes, in the science building next door," Daphne said, motioning to the left with her head.

David swallowed hard and suddenly looked a little nervous. "Can I take you to lunch afterward?" he asked.

Daphne raised her eyebrows in surprise. "Um, y-yes," she stuttered. David smiled broadly showing his perfect teeth. "Great. I will meet you outside the science building at noon. Does that work?"

"Of course," she replied, returning his smile. The two of them stood in silence for a moment, both grinning from ear to ear. David let out a nervous laugh. "Okay, I'll see you then."

"Bye." Daphne waved, and they both parted, going opposite directions down the hall.

Daphne couldn't believe what had just happened. David Delooté. David Delooté had asked her out! How many girls wished for that?

As she pushed open the doors to exit into the sunshine, Daphne recalled a girl's night out party last Friday where David Delooté's name had come up. "What a hottie!" "What an athlete!" "Wow, so rich!" "Have you seen the car he drives?" Daphne had learned David's dad owned the power plant and was the richest man in all of Brocksville. Apparently, he wanted his children to work for themselves, so all of his five children, David being the youngest, had attended college. One girl at the party, however, vehemently spouted that all the Delootés were nothing but weasels and crooks. Nobody else believed her, and Daphne didn't either. *Some jealous person always tries to undermine another's success.*

Daphne was so caught up with her thoughts about David she did not hear someone behind her calling her name.

"Daphne! Hey, Daphne!"

Daphne whirled around to face the voice as she realized this must have been the third or fourth time he had spoken.

Totally shocked, she recognized the last person in the world she expected to see.

"Tom?" she gasped.

Tom cracked a smile as he walked towards her. The wind rustled through his fiery hair and his tan jacket ever so slightly. "I was hoping to see you around here. How are you, Daphne?"

"I—" Daphne cleared her throat. "I'm good. What are you doing here?"

Tom stuffed his hands into the pockets of his jacket and inhaled deeply. "Well, now that it's spring we were finally able to bury my pa."

"Oh, that's right. How did that go?" she asked sympathetically.

"It went well," replied Tom casually.

Silence.

"What are you doing here on campus?" Daphne didn't know what else to say.

"I'm looking for a place to live. I'm going to attend school here."

"Oh!" Daphne cried in pleasant surprise. "You got in? You're going to Brocksville?"

Tom smiled a little shyly and nodded.

"That's…that's incredible, Tom. Good for you."

"Thanks," Tom replied, but now his expression grew soft and thoughtful as he focused his gaze on her.

Daphne felt chills run down her spine as she recognized that look.

"You...you look amazing, Daphne," Tom said, trying to sound casual.

"Ah, yes, you probably would think that now since you knew me before." Daphne pointed with both hands to her face. "It's an off-season right now. My skin has been pretty clear lately," she said with a slight smile.

Tom raised his eyebrows as if confused. "Oh," he said. "I didn't—" and then he shook his head at the ground and glanced back up at her. "It's not that. You...It's just great to see you, Daphne."

"You, too," she said brightly. "I wish we could catch up more, but I have to go take my last final."

"Can I take you to lunch when you're finished?" Tom asked.

Two date offers in one day. This is new.

"Well, actually, I...I already..." she hesitated.

"You already have a date?" Tom finished for her, looking not at all surprised.

"Yes," Daphne admitted.

Tom cocked his head to one side. "What's his name?" he asked, feigning casualness.

"David Delooté."

Tom's eyes abruptly bulged, and for a brief moment, his face held a look of horror. Quickly he smoothed out his expression as he cleared his throat. "Well, have fun. Good luck on your final."

"Thank you. I'll see you later."

Tom nodded, and Daphne spun around quickly and ran toward the front doors of the science building. She didn't quite know why she was nervous. Was it because she was having lunch with David or because she had seen Tom again? Maybe she was just anxious for her last final of the semester to be over.

Three hours later, Daphne swiftly unlocked the door to her dorm and ran through her rectangular kitchen, down the hallway with the long vanity, and into her tiny bedroom. Out of breath, she plopped her heavy backpack down on her bed and almost immediately plopped herself right next to it. Her roommate was lying on her stomach across her bed on the other side of the small room. Laurel's feet were up in the air and crossed at the ankles. She had long, smooth, tan legs. She was staring at a textbook and was deep in thought. She hardly seemed to notice Daphne's presence. Without looking up from her reading, she muttered, "Hey, Daphne."

"Hey, Laurel."

"You all finished with your finals?"

"Yes!" Daphne exclaimed as she scooted onto her bed so her back was against the wall. "Should I let you study?"

"No," said Laurel as she slammed her textbook closed and got into a sitting position. "I'm burned out. Besides, nothing I try to cram into my brain at this point will make much of a difference." Laurel shifted onto her bed so her back was also against the wall and the two girls were facing each other across their miniature room. This was common for them when they talked with each other, almost like a ritual.

For a moment, Laurel scrutinized Daphne's face. "This glow of yours is more than just the satisfaction of doing well on your finals. What's going on with you?" Laurel was curious.

"I'm not glowing," Daphne protested, trying not to smile too big.

"What are you grinning about?" Laurel pressed.

Daphne shrugged, leaving her grin in place. "It's a secret."

Laurel cocked her head to one side, giving Daphne a dis-approving look.

"What?" asked Daphne in a high, excited tone.

Laurel's eyes bulged. "It's a boy, isn't it?" she said in her that-is-out-of-this-world voice. Laurel slid her textbook to the side and lay on her stomach, facing Daphne, putting her chin on her fists. "Tell me everything. Don't leave out a single detail," she demanded.

Daphne smiled brightly and flipped some hair behind her back. "It's nothing."

Laurel rolled her eyes. "It never is, according to you," she declared. "How about you start with his name?"

Daphne pursed her lips, trying not to appear too pleased. "David Delooté."

Laurel let out an audible gasp and then she smacked her bed with her palm. "Get out!" she exclaimed. "Are you serious?" she cried, her voice creeping to an extremely high squeal at the end.

Daphne nodded and covered her mouth as she tried to keep in the uncontrollable giggles escaping her lips.

"No way!" Laurel cried again in the same high squeal. This time she swung her legs around to the ground so she was sitting on the edge of her bed. She looked very proper as she sat up tall with perfect posture. Her entire expression and body language said she was alert and intensely focused. "How do you know him?" she asked.

"He's in Professor Harper's class with me."

Laurel slammed both her palms down on the bed again with giddy surprise, her eyes getting bigger by the second. "David Delooté was in your English class all semester, and you didn't even tell me?" Laurel squeaked.

Daphne giggled involuntarily again. "I didn't think anything would come of it," she admitted.

"Did he ask you out?"

Daphne nodded unable to keep the smile off her face. "We went to lunch."

This time Laurel put her hands on her lap and leaned forward. "Get out!" she squealed.

Daphne laughed out loud. "Crazy, isn't it?'

"No!" Laurel exclaimed, standing up now. "He is only the handsomest, richest guy on campus! Of course, he would want you!"

Daphne rolled her eyes. "That makes zero sense, Laurel."

Laurel just returned the eye rolling, just more dramatically as she let out an irritated sigh. "You're the one who makes zero sense, Daphne," Laurel countered. "When are you going to stop being so anti-you?"

"I'm not anti-me," Daphne protested. "I just know what guys are all about."

Laurel's eyes remained huge as she put one hand on her hip. "Oh, really? Well, please enlighten me because I would love to know!"

"They only care about looks," Daphne announced.

Laurel rolled her head as she took a few slow steps towards the dresser on the south wall. "Oh, Daphne. Not all of them."

"Yes. All of them," Daphne confirmed sternly.

Laurel turned to face her again. "Well, okay, they do, but that's not all they care about. Not all guys are pigs."

Daphne put her head back on the wall as she spoke. "Then how do you explain this? A few months ago my face was completely covered with acne and not a single guy looked at me. Now that my complexion is sometimes almost entirely clear, guys ask me out for lunch? I don't think that is a coincidence."

"But it is," said Laurel pacing a little now as if she were giving a lecture in a classroom. "The only reason they didn't ask you out before was because you were too self-conscious and never spoke to anyone. They ask you out now because you are a little less so and you smile back occasionally."

Daphne shook her head, feeling somewhat irritated Laurel was saying this to her.

"Besides," continued Laurel, plopping back down on her bed, "guys did talk to you a few months ago, and they liked you, too. You were just too blind and stubborn to see it because you thought such a thing couldn't be possible."

"Such a thing wasn't possible," Daphne protested a bit sourly.

"*Ugh!*" Laurel groaned in frustration, throwing her hands up in the air. "Sometimes you're so difficult. Guys liked you then, too!"

Daphne felt like glaring at Laurel but tried not to. She hated when Laurel did this. She was such a wretched, good friend. She always said things to make it sound like Daphne and she were on the same level. But it wasn't true. She couldn't accuse Laurel of lying because Laurel genuinely believed what she said. All Daphne could do was try to prove her otherwise. "Name one person who liked me when I was a pizza face," Daphne insisted.

Laurel scowled deeply at her. "I hate that phrase."

"Sorry. Name one person," she repeated.

"Well, let's see," Laurel said trying to think as she crossed her legs on the bed. "Oh, yes. That redheaded guy at the cabin you were stranded with who liked you so much he wanted to marry you. I think he certainly counts, don't you?" Laurel asked, a little bitterly.

Daphne felt an unexpected chill race up her spine. "I was a rebound to him," Daphne clarified.

"Hmm," said Laurel, cocking her head and pursing her lips as if she was deep in thought again. "Guys do rebound for sure, but," she said slowly, "they generally don't go as far as *proposing*." This time Laurel looked Daphne straight in the eye.

Daphne slowly blew out a gush of air. "I saw him today," she confided.

Laurel perked up and furrowed her brows together. "Who? Your cabin boyfriend?"

Daphne nodded. "On campus."

"What is he doing here?" Laurel questioned.

Daphne shrugged. "He says he's going to school here next year and was looking for a place to live. I think it's great, actually."

"You want him to—" Laurel began.

"Not like that, Laurel. I'm just glad he's started to make decisions for his life."

"Is that why you said no to him? Because you thought he wasn't going anywhere?"

Daphne shrugged. "Not exactly. It was mostly because of me."

"What about you?" Laurel asked carefully.

Daphne didn't want to have such a serious conversation at the moment. "I don't know. I don't deserve someone like Tom Multon," she said, trying to sound casual. She was never going to let Laurel know Tom was an alcoholic. Her friend could be a bit judgmental sometimes. Laurel sighed and slouched as she looked sadly at Daphne.

"And to get married! We barely knew each other."

"Sometimes people know right away," Laurel pointed out.

"Well, I didn't know," Daphne admitted.

Laurel nodded thoughtfully. "You must have made the right choice then. I'm only sorry you will see him around sometimes now."

"Why do you say that?" Daphne wondered. "It's good he is doing this."

"I know," Laurel agreed, "but you were so sad when you first came back from his cabin. I don't want that to happen to you again."

Daphne smiled half-heartedly. "Thanks, but I'll be okay. I've moved on."

"I wish I could hear more about your date with David, but I have to go take my last final," Laurel declared.

Daphne shrugged. "It was a typical date for me. I can summarize it in two sentences."

Laurel raised her eyebrows as she started stuffing her backpack with notebooks.

"He looked gorgeous and made a lot of jokes. I blushed practically the entire time," Daphne confessed.

Laurel smiled back. "It sounds like it's going somewhere," she teased.

Daphne chuckled and shook her head as she heard a knock at the front door.

"Will you come to the door with me?" asked Laurel. "That way I won't feel bad leaving the conversation if you're here to stay and talk."

Daphne slid across her bed and onto her feet. She followed Laurel all the way into the kitchen. Daphne stood a few paces behind as Laurel opened the door to welcome their visitor.

"Hi." Laurel's voice was saturated with sweetness, so Daphne knew their guest was a guy. He was sure to be disappointed when he discovered Laurel had to leave and would be stuck with her instead.

"Hi," replied the man. "Is Daphne here?" Daphne's heart jolted at the sound of this voice. She stepped aside to see if her ears were telling the truth. They were. Tom's eyes turned to Daphne as she came into his view. "Oh, there you are," he said with a warm smile.

Daphne tried to greet him but choked on her words.

Laurel took this opportunity to introduce herself. "I'm Laurel," she said, extending a friendly hand towards him. "I don't believe we've met."

Tom peeled his eyes off Daphne and met Laurel's gaze again. "Oh, no, we haven't." He shook her hand. "I'm Tom."

Laurel glanced back at Daphne with a look of utter shock. Daphne raised her eyebrows in return.

"Well, I have to run off to my last final. It was nice to meet you, Tom," declared Laurel in her sweetest voice.

Daphne mentally winced as she felt an unexpected, yet forceful scorch of jealousy burn her. Now that Laurel knew he was Tom, she knew Laurel would never purposefully try to flirt with him or invite his attentions. Daphne also knew after seeing Laurel next to her, Tom would fall for her friend, just like every other guy.

As Laurel slid out the door, she turned her head to look back at Daphne and gave her an intense look Daphne interpreted as: *you better tell me everything later!*

Daphne nodded and Laurel promptly shut the door behind her, leaving Daphne alone in the now awkward space of Tom Multon.

Chapter 20

Out of Reach

Tom made the first move to speak since all Daphne could do was stare at him like an idiot.

"Are you mad I came here?" asked Tom, his brow furrowed.

"What? No, of course not. Why would you say that?" Daphne wondered.

"Because you look mad," Tom clarified.

Daphne laughed a little nervously, realizing the lingering jealousy of Laurel was probably showing as anger on her face. "I'm sorry. It's not you," she explained. *Then again, maybe it is. What did Tom come here to do, break my mended heart?*

"What are you doing here, Tom?" Daphne inquired.

Tom shrugged casually, but Daphne could see her words bothered him. "I wanted to see you," he admitted. "Can I sit down?" he asked, motioning to a chair at the kitchen table.

"Oh, sure," replied Daphne. "I'm sorry. My manners are awful today."

Tom laughed lightly at that as he scraped a cheap chair across the linoleum floor. "No need to worry about that, Daphne. It's just me."

Daphne sat across from him and rested her arms out on the table.

"Look, Tom, let's cut to the chase," Daphne blurted.

Tom raised his eyebrows as high as they could go as he stared back at Daphne. "Let's do that," Tom agreed, "but you will have to explain it to me because I haven't a clue."

Daphne lifted an arm and pointed a finger at him. "My heart had a lot of mending to do after you, and if you think you can just waltz in here again and make more scars, then you better leave right now."

"Wow, Daphne. That was very direct," Tom announced, surprised.

Daphne leaned back in her chair casually. "I had to get it out. You know I'm not good with small talk."

Tom stared softly at Daphne with a gaze she readily recognized, but it was different somehow this time. Why?

"I promise, Daphne, I'm not here to give you more scars," Tom said solemnly.

"Then tell me the reason," Daphne demanded.

Tom sighed and leaned back in his chair as well. "For some reason, girls have this way of analyzing every possible purpose behind what someone says or does. I'm a simple man, Daphne. I wanted to see you, and that's why I came here. Nothing more."

Daphne stared back at Tom. She knew he was telling the truth. "Well, in that case," she said with a grin as she leaned over the table, "tell me how you have been these past few months."

***

Tom didn't know how long he and Daphne had talked, but it almost seemed like they were right back to where they left off—minus the kissing and snuggling and stuff, that is. Tom loved how Daphne roared with laughter at his story of a hunter twice his size who had brought good tidings of fish and rabbits. He loved how she rested her chin in her hand, looking utterly fascinated by another story of his finding a new set of moguls for snowmobiling. He told her about his progress on a rocking chair he was making for his ma. Daphne seemed enveloped in all of it. Suddenly, he realized how rude his manners were.

"I'm sorry," said Tom. "I'm doing all the talking." Of course, Daphne would say nothing about it, considering how selfless she was.

Daphne shrugged. "I don't mind. I just realized how much I miss your cabin and going on adventures."

"Tell me some of your adventures here," Tom suggested.

Daphne shrugged again. "There's not much to tell."

"Ah, come on. I know you can come up with at least one good story. The dorms must be full of them."

Daphne pursed her lips thoughtfully for a moment and slapped her palms lightly on the table. "Okay, I've got one." Her broad smile was already forming on that beautiful mouth. "A couple months ago..." she paused as she was already chuckling to herself. Tom couldn't help but smile at that. "You know, I better skip this one because it will only be funny to me."

"No way. You have to spill now," Tom persisted.

Daphne laughed a moment longer before she continued. "We have a friend, Gary, who lives downstairs. He is the *hairiest* man you have ever seen. I mean a regular hairball!" Daphne claimed, trying not to laugh but failing.

Tom cracked a smile.

"For my 22nd birthday, he decided his present to me would be..." Daphne burst out into laughter and couldn't continue at all. Tom couldn't help but chuckle as he witnessed the laugh attack in front of him. "What was it?"

Daphne's face was scarlet red, and through her sniggers, she managed to squeak out, "He shaved '22' on his chest!"

Daphne slapped the table with one hand as she sustained an uncontrollable, inaudible laugh.

Tom laughed along with her at this, but Daphne was right: it wasn't as funny to him as it was to her. In fact, he was feeling a little jealous. Why couldn't *he* produce such a hilarious reaction out of Daphne?

Tom smiled at her sadly as Daphne eventually calmed herself. "I'm sorry," she apologized. "I warned you only I would think it was funny."

"It was funny," Tom agreed.

Daphne stared at Tom a moment, suddenly looking ashamed. "It certainly wasn't as nice as your present, however."

Tom raised his eyebrows. "Did my present make you laugh like that?"

Daphne smiled shyly. "Well, no, but it was much more beautiful. You obviously put a lot more thought and time into it. I appreciate it. I still have it, by the way."

Tom nodded as he recalled the small wooden angel he had carved by hand and mailed to Daphne a couple of months prior. The angel, of course, represented Daphne. He had been afraid of doing something too big considering things were over between them, but he had to do *something*. Tom suddenly felt very awkward, like Daphne could see through him and sense he still loved her. He promised himself he wouldn't let that happen...not yet, anyway.

The silence was far too thick, but he didn't know how to break it. He gazed up at Daphne, which didn't help with his speech. She was so beautiful! Sure, her skin had obviously cleared up a lot, but that smile was what captivated him. How he had longed for her all these months, and now here she was right in front of him! In that very same, stark moment, he never felt farther away. He knew she didn't love him for certain now. He had fancied himself into thinking when they saw each other,

Daphne would somehow leap into his arms again. *What a fool I am.*

Amid these self-pitying contemplations, Tom noticed the expression on Daphne's face had changed. She looked sad, too.

"What is it?" he asked.

Daphne raised her eyebrows quickly. "What? Oh, it's nothing," she said, batting her hand.

Why is she lying to me? Oh, well. He wasn't going to force the issue. "Hey, I've been meaning to ask you how your date with David Delooté went." Tom could hardly speak that disgusting name without spitting. Daphne apparently didn't know what a scumbag that guy was. Tom recalled David and his older brother, Mitch, stealing Tom's new bike in junior high school. His parents had probably saved up for months to buy it. Tom had seen the boys' very act. He had run outside yelling, trying to catch them, but Tom couldn't outrun the bike. The police had believed their story rather than his. Tom figured it was probably because they had paid someone off. Filthy rich scumbags.

Tom also knew Mitch was known to play girls in the dirtiest way in college. Mitch had lived down the hall from Tom a few years back when Tom had gone to college. He had had a different sleazy girl with him every night. Tom had been repulsed by Mitch's nasty behavior and loud, crude speeches.

Now Mitch was a lawyer and supposedly a good one. *He probably paid someone off to get that far.* It was true Mitch's baby brother could be different now, but Tom still didn't trust him.

With sudden alarm, Tom realized he had been so involved in his thoughts he hadn't been listening to a word Daphne was saying. She had now asked him a question, and he had no idea what it was.

"What was that?" Tom asked, chagrined.

Daphne stared at Tom with a disparaging look. "Have you been listening to me to at all?"

Tom tried not to look too guilty and come up with a way to dodge her question, but he hesitated too long.

Daphne sighed and shook her head. "It doesn't matter. Do you want something to eat?"

"No, thank you. I'm all right," he replied. Tom frowned, wishing he had listened, even though it was true he really didn't want to hear about her date with the despicable David Delooté. "I'm sorry, Daphne. I got distracted thinking about David's brother. I knew him when I was in college. He wasn't a very good guy."

Daphne stood up from her chair and walked to the kitchen counter behind her, opening a cupboard door. "That doesn't mean David is the same way," she noted, pouring herself some cold cereal into a bowl.

"I know," Tom agreed, wondering if this were a regular afternoon snack for her. "But. . ."

Daphne finished pouring and looked up at him, raising her eyebrows. "But what?"

"It worries me," Tom confessed. "I would hate for you to be with someone like that."

Daphne furrowed her brow at him and walked a couple of steps to the refrigerator and pulled out some milk. "I'm a big girl, Tom," she told him.

"No, you're a little girl," teased Tom. After the bad joke, Daphne glared at him and she started to eat her cereal.

A knock sounded on the door and immediately a visitor walked right in. "There's my girl!" he called to Daphne with outstretched arms.

"Apparently, you are also *his* girl," Tom muttered under his breath. Luckily, the noisy reunion between Daphne and the stranger no one heard his words but himself.

The man was tall and lanky with bright blond hair. He lifted Daphne off the ground when he hugged her and didn't let her go for a long moment. Tom was happy to notice it did seem like more of a friendly hug than a passionate one. Even still, the jealousy seethed inside him.

"Okay, you can let me go now. I can't breathe," Daphne choked out.

The man gently let her down on the ground and patted her on the head. "That's because you are such a little thing," he noted.

"Told you," Tom muttered softly, but this time the words were audible.

The two of them turned their heads towards him. "Oh! Another male visitor for Daphne, huh?" the man said with a bright, white smile. "They come by the dozens these days."

Daphne smacked the guy's arm with the back of her hand. "Whatever, Jeremy."

"Ow!" Jeremy whined. "For a little thing, you're kind of tough."

Daphne rolled her eyes. "Tom, this is my friend, Jeremy. Jeremy, this is Tom," she introduced them before taking another bite of cereal.

"It's nice to meet you," said Jeremy, holding out a friendly hand.

Tom stood up a little to reach across the table where they both shook hands firmly and promptly released.

"What would you like for dinner tonight, sweetheart?" Jeremy asked Daphne.

Tom's blood began to simmer at the sound of the term of endearment for Daphne and his offer.

Daphne sat down at the table, seemingly unaffected by it. "You're making dinner?"

"Yes." Jeremy reached into a low cupboard and pulled out a frying pan.

Tom wondered what kind of friend this was. He was obviously very comfortable in this dorm.

"I see you have already done *your* cooking," Jeremy said to Daphne, gesturing to her cereal.

Daphne smirked at him but continued chewing.

Tom was growing more uncomfortable by the minute. Abruptly, he stood up, causing his chair to screech across the floor. "Well, if y'all are having dinner together, I guess I better head out."

Jeremy half turned around from his position at the stove and began saying something to him at the exact moment Daphne spoke. "Oh, no, you don't have to go," she rushed. A sudden look of alarm was on Daphne's face. Her eyes were as wide as ever, and she shook her head ever so slightly at him.

Tom hesitated a moment. "Uh, what was that, man?" he asked Jeremy.

Jeremy half turned to face him again as he cracked an egg into the pan. "Oh, I was just saying that I cook for Daphne's second and third boyfriends all the time. It's okay with me as long as I'm always the first," he said with a shrug and a wink at Daphne.

"Stop saying things like that!" Daphne objected with her mouth full.

Jeremy laughed. "Ah, come on, Daphne! I'm just letting him know about his competition."

Tom groaned to himself, wishing he could either say something smart, vanish from the room, or punch the skinny dude.

"You know very well *I* am not the one you are after in this dorm so stop pretending like you are," Daphne insisted, her mouth empty this time.

"I'm not pretending anything! I'm after every girl in this dorm."

Daphne rolled her eyes again but said nothing since her mouth was full again. After she had swallowed, she patted the table across from where she was sitting. "Come on, Tom, sit down. I don't want you to go."

Tom took a deep breath. That was a *little bit* encouraging, at least.

Jeremy turned to speak to him. "Other guys will be here later to eat, too, I'm sure. It doesn't have to be weird," he said thoughtfully.

Daphne was still staring at him and patted the table again.

Tom sighed and sat back down in his chair.

***

Daphne was glad Tom decided to stay. She couldn't stand being with Jeremy alone. He began humming and singing to himself loudly as he made himself at home and raided the girls' kitchen.

Tom leaned over the table and whispered, "Are you just being nice to me, or do you not want to be alone with this guy?"

Daphne swallowed before she spoke. "I *really don't* want to be alone with him."

"Why?" Tom wondered.

Daphne shrugged. "He never goes away unless I have a reason to leave."

"You have a lot of beaus," Tom assumed.

Daphne shook her head hard. "He doesn't like me like that. We're not quite sure who he likes, but he's always here. We even added him to the weekly chore chart," she declared, motioning to the wall on her right.

Tom glanced over in that direction and chuckled to himself. "So, Jeremy's got vacuuming duty this weekend?"

"You better believe it," Daphne confirmed with a grin.

"Did somebody say my name?" asked Jeremy.

"Yes, I was just telling Tom how you're basically a room-mate."

"Somebody's got to feed the lovely ladies here," Jeremy replied.

"You've taken up that venture entirely on your own," noted Daphne.

Jeremy dried his hands on his apron and grinned fully. "Yes, but it's a good venture."

"Which girl are you after, Jeremy?" asked Tom.

Daphne turned to him in surprise.

Jeremy shrugged. "I already told you. All of them."

"*Laurel*," Daphne mouthed to Tom.

Tom raised his eyebrows at her. "Laurel?"

"Hey, did you—" Jeremy began but was interrupted by the loud opening of the door.

"Did someone say my name?" Laurel said as she rushed through the door.

"Hey, Laurel," said Daphne and Jeremy in unison.

"Hey, I'm all finished with finals!" Laurel exclaimed. She took a fleeting glance at Tom. "Oh, hi, again," she said to him. Tom raised his hand in a friendly wave.

"Oh, Jeremy! Are you making dinner?" Laurel squealed in an overly excited voice.

"I'm always at your service, sweetheart," he declared. Laurel began jumping up and down and clapping her hands. "Do you think you could make some food for, let's say…fifty people?"

Jeremy raised his eyebrows. "Are we hosting a party?"

Laurel clapped her hands together and squealed in delight again. "I'll help! Whatever you need."

"For fifty people, it will take more than just us," Jeremy pointed out.

"Well, what are you making?" asked Laurel as she rubbed a hand up and over Jeremy's shoulder and looked at his invention in the frying pan.

Daphne couldn't help but notice Tom's eyes on Laurel as she and Jeremy conversed. *This is one sure way to get him completely over me. Simply put Laurel in front of him.*

Laurel spun around to face them. "Will you two help with dinner?" she asked excitedly.

"You better have Tom here be the head chef," suggested Daphne. "Whatever he brews up transforms into a masterpiece."

"Really?" Jeremy asked.

"Oh, that's right!" cried Laurel. "I heard about your *amazing* culinary skills!"

Laurel shot Daphne an apologetic look. Daphne knew why. Laurel was flirting with Tom but didn't want to hurt Daphne's feelings. Daphne knew, however, it was nearly impossible for Laurel to stop herself from flirting with a good-looking guy. Daphne wasn't mad at her. It was the way Tom looked at Laurel that made her want to run away.

Tom stood up. "Well, I don't know if I'm that amazing, but among the four of us, I think we can make this party happen," he beamed cheerfully.

Chapter *21*

Party Time

Before the small— or so they tried to be—group of friends had their fried steak and burgers ready, Daphne's and Laurel's small dorm room was jam packed with noisy bodies. Tom was glad he was busy with the homemade fries and didn't have to mingle too much with the crowd. He never knew how to act in these situations when everyone was wild. That heinous David Delooté was here with all the ladies fawning over him. *Ridiculous.*

Daphne came into the kitchen frequently to check on Tom and see if he needed anything. He knew she just wanted to make sure he didn't feel taken for granted, and he was grateful for that. However, at the same time, he wished she were coming in to see *him.*

"It smells delicious!" Daphne commented as she came to observe the simmering fries.

"Thanks," Tom started to say, but David, who had followed Daphne into the kitchen, beat him to it.

"Yes, everything looks and tastes incredible," David agreed. "I can't wait to try those fries. Did you hire this guy, Daphne?"

Tom clenched his teeth together, but fortunately his back was to them so neither Daphne nor David saw his response.

"No, this is my friend Tom," said Daphne. "He's doing this all *pro bono*."

Obligingly, Tom turned around enough so he could see them. Luckily, he had to keep his hands busy so he didn't have to shake hands with the slimy bike thief.

"Hi, I'm Tom Multon," he said a bit stiffly. "I believe we already know each other."

David's face looked surprised, and his cheeks turned a bit ruddy. *Probably from all the scandal about him.*

David cleared his throat and tried to act unaffected. "Ah, you're right, Daphne. Did you know Tom and I went to junior high school in the same little town just outside Brocksville?" he asked.

"No, I didn't know that," said Daphne, glancing back and forth between the two of them. "All Tom told me was that he knew your brother."

David's face was now unmistakably red. "Yeah, well I'm different from Mitch," David insisted, looking directly at Tom.

"I never said you weren't," Tom bantered back. Tom glanced at Daphne who was taking in this encounter with very curious eyes.

"Of course you're different," declared Laurel, who had just walked up beside David. She rubbed a hand up his arm and over his chest. "You're *much* better looking."

Yuck. David spouted back some sort of sweet nothings, and Tom was grateful he had to turn his attention to his cooking.

This Laurel friend of Daphne's could not keep her hands off anyone, even this two-faced weasel. He couldn't deny Laurel was quite striking to look at, but the way she flaunted herself around as if she were princess of the palace made her much less attractive. *Oh, well. Not my business.*

Tom flipped the last of the fries one more time in the pan. They were now crisp and ready to serve.

"Hey, Daphne, would you mind helping me with this?" Tom asked.

"Sure," Daphne said readily. The two of them started placing hot fries on several more serving plates, dropping them quickly so as not to burn their fingers. David came up close to Daphne and whispered something in her ear, too softly for Tom to hear.

"Of course," Daphne told him. Thankfully, the dreaded creep left with Laurel and headed into the living room.

"I really appreciate your doing this, Tom. I know it was a lot of work, and I hope you didn't feel obligated."

"Not at all," Tom said as he opened the fridge to grab one more bowl of potato salad.

"Is that the last of it?" Daphne inquired.

"The only thing left to do is cut up the rest of the tomatoes and onions for the burgers," Tom replied.

"I can help with that," Daphne offered.

"Thank you," said Tom, sliding a cutting board over to her. "You're always so willing to work, Daphne."

Daphne shrugged as she grabbed the knife still lying on the table. The two of them started slicing vegetables side by side in silence. Tom was glad to be next to Daphne, and he wished he could think of something to say. But just like always, when he wanted to talk to a girl, his tongue was stuck.

"Why don't you ask Laurel out?" Daphne asked suddenly.

"What?" Tom turned to look at her in surprise and then back to his knife.

"You heard me. Why don't you do it?"

Tom cut a few more slices before he responded. Did Daphne suspect Tom's intentions towards her and was now trying to divert him to Laurel? Did she really not want him that much? "I'm not interested in Laurel, Daphne," Tom admitted.

"Oh, is that so?" asked Daphne, feigning casualness.

Tom looked up at her again in confusion.

Daphne stared back at him with a bit of an accusing look. "You were staring at her for a full minute when she came to talk to David."

"I was not," Tom contradicted her. *Drat! Was I?* Tom wracked his brain back to just a minute ago. He hadn't consciously done it. Did Daphne care about that? Tom felt a spark of hope spring within him.

Carefully, Tom continued to slice another tomato. "Well, if I was, it's because I was thinking about what a nasty flirt she is," Tom offered truthfully. However, now he wondered if he shouldn't have spoken this way to her about her friend.

"Are you saying you don't like flirting, Tom?" Daphne questioned, trying to sound like she was teasing. "I doubt that."

Tom shrugged. "Not that kind of flirting."

Daphne fell silent. Tom scrutinized her face, but unfortunately, it was unreadable.

"Are you done here?"

Tom looked up to see that despicable Delooté again.

"Yes," Daphne answered.

"Great," said David, with an ugly, charming smile. He walked around the counter holding out his hand to Daphne. "This party is dull without you."

Daphne turned towards Delooté. Tom was unable to see her face. Somehow or another, they were holding hands as Delooté led them into the crowded living room.

Tom clenched his teeth together again. He hated that guy. He hated him now more than ever.

***

"Hello, everyone!" David called out to the crowd, holding a drink high in his hand. Most of the voices in the room died down. "I would like to make a toast to our hostesses!"

Now all eyes were on him. Seeing this, David smiled his impossibly gorgeous smile and raised his glass. "Where are you, ladies?"

Daphne's roommates all raised their hands. David noticed Daphne did not raise hers, so he clasped her hand in his and raised it up. "To the lovely ladies of dorm D4!"

Cheers rang around the room and people clapped excitedly. Almost immediately afterward, the noisy chatter resumed.

David knew everyone at the party, and he dragged Daphne around with him, rarely letting go of her hand. He introduced her to them all. Most people were friendly and even giddy with the encounter. Daphne figured it was because of the novelty David was. Even the guys were jovial in their greetings and slapped him on the back. Daphne was happy to see her guests enjoying themselves...probably because they were all drinking. Daphne was disappointed Laurel had insisted on serving alcohol. She didn't want to deal with any of the aftermath in her own dorm room. Besides, drunkards often exuded less intelligence than a rat, and they most certainly smelled like one. Oh, well. There was no stopping Laurel when she wanted something. Daphne was fairly certain Laurel wanted David Delooté. Daphne was fine with this, of course, and was trying to give Laurel plenty of opportunities to flirt with him. Much to Daphne's surprise, David kept coming back to her. Even with Laurel's supple fingers massaging his shoulders, David didn't let go of Daphne's hand.

Daphne occasionally risked a peek at Tom. Each time she found him eating and conversing comfortably with those around him. He never took a single drink. One time, however, when she peeked at him, she caught him looking at her. He smiled shyly and immediately looked to the girl beside him.

Making the situation even more awkward, Daphne found David staring at her when she tore her eyes away from Tom. Daphne felt her cheeks turn red.

David smiled a gorgeous smile and carressed the top of her hand. "You throw a great party, Daphne."

"Thanks. You are the life of it by the way everyone fawns over you," Daphne pointed out.

"Nah," David dismissed, batting his hand and then sipping his drink.

"Of course, you are," Daphne persisted. "Everyone loves you."

David stared at Daphne's eyes directly. It was impossible to look away. His eyes were so blue it was like being pulled right into the ocean. "All right," he conceded. "I'll agree I'm the life of the party if you'll agee you're the beauty of it."

Daphne laughed out loud and blushed deeply. "That might be going a little too far."

David shook his head, still looking right at her. "It's quite the understatement, actually."

Daphne smiled, blushing again. "Um, thank you."

David smiled back and took another drink. "Don't you hear that every day?"

Daphne shook her head, not knowing what to say.

"Well, you should," he said, beaming at her and setting his drink down again.

David rubbed his hand over Daphne's again. Their hands had been together so long they were both starting to sweat, but David didn't seem to mind. "Hey, let's take a break from the crowd. What do you say?"

Daphne raised her eyebrows in surprise. "Where would we go?"

"Oh, just outside. I need some fresh air after being with all this bad breath in here."

"I can't argue with that," Daphne agreed.

David looked very pleased and stood up, pulling her with him. As he led her out of the room, Daphne felt Tom's stare burning right through her back.

***

That evil, conniving, revolting Delooté! Tom shouted in his head. *I can't believe Daphne is falling for such a fake!* Tom hated they were out of his sight. The way Delooté had been looking Daphne over all night with his sleazy eyes left Tom seething in his seat. When he saw that scumbag again, he was certainly going to let him have it! Tom wasn't exactly sure how, but he was going to do it!

Chapter 22

Face–off!

David led Daphne across the street from their dorm building into a small park. Daphne was starting to feel a little nervous about being alone with him, but her nerves subsided when he led her to the bench by the road.

The bench was facing the sloped hill at the entrance of the park. A couple of small bushes were behind them. The fresh air was nice, and Daphne took a deep breath, taking in as much of it as she could.

"Fresh air at last, huh?" David sighed, sitting beside her. In doing so, he immediately put his arm around her and pulled her close to him. Daphne was surprised David was moving so quickly, but she couldn't deny she liked it. The fact such a gorgeous man was holding her seemed almost unbelievable.

David stroked her upper arm gently with his fingers as they sat in silence and stared at the park below them. Everything looked green and inviting, so calm. It was quite the contrast from where they were only a minute ago. Daphne couldn't help but wonder what Tom was thinking. After seeing him again, she had to admit an old flood of emotions came back to her. She knew if it were Tom sitting next to her, he would be a bit more shy about this, not so sure of himself.

"What are you thinking about?" asked David.

Daphne jumped a little in her seat. David laughed lightly. "You really must have been deep in thought. What's on your mind, beautiful?"

Daphne blushed again at his pet name. "Actually, I was just thinking about how confident you are."

David raised his eyebrows, looking pleased. "Oh, well, that's sweet of you."

"And what has the famous David Delooté been thinking?" Daphne asked.

David smiled. "Am I famous?"

"Absolutely. You know that already."

David grinned again, his eyes shining in the pale moonlight. "You're famous, too, you know."

Daphne laughed out loud. "For what?"

"For your good looks," he said thoughtfully.

Daphne chuckled some more, shaking her head. David lifted one hand up to her face, directing her sight into his. "It's true, Daphne. I, for one, haven't been able to stop thinking about you all day."

"Really?" Daphne whispered.

David nodded solemnly. For the first time, he looked a little nervous. Slowly, but surely, he tilted his head and pressed his lips against hers and began to move them in a soft, unfamiliar way.

At first, Daphne was too shocked to move. *This is too soon!* David persisted, and Daphne finally gave in and began kissing him back.

***

"Are you okay?" asked the girl beside Tom. He couldn't remember her name. He had only been half listening to their conversation because he was too distracted and abhorred at seeing David make Daphne blush. Now he couldn't stop thinking about it since they had left the room. He knew it was rude, but Tom found it impossible to keep his mind on her jabber about being top in her literature class, or maybe it was linguistics, he couldn't remember. All he could think about was his anticipation of seeing Daphne and the devil come back.

Tom was momentarily distracted by a new game of arm wrestling at the other end of the room. Both guys were wimps.

"Hey." Tom felt someone elbow him in the side. It was the girl again. "Are you okay?" she repeated.

"Oh, yeah, I'm sorry. I've been watching the arm wrestling," said Tom, pointing to where the competitive boys were.

"You should get in line for the next one," the girl encouraged.

Tom shrugged. He knew he could beat both of them, but he didn't care.

"I can't believe you made these burgers!" exclaimed the girl. "They are seriously the best I've ever had!"

Tom smiled back at her. "Thanks. They are my specialty."

The girl sweetly started to say something else, but a booming voice from the other side of the room was so loud he couldn't hear what she said. "Hey, Delooté! You're back! Come join in the wrestling!"

Tom glanced up to see Delooté and Daphne standing hand-in-hand by the dorm room's front door. "I'm game," he called. David looked at Daphne and pulled her toward the other end of the room where the crowd of anxious contestants gathered.

"Wrestle me," suggested one large guy.

"No way, Schatz. When you wrestle at school, you wrestle people who are your same weight. You're twice the size of everyone here put together. I'm not wrestling you, but maybe a fellow basketball player," said Delooté as he scanned the room.

"I'll challenge you," Tom called loudly from his seat.

All heads in the room turned to face the chef who hadn't said much the entire evening.

"There you go, man," said the huge man Schatz. "He's about your weight; he's a perfect match."

Delooté's bright eyes glared at Tom. "All right," he agreed. "Whoever wins gets the next date with Daphne."

Tom's mouth hardened, and his heart raced with the challenge. "Daphne can date anyone she wants," Tom declared, "but I'll beat you anyway."

David smirked at him and looked like he would have spit if they were on the court. He glanced at Daphne, who appeared completely stunned, and then back to Tom. "In your dreams, Texas," David mocked in a poor impersonation of Tom's accent. He was happy to see Daphne elbow him in the ribs for that.

That is it. Tom would not go easy on him.

***

Daphne couldn't believe this. As the two men lay on the floor with their elbows on the ground and hands ready to clasp together, a few girls had come to whisper fiercely into Daphne's ears.

"They're fighting for you!"

"Which one do you like better?"

"Isn't that romantic?"

One girl even dared to say, "I can't believe David Delooté wants to date you!"

Daphne couldn't respond to any of them. Her eyes were glued to the two men in front of her. What would happen if David won? Poor Tom! Daphne also knew if Tom lost he would take it much more gracefully than if David did.

Everyone else in the crowded room had taken an interest in this particular challenge since the two men had obviously displayed their distaste for each other. They were grasping hands now and the big man, Schatz, who took it upon himself to be the judge, had his massive hand over theirs and began to count. "One, two, three!"

Immediately both men pushed against the other. Both of their biceps bulged and flexed. Daphne saw David's face cringe with exertion. Tom's expression was hard but not as stressed. Tom was a little in the lead. Abruptly his face hardened, and a vein in his head popped out with a new rush of determination. Slowly, but surely, Tom pushed David's arm backwards to the floor.

Now that it was over, Daphne realized she wasn't surprised. How many times had she seen Tom lift piles and piles of wood with ease or heft an animal three times his size out of the buried snow? Maybe that hadn't been such an even match after all.

There were a few cheers and automatic "Oh's!" Most of the crowd was a bit awestruck since they had been anticipating David's victory. He had lost within thirty seconds. The relative silence was a bit stifling, but a few brave people broke it by saying, "Good match, good match." At this, others started to clap, repeating, "Good match, good match." Most people then busied themselves with clattering glasses and small talk.

Both men stood up. David's face was hard and beet red. Tom no longer looked like he wanted to punch the guts out of David, and he held out his hand to him. David refused it. "I always knew you weren't natural," David spit, still breathing hard. He got right in Tom's face and whispered something fierce Daphne couldn't hear.

Schatz put a large hand on David's shoulder. "Come on, Delooté, some guys are smashing bottles outside. Let's go."

David said something else angrily in Tom's face. Tom's expression was hard, but he didn't flinch. For the first time, David left Daphne alone and escaped out the door with Schatz following closely behind.

Daphne just stared at Tom, who was making an effort to act casual. He felt her stare and gazed back at her for a long moment. Kelsy, a short, spunky, curly-haired girl, slapped him on the back. "Way to go!"

Tom blinked and turned towards her and smiled politely.

"Do you lift weights or something?" she asked in a high voice.

Tom shrugged. "I'm a mountain man. I lift a lot of things. Excuse me, please." Immediately Tom took a few brisk steps to where Daphne was standing. Daphne's feet were still frozen, and her eyes were still glued on Tom. "Hi," he said when he reached her side.

Daphne swallowed hard. "Hi."

"I knew beating him would make him mad, but I did it anyway. I'm sorry."

Daphne shook her head. "Oh, no. That's...that's fine."

Tom deliberated for a moment. "You don't have to tell me this if you don't want to, Daphne, but...do you like him?"

"Yes, Tom, I do."

Tom looked down at the ground and rubbed his mouth. "Okay, Daphne," he said to the floor, "but..."

"But what?"

Tom looked back up at her. "You should be careful, Daphne. I don't trust him."

Daphne didn't like this. She loved the way she had felt with David in the park a few minutes ago, and now Tom was trying to pull her another direction. It wasn't fair. "Why are you saying this, Tom? You think if you can't have me, no one else can?"

Tom's face filled with surprise and a little hurt. "No, of course not, Daphne. I've always wanted you to be happy. I'm just worried about you."

Daphne was upset now. "Why, Tom? It doesn't make sense!"

Tom took a quick breath. He looked careful and earnest now. "He might be dangerous, Daphne."

"And how is that?" Daphne was definitely challenging him now and was just realizing she was raising her voice a little too much for this conversation to remain a private one.

Tom placed his hands on either side of Daphne's arms. He looked her directly in the eye and spoke urgently. "I've heard him talk about you, Daphne, and it's not what a good man would say. I don't like the way he looks at you, either."

"How does he look at me?" Daphne whispered angrily.

Tom frowned but kept his intensity. "Please, Daphne. Don't make me explain it."

Daphne shook Tom's arms off her. "I won't," she said, coolly. "I don't need you to. I can take care of myself."

"That's true, Daphne, but you can't protect yourself from every kind of creep all of the time."

Daphne felt like yelling at Tom, but fortunately, she didn't. "David is not a creep," she said in a low voice. "I don't need you to protect me from him, nor do I want you to talk to me about it anymore."

Tom's eyes rolled in frustration. "If you would just listen to me, Daphne, you would be reasonable like I know you can be. Don't fall for his tricks."

"Oh, and you didn't play tricks, Tom? You *always* led me on," she accused, jabbing a finger at his chest.

Now Tom's calm was beginning to crack. "I was never deceitful in any way," he contradicted bitterly. Tom sighed heavily. "I'm sorry, Daphne. I just...I'm sorry," he said, scratching his head. "I better go. Thanks for the party." Without waiting for a response, he swiftly walked out the door.

***

The adrenaline pounding inside Daphne prevented her from doing much of anything for the remainder of the night. She couldn't sit still, nor could she be productive. She couldn't go home since was already home. She wished she could just run into her room and hide, but there was a couple making out in there. Oh, how could she have been so rude to Tom!? She had accused him, again, of being deceitful when she knew very well he never had been. She said it to be hurtful because she was angry. She *had intentionally been* hurtful...to Tom! The sweetest man alive! Daphne slumped in her chair, feeling more ashamed than ever.

And now Tom was gone...again, and so was David. To Daphne's surprise, Laurel didn't even come to her rescue and save her from her awful feelings. Daphne scanned the room for her friend. Ah, there she was playing ping-pong with a guy Daphne didn't know. Several other people were surrounding their game and cheering Laurel on. Laurel did seem to have taken an interest in David. *I wonder what she will say when I tell her he kissed me tonight.*

Out of the blue, Daphne felt an elbow brush across her knee. David was kneeling in front of her chair with a drink in his hand. "Hey there, beautiful." His speech was slurred, followed by giggles and hiccups.

"Are you drunk, David?" asked Daphne, a bit disgusted.

"Of course, not," lied David, hiccupping again. "I do want to ask you a que—"

"Why, David, I've never seen you so...free," said a new voice beside them. Daphne turned her head to see Laurel sitting next to her.

David smiled and pointed a raised finger at Laurel. "You're smokin' hot," he said sluggishly.

Daphne groaned to herself, but Laurel put a hand to her chest and feigned flattery. "Oh, David, just listen to you!"

David smiled stupidly again and now pointed to Daphne. "But Daphne here is—" he paused to lick his lips. "Daphne is mighty fine, too, and she's a g…good girl, you know what I mean?" David slapped his thigh and laughed grotesquely.

This time both Daphne and Laurel stared at him. David lifted his chin some more as if he had just thought of a great idea. "I have a question for you, Daphne," he said. "Will you—" He paused as he let out a high laugh. He swallowed again. "Will you marry me, Daphne?"

Daphne felt her jaw drop, as several others around them gasped, gaped, and giggled. "No way I am going to talk to you until you are serious, David."

David raised his finger and pointed it at her again. "Oh, I'm serious," he said very slowly and with some difficulty.

"Ugh," Daphne muttered under her breath. "I'm going to bed," she said to Laurel. "I'll help you clean up in the morning."

Laurel nodded as Daphne quickly stood up to leave.

"Wait, baby! Don't leave!" David called to her listlessly.

Daphne shook her head and pushed open the door leading to the hallway.

Chapter 23

Skin–deep

The sun was hot. Daphne opened her eyes and squinted in the bright summer light streaming through her bedroom window. She had definitely overslept. Daphne reached out to pull back the blanket covering her alarm clock: 10:30 am. Daphne stretched and yawned and then sat up a little bit to see if Laurel were still sleeping. Laurel was gone. She had even made her bed already. Daphne slowly slid her legs over the bed and planted her feet on the floor. Her body was so stiff it felt like she had been in bed for days.

Finally, she shuffled out the door, down the hallway, and into the living room where the party had been. She found Laurel up and dressed and tossing bottles and soda cans into a large, black garbage bag.

"Morning," Laurel said without looking up.

"Hey," Daphne said, rubbing her eyes. "I can't believe you're up already. You went to bed a lot later than I did."

"I know," said Laurel as she continued to pick up more trash. "I couldn't sleep."

"Where is everybody else?" asked Daphne.

"You mean our roommates?"

"Yeah," said Daphne, yawning again.

"They're dead asleep. I doubt we'll see any of them before noon."

Daphne nodded lazily. "Well, why don't you take a break, and we'll get some breakfast."

"I already ate," said Laurel curtly as she continued to walk around and drop random things into the plastic trash bag. Laurel was still not looking at her and was definitely not her giddy self as she usually was the day after a party.

"Is there something wrong?" Daphne asked.

"Yes," she said, still moving quickly.

Daphne paused for a moment, waiting for Laurel to continue, but she never did.

"What is it?" Daphne asked.

Laurel shrugged, still making her rounds. "I'm not used to feeling the way I do right now."

This was going to be harder than Daphne thought. Laurel was usually pretty open with her. Daphne slowly walked towards Laurel, collecting some more trash on the way. "Well, how *are* you feeling?"

Laurel shrugged again. "Awful," she said, choking on the word.

Daphne stood straight up and looked at Laurel until Laurel stopped in her place and looked back. "Did something happen last night?" Daphne asked carefully.

Laurel nodded. Daphne waited for her to continue.

Laurel looked down at the garbage sack as she spoke a little forcefully. "Well, at first I was mad David liked you instead of me." She turned to Daphne and smiled apologetically. "I'm sorry for that."

"I didn't know you liked him, Laurel," Daphne felt the need to defend herself. "At least, not until after—"

"Well, I don't anymore," Laurel interjected sourly. "Not after last night."

"What do you mean?" Daphne questioned warily.

"After you went to bed, he and his friends were being so...so *gross*!"

"Gross as in they were belching or—"

"No!" Laurel exclaimed, shaking the bag. She sounded irritated. Her voice was shaky when she continued. "They were gross to *me*, like, they were—" Laurel shook her head, put one hand over her mouth, and started to sob.

"Laurel!" Daphne cried in surprise. Immediately she walked over and hugged her friend. Laurel buried her face in Daphne's shoulder. "They were *so* awful, Daphne. *So* awful."

Daphne was at a loss for words. "David, too?"

Laurel nodded into her shoulder.

Daphne took a deep breath but instantly jumped at a sudden knock at the door. "I'll get it," she offered. Laurel stepped back and wiped her eyes.

Daphne felt a little embarrassed to be answering the door in her pajamas and disheveled hair, and to make her humiliation even worse, there stood the most handsome man alive: David Delooté.

Daphne couldn't help but blink and gape for a moment.

David stood behind the threshold smiling shyly. "Hi, Daphne."

Hi was all she could say.

"May I come in?" he asked.

"Um—" Daphne deliberated. She still was unclear about a lot of things concerning the man in front of her, especially considering what Laurel had just revealed.

David looked like he was worried or concerned. "Never mind. I understand if you don't want me to. I just came here to apologize."

"You need to do a lot more than that!" yelled Laurel from inside the room. Daphne's eyes bulged in surprise, but she didn't turn around. It wasn't very often Laurel yelled, especially at a cute guy.

David's face turned dark red and full of shame. "I came to apologize to you, too, Laurel," David said a little louder.

"You can apologize to the police when I report you!" Laurel yelled again.

David clenched his teeth together. "May I please come in?" he whispered to Daphne.

Daphne scrutinized him a little more. He did look sorry and ashamed. Daphne wished she knew exactly how bad it had gotten last night. "Are you sober?" she questioned him.

David sighed and nodded.

"Do you usually get that drunk?"

David shook his head emphatically. "I promise I don't. I'm so sorry, Daphne. I was just so mad—"

Daphne raised her eyebrows. "Mad at what?"

David swallowed hard, looking more embarrassed by the minute. "I was mad at your friend Tom."

Daphne folded her arms across her chest and leaned against the threshold, giving him a challenging look. "Losing a silly arm wrestle hurts your pride so much you have to get wasted a minute later?"

David sighed. "That's not the only reason."

"What other reason is there?" Daphne asked smugly.

"Because...," David turned his head to look down the hall and then back to Daphne, "because he likes you and I...I like you, too," he said solemnly.

Daphne shifted in place a bit. "I thought you liked competitions."

David smiled a little at that. "I do, but..." He sighed again. "I don't know what else to say except I'm sorry, Daphne. I really am."

Daphne studied him a moment longer. He did look sincere. Daphne sighed and relaxed her snooty stance.

David recognized her barrier coming down. "May I please come in now? I should apologize to Laurel, too."

"You can come in if you promise to tell me what happened later," said Daphne in a quiet voice,

David nodded solemnly. "I promise."

Daphne opened the door wider and let him glide past her. They both glanced around for Laurel and eventually found her at the far end of the room, looking out the full-length window with her back to them. "You can skip it, David," Laurel said sternly. "I never want to see your face again."

Again, Daphne was surprised at Laurel's forcefulness. David took a step towards her so his toes were touching the carpet that led into the living room. He stopped right there.

"Laurel, I am so, *so* sorry. I cannot tell you how sorry I am. I...I was drunk and—"

"Yeah, I noticed!" Laurel interrupted.

Daphne was growing more uncomfortable with this, so she decided to sit down at the kitchen table.

"I didn't know what I was doing!"

Daphne rolled her eyes, but David didn't see. "What *did* you do, David?" Daphne wondered out loud.

David turned to face her quickly. "I didn't *do* anything. It was just what I said," David explained. "What I said was so wrong, Laurel, so wrong," he confessed, turning back to Laurel, who was still looking out the window.

No one spoke for a long moment.

"Laurel, these other guys were saying stuff about a bunch of girls, and in my drunken stupor, I was just repeating what they said. I don't even remember what half of it was."

Daphne rolled her eyes again, and Laurel scoffed but didn't turn around.

"Laurel, do you believe me?" David asked.

Laurel waved a dismissive arm at him. "Sure, whatever."

David sighed and stepped closer to Daphne. "Please, forgive me for this," he whispered. "Can I see you later today?"

"I don't think that's such a good idea, David," Daphne said.

David rolled his head. "Oh, come on. I made a mistake, and I'm apologizing. What else can I do?"

Daphne shrugged. "Nothing, I guess. I don't think you and I need to be spending time together anymore."

David walked around the table and leaned in towards her. "Daphne, please don't do this to me. You know I really like you." Those gorgeous blue eyes were staring at her, pleading.

In that brief moment, Daphne began to reason with herself. *Laurel usually lets guys say really, really stupid things to her and somehow is always okay with it. She's never been upset like this before.* Daphne was beginning to believe Tom had been right. Maybe this very attractive man was dangerous.

"You don't even know me, David," Daphne noted.

"I want to get to know you better," David pressed. Daphne looked into his eyes again. They were certainly beautiful, but something was missing underneath. No light was in them, just bleakness.

"I'm sorry," Daphne apologized. "We need to go our separate ways."

Shock flooded David's eyes and Daphne sensed a wave of resentment as bitterness swept over his face. "I'm not giving up on you!" he whispered, but the whisper sounded more like a threat than a promise. Daphne felt chills run down her spine as David Delooté spun around and aggressively walked out the door.

***

Tom was restless. He had been walking around the park for over an hour now. He wanted to go see Daphne but wasn't sure if it was a good time. Then he saw her, as if fate had planned it, sitting on a park bench a few feet ahead of him. She was sitting with Laurel. They appeared to be having a very serious conversation. Tom instantly wanted to jet out of there as fast as he could, but he also wanted join them.

At that moment, Daphne looked up and saw him staring at them. She looked surprised to see him, but not angry. Tom would count that as a good thing. Laurel turned around, too. Tom was shocked when he saw her face. She had obviously been crying hard. Tom involuntarily took a step back. *Now would probably be a good time to retreat.* He certainly didn't want to interrupt whatever this was. Daphne stunned him by motioning him to come over to them.

He threw her a questioning look, but that only encouraged her further. "Come here!" she called.

Hesitantly, Tom took a few steps and closed the large space between them. Tom had no idea what to say, so he was grateful when Daphne spoke first. "Tom, would you help us with something?" she asked.

"Sure," said Tom. He glanced at Laurel. "Wh-what happened?"

Laurel didn't speak but just continued to sob. He turned to Daphne for an explanation.

"It's a long story," explained Daphne. "We were wondering if you would write a report to the police for us as an additional witness."

Tom's jaw dropped. "Witness to what?"

"I don't want to be here for this," Laurel admitted. "You can tell him without me."

"Are you going back home?" asked Daphne.

Laurel nodded, and the two girls leaned in and gave each other a warm hug. "Everything's going to be okay," Daphne assured her.

"Thanks," said Laurel, sniffling. Without another word, she scurried off past the large pine that led into the quiet street.

"I didn't want to interrupt you two," Tom told her.

"Not to worry," said Daphne, patting the bench beside her. She began speaking with urgency before Tom sat down. "Tom, I'm so sorry for what I said to you last night! I was really, *really* wrong! I only said it because...well, never mind. I hope you're not still mad at me," Daphne announced. She gazed at him with a sincere, imploring look. It almost made Tom's heart stop.

Tom shook his head. "I shouldn't have challenged Delooté, but my ego got the better of me."

"No, Delooté's ego got the better of *him*," Daphne countered.

Tom leaned forward and put his elbows on his knees as he looked at Daphne. *What did that devil do?* "What do you mean? What happened?"

"He got drunk last night and turned into an entirely different person. I could blame it all on you if I were foolishly in love with him," Daphne said, but then she flashed Tom a smile to let him know she wasn't.

"What did I do that could have merited that blame?" Tom asked playfully, unconsciously moving closer to her.

"You beat him in an arm wrestling contest," Daphne said matter-of-factly. "That obviously hurt his pride."

"He was so embarrassed he got drunk?" It was an easy assumption to make.

"Mmm-hmm, and unfortunately, he humiliated himself even more, although he didn't care about that at the time."

Tom tried not to smirk at this. He would have loved to have seen that hateful man act like a fool.

"Not funny, Tom. It was awful," Daphne declared.

Tom was suddenly worried at Daphne's serious tone. He shouldn't laugh at something he knew quite well could lead to something terrible. "I'm sorry. What...what happened next?" he asked, hesitantly.

"Well, in his drunken stupor he decided to propose to me," Daphne said wryly.

Tom felt his jaw stiffen. *That sloth of a man marrying Daphne?* Tom would gut him first.

"After that foolishness, I decided I better leave the party and go to bed."

Tom nodded. Good for her.

"This morning Laurel told me what he said to *her* after I left, and—"

"And?" Tom prodded.

Daphne shook her head and swallowed hard. "It was beyond horrendous, Tom. She and I are going to report him to the police this afternoon."

Tom stared blankly at Daphne as he soaked in what all this meant. He felt his blood run cold. "Did he do anything, Daphne?" Tom said in a low voice.

Daphne shook her head. "No, but we're going to report him anyway."

Tom nodded. "Of course, you should. I just want to make sure you tell the police everything."

"We will," Daphne assured him.

Tom stared at Daphne's lovely face a little longer. "Did he do or say anything to *you*, Daphne?" Tom asked carefully.

Daphne shook her head again. "No."

Without thinking, Tom grabbed her hand in earnest. "Are you sure?"

To his surprise, Daphne did not pull away. "Yes. I'm positive."

This response only made Tom press the issue more. "Daphne, just think for another moment. Is there anything at all he has said to you that...that bothered you or worried you?"

"You mean besides his ludicrous, drunken proposal?" Daphne said disdainfully.

Tom scoffed. "Yes, besides that."

Daphne looked thoughtfully to the sky and watched some flying geese for a moment. "Yes," she finally said.

Tom felt his entire body stiffen with anxiety as Daphne said nothing else. He looked down at his hand that Daphne was now tightly clutching. He realized this might be something very hard for Daphne to say. "You can tell me," he said softly.

"He came to our room again this morning and—"

"Was he sober?" Tom interrupted.

"Yes," Daphne said. "He tried to act apologetic. At first, I believed him but then—"

Tom patted her hand in encouragement.

Daphne was looking at the trees now and appeared almost to be talking to herself. "But then I realized I didn't want to be with someone who would ever do something like that regardless of how handsome or rich he was."

Tom felt his jaw tighten again.

"I told him we needed to go our separate ways and then he—"

"And then he what?" Tom whispered fiercely.

Daphne cocked her head. "He said he wouldn't give up on me, but the way he said it was like. . .almost as if he were threatening me," she finished as she glanced up at Tom with a concerned look.

At that moment, Tom knew David was up to something. *Something is not right.*

"Don't ever be alone with him again," Tom warned.

Daphne nodded.

"I'm serious, Daphne. Promise me."

"I promise."

"Let me know if he ever says or does anything like that again; anything at all and you let me know. I'll come running if you need me."

Daphne smiled a small smile. "Thank you, Tom. You've always been so good to me."

The ache Tom had felt all these months away from Daphne now swelled all the more. "And I always will," he promised.

***

"Is that all, Miss?"

"Yes, thank you," said Daphne to the cashier as she grabbed her apple juice and headed out the door of the gas station. The chime on the door rang, and she headed out into the bright light.

"Hey there, beautiful."

Daphne jumped in surprise. There he was. The most handsome devil of a man.

"You're at a gas station with no car?" David asked.

"I just stopped in to get a drink," Daphne said. She wondered why she was standing there answering his question. She should be giving him the cold shoulder and walking away at the very least.

"Why don't I give you a ride home then? I've got a nice lift," he said, motioning to his sleek, red Beamer parked next to them.

"No thanks, David. It's a nice day. I'll walk."

"Ah, come on," David complained. "Let me be a gentleman."

Daphne stared at his blue eyes. Although they were bright in the sunlight, they seemed to have a dark cloud looming over them. He looked as if he were trying to be casual, but his jaw looked stern and mean. His stare didn't leave Daphne's face, and she felt a frightening chill run through her as she remembered Tom's warning: *"Don't ever be alone with him again."*

"No, thank you," Daphne muttered again as she took a step towards the curb that led into the parking lot. David caught her arm in a hard grip. Daphne grimaced at the sting of it. "Don't be that way. Let me get the door for you," he leered as he pulled Daphne alongside him to the passenger door of the Beamer.

"Let go of me!" Daphne said through her teeth.

David leaned into Daphne and whispered into her ear. "One thing you need to learn about me, princess," he sneered, tightening his grip on her arm, "I don't take no for an answer."

"Until you met me!" Daphne said loudly, pushing David with her free hand as hard as she could.

At that moment, a man came out of the gas station, looking pointedly at the two of them. David took a step back, loosened his grip a bit, and forced his face to be smooth.

"Come on, babe, don't take your angst out on me," he chided loudly.

Daphne glared at David and turned to the man who had come outside and was walking past them now. "Will you call the police, please?" she yelled.

The man raised his eyebrows high.

David laughed lightly and rolled his eyes. "All I did was say hi to another girl, and she's ready to turn me in," he lied.

Daphne opened her mouth to protest, but David gripped her arm again, and she grimaced just long enough to give the man enough time to step into his car and drive away. She screamed after him, "Please, call 911! Daphne Zollinger!"

Seriously? Is he not going to help me at all?

David smirked at Daphne's shocked expression, and with a great heave, he pushed her into the car. Daphne smacked her head on the way in and fell back onto the gearshift. She immediately sat up to get out, but David had already slammed the door shut and locked it. Daphne fumbled to find the lock on the door, but David was already in the driver's seat and driving away.

Daphne's head was whirling. *What was she going to do?* She thought about jumping out of the car, but David was already going forty miles an hour and speeding up steadily.

"You never answered my question, Daphne. I want to marry you."

"Oh, shut up!" Daphne yelled.

David nodded calmly. "I thought you might disagree. I already told you I never take no for an answer, so you are going to accept me, one way or another."

Daphne scoffed but said nothing.

"You see, Daphne," David said in his smooth voice. "I am one who likes to have everything. And not just money either. In fact, that is why you are going to marry me. I need people to see I care about more than money. Since you're not rich and have a good reputation, everyone will have to agree I care about having a good relationship and a happy family. I won't be like my brother, like your boyfriend accused me. You see, people don't like my brother because they think he's not a good man. People like me, and marrying you will secure that. Now I will be the wealthiest, handsomest, most respected man in all of Brocksville, maybe even beyond. Don't worry. I have enough money to buy me any job I want." Then he let out a maniacal laugh. "It's funny. People claim to have good morals, but once you put a few thousand dollar bills into their hands, they will do anything."

Daphne was getting angrier and more aggravated by the minute. At the moment, she cursed herself for deciding to pay off her small student loan rather than buying a cell phone. She knew Tom would help her, but she had no way of letting him know!

"Besides," David continued, enjoying hearing himself talk. "You're a good girl, and I know you will take care of the kids while I'm off...doing whatever I want."

Daphne clenched her teeth together. She *was* going to get away from this scoundrel.

"Oh, and by the way, I don't know if you heard," David said. "Laurel dropped her charges against me. She confessed she was just furious and drunk with jealousy so she accused me falsely."

"What?" Daphne gasped under her breath.

David laughed greedily. "You're going to do the same thing if you know what's good for you."

"I'll never do it," Daphne vowed in a quiet voice.

"Sure, you will," said David as he stopped his car in front of his custom-made home. He turned to her and stared at her darkly. "I know you will."

***

Tom arrived at the police station about ten minutes after noon. He had come as quickly as he could after he had worked his first shift at the local hardware store. He knew Daphne was planning on coming around this time, and he hoped he hadn't missed her.

He walked up to the front desk and asked for Daphne Zollinger.

"Are you here as a witness to her claim?" the lady asked.

"Um, well, I could probably help with some details," Tom offered.

The lady nodded. "She's in an office with one of our lawyers. I'll take you back."

"Thank you," said Tom as he followed her through some winding hallways. They stopped in front of a large office with tall glass walls. The lady knocked at the door and then opened it without waiting for a response. She walked in but didn't shut the door.

"Excuse me, Drew. Oh, did your client already leave?" Tom overheard her say.

Drew started to answer, but Tom did not hear. He was distracted by a couple of officers walking rapidly past him.

"The man at the gas station said her name was Daphne Zollinger. She was with someone she apparently didn't trust and begged him to call the police."

Tom flipped his head around as he heard Daphne's name.

"Said they drove off west on Balboa Avenue," the officer continued.

"I'm sorry, sir. Your friend has left already," said the front desk lady.

"Yeah," said Tom as he pivoted and sprinted out the door.

Chapter *24*

Filthy Blood

Daphne stared at David's face on the ground, bleeding. Her hands were still shaking, and her palms were oozing blood from one of the broken pieces of the glass vase she had thrown at David's head. She knew she should move, get dressed, and get out of his bedroom, but she couldn't stop staring at the bleeding, unconscious man. *How did I not see it? How did I not see the evil in him before?*

Suddenly, there was a vicious pounding at the front door. Daphne jumped. "Delooté!" someone was shouting.

The adrenaline that had just filled her chest moments before now came rushing back. As quickly as she could, Daphne slipped her clothes back on as the pounding and screaming continued. Daphne stumbled to her feet and held herself up by holding onto the walls. The blood from her hands smeared over the white-painted surface. Abruptly, the front door burst open. The fright of it caused her to lose her already-shaky footing and fall into the hallway.

"Daphne!" a man hollered to her.

Daphne glanced up to see Tom running toward her. Before Daphne could get to her feet, he was already kneeling by her side. "Daphne, are you okay?" Tom asked anxiously.

This question seemed so odd at the moment. All Daphne could do was stare back at him. His current countenance was unfamiliar to Daphne—full of utter shock, anger, and irrepressible worry.

"Daphne," Tom said intensely, placing his hands on either side of her face. "Are you all right?"

Daphne stared back into Tom's eyes for a moment and then shook her head. "No," she whispered.

The worry in Tom's eyes grew all the more urgent. "Where's the devil?" he whispered fiercely.

Daphne motioned with her head to David's bedroom. Tom looked over his shoulder, but at that moment, two officers stepped into the doorway. "Excuse me. Are you Daphne Zollinger?" asked one of them.

Both Daphne and Tom glanced in their direction. "Yes," Daphne croaked.

"Did this man hurt you?" said the tall one, pointing at Tom.

***

Tom couldn't believe his ears. *They think I'm the devil?*

"No, he came to help me," Daphne croaked again.

"I'm the one who just called you," offered Tom.

"Then where's the culprit?" asked the short one.

Tom half turned and pointed to the bedroom. "In there."

The two officers walked down the hallway and into David's bedroom. "Four-One-Two, we need an ambulance at 54 South Brundage Street," said an officer into his radio.

"His heart is beating, and he's still breathing," said one of them from inside the room. The short one walked out into the hallway. "Which one of you did this to him?" he asked.

"I did," Tom and Daphne said in unison.

Daphne glared at Tom. "*I* did," she repeated defiantly. Tom groaned internally. He wished he could take the blame for it. But then again, he was proud of Daphne for doing what she did.

"It was clearly out of self-defense, officer," Tom protested.

"We'll need you both to come down to the station with us and answer some questions," said the tall one, as he ducked out of the bedroom.

"Can't I have a few minutes to talk to her first?" Tom asked him.

"I don't want to talk about it, Tom."

Tom glanced back at Daphne. Her face was pale with distinct slap marks across her cheeks. The sight filled Tom with rage. He stared into her eyes that were full of shock and dread. Her once neat ponytail was now a jumbled mess, and upon examining it, he found some blood in her hair on the side of her head. Tom stifled a gasp and reached his hand up to touch it. Daphne flinched, causing Tom to worry all the more.

"What happened to your head?" he asked.

"It's just blood from my hands," Daphne explained as she flipped her hands over so her palms faced upward, exposing the cuts there.

"What's that from?" Tom wondered.

"Come on, kids. We need to go," urged the tall one.

Daphne started to get to her feet. Tom assisted her by putting his arm around her waist. Daphne winced in pain. Tom shot her a questioning look, but Daphne just ignored him, shifted out of his embrace and walked towards the door. *What did that devil do to her?*

Tom wanted to talk to Daphne on the way to the police station, but he knew she didn't want to, especially with the officers in the front seat. He tried to hold her hand a couple of times, but Daphne refused that as well. Usually, that would hurt Tom, but under the circumstances, he was not offended. He probably needed to give her space for a while. Now, more than ever, he didn't want to leave her side. She was too beautiful for her own good, and she needed protection from that—Tom clenched his teeth. He couldn't even think about David Delooté without his blood boiling.

At the station, Tom wasn't allowed to be with Daphne as they asked her questions or as she wrote her report. Tom was finished before Daphne was. He sat in the waiting room until she came out. When she finally did, she looked even worse than before. Tom stood up abruptly and rushed over to her.

"I'm all right," she claimed. "Officer Brown and Officer Wyatt are going to take me to..."

To the hospital, Tom thought.

Daphne pursed her lips and looked away from him. "To where I need to go. And then they'll take me to my grand-mother's house in Sunland."

Tom furrowed his brow. "Well, I can do that," he offered.

"We have advised her not to be without police protection for a time," said an officer behind her. Tom hadn't noticed his presence until that moment. Next to him stood a shorter female officer. The two officers going with Daphne eased Tom's anxiety a little bit.

Tom took a deep breath, looking at Daphne's puffy eyes. "May I visit you in Sunland?"

Daphne nodded and turned to follow the officers out the door.

"Wait!" Tom cried.

The three of them twisted around.

Tom took a step forward and spoke in a low voice. "I'm here for you, Daphne. Whatever you need."

"I know," Daphne whispered, "but you're going to have to give me some space for a while. Confiding in you is going to be very difficult now."

Tom felt confusion smother his face. *What did she mean by that?* Without another word, Daphne walked out the door. This was far worse than the last time she walked out on him—or rather he walked out on her. That horrible, empty, hopeless feeling he had felt then was nothing compared to this. Something had died in Daphne. That Delooté devil had changed the most beautiful girl in the world. Tom would make sure he paid for whatever he did. Yes, he would pay. If Tom had anything to do with it, David Delooté wouldn't see the light of day for a long, long time.

***

Tom was sitting across the office desk of the private detective he had hired. The detective was giving him a play-by-play of what he thought had happened in David's room based on the various evidence of chaos he found—lamps turned over, blood smudges in the carpet and on the wall. Tom still couldn't believe it. It just couldn't have happened. Not to Daphne.

"How long will it take for the DNA results to come back from the lab, Detective Lawson?" Tom inquired.

"Oh, just call me Craig," the detective insisted.

"How long, Craig?"

"Just a couple of days."

Tom inhaled deeply. "Do you think we have a case against him?" He hoped.

Craig was still jotting something down on his notepad when he responded. "Absolutely. You've given me some excellent sources." He put away his pen and looked up at Tom with his glasses still down on his nose. "It's splendid you have a few people from the party willing to give testimonies."

Tom nodded. "It was really good of the man who saw them at the gas station to give one as well."

Craig put his glasses back up over his eyes. "Yes, I believe we are well on our way to some convicting evidence."

Tom tried to smile at the detective's well-intentioned, encouraging words, but he still worried.

"It would also help if that other girl agreed to testify," Craig mentioned. "What's her name?"

"Laurel," Tom told him. "Yeah, I know. I'll talk to her. Look, Craig, I heard Judge Bridges is scheduled to be the judge on the day of trial, but I don't trust him. Do you think you could look into him for me?"

"Sure thing," said Craig, jotting down another note.

***

Tom lay in bed and stared. He had never felt more anxious in all his life. Tom prayed Daphne would find comfort where she was. He prayed and prayed that she would know how much he cared about her. He had already found out where her grandmother lived in Sunland, but he wanted to give her space as she had requested. At the same time, he didn't want her to be alone for another second.

That's it. He was going to see her after he had everything taken care of. Once more he prayed that everyone to whom he had spoken would testify against Delooté in court.

Tom thought back to earlier that evening when he had gone to visit Laurel to ask her if she knew anything that might have led up to the "incident" with Daphne. Laurel been very reticent, very unwilling to open up. He had asked her direct questions: "Did you talk to David today besides this morning?" and "Did you file the complaint on him?" Laurel shook her head and wouldn't say a word. Then Tom realized Laurel hadn't a clue as to what had happened to Daphne, so he told her what he had witnessed. Laurel was beyond shaken. She had paced around the room with her hand over her mouth, fighting sob after sob. Tom had tried to console her and attempted to convince her if she told the police all she knew, David's crimes against Daphne and her could be rectified.

"Is he in jail?" she finally asked.

"He was, but his parents bailed him out." Tom grimaced at that. Only the Delooté's would have $25,000 on hand to bail out their twisted son. "But he will be again soon if everyone who knows anything will speak up about it."

Laurel shook her head. "If...if I say something he...he will—"

"Did he threaten you?" Tom questioned.

Laurel didn't say anything, but Tom could tell by the look in her eyes the answer was yes.

"Don't worry, Laurel. He's not going to get away with anything this time. You can testify against him. You can do it."

Laurel covered her mouth and began to sob again. Tom was getting the feeling the situation with Laurel was worse than he knew.

"That two-faced, mongrel," Tom seethed under his breath.

Laurel nodded but said nothing.

"I'm trying to get a court date with Judge Ruby. The Delootés are trying to get Judge Bridges, but—"

"They'll pay him off," Laurel interjected.

"Yeah, I know."

"Doesn't Daphne need to set that up?" Laurel asked through her tears.

"Not necessarily. She just needs to show up in court," explained Tom.

"Do you think she will?" asked Laurel.

"I'm sure of it," Tom pledged.

Laurel turned her gaze out the window. "She's a lot stronger than I am," Laurel whispered.

"You can do it, too, Laurel," Tom encouraged. "You can do it, too."

Tom wished he could do something else to console her. He asked her how he could help.

"I need to be alone so I can think," she said.

Tom nodded. "Keep your doors locked," he told her.

"I will," Laurel promised.

Tom went to leave. When his hand reached the doorknob, Laurel called to him. "Tom?"

He turned around to face her.

"Are you still in love with Daphne?" she asked.

Tom swallowed hard before answering. "More than ever," he said.

Tom's thoughts now brought him back to the darkness of his friendless room. He had to solidify a court date with Judge Ruby. Tom knew his pa had trusted her. His pa had never told him why, and at the time, Tom didn't care to ask. If his pa had trusted her, then so did he.

Hastily, Tom picked up his phone and dialed his hired detective's number. "Hello, Craig? Did you find anything on Judge Bridges yet?"

"Oh, sure, there was plenty to find," Craig replied. "It'll take a long time for an actual conviction of a judge, but while the case is under review, we should have no problem getting another judge for your girl's trial."

"How about Judge Ruby?" Tom suggested.

"Sure, she's an excellent choice," Craig agreed. "I'll take care of it in the morning."

"Excellent! Thank you!" Tom cried.

Tom's heart beat rapidly with excitement and hope as he ended his call. Even still, he knew the fight wasn't over. Tom was going to find all the honest people in the world he knew who could help him with this. Daphne deserved justice, and so did David Delooté.

Chapter 25

Exposed

Tom slammed his fist down hard on the desk, causing the receptionist in front of him to jump in her seat, and the pens tumbled out of their cup next to her. "Do you have any idea what kind of a man Bridges is?" Tom whispered fiercely, leaning close to the woman.

The woman jolted her head back, shocked by Tom's reaction. "I—"

"Never mind," Tom curtly said as he crinkled up the paper on the desk that stated the officials in the court.

Utterly livid, Tom stomped his way out of the courthouse and down some long steep stairs leading to the street below. *How did this happen?* After all the phone calls he had made and all the promises people had made to him, how could Judge Bridges *still* be the judge?

Tom snatched his phone from his pocket and angrily punched in a phone number. He had to do it three times since his fuming fingers kept missing the correct digits.

"Hello, Tom," came the voice on the other end, "I know you're angry with me."

"You bet I am, Craig!" Tom shot back. "You told me you were certain you could find evidence Bridges had been bought out!"

"I know, and I did find it, but—"

"But what?" Tom nearly yelled into the phone.

"It's gone, Tom. I don't know how, but all my documents are gone."

"What do you mean they're gone?" Tom shouted.

"I mean they're missing," said the frantic man. "My hard drive is wiped out, and my paper copies have vanished. I had them locked up, but they still disappeared."

Tom bit his lip as he ducked his head. Dread and despair flooded his chest. *It cannot end this way. It cannot.*

"I can't afford to hire another detective," Tom mumbled, mostly to himself. "I need money for a lawyer."

A moment of silence passed, "I would lend the money to you if I could, Tom."

"I'm sure you would," Tom whispered again. "Thanks, anyway."

"Good luck to you. I'm so sorry about all of this."

"Yeah," Tom said as he ended the call.

Tom was rubbing his head hard as he began pacing back and forth. An abrupt ring made him almost jump out of his skin. He sighed when he realized it was his phone.

"Hello? Jenny?"

"Tom, where are you? I have something for you."

"What do you mean? Are you here in Brocksville?"

"Yes, I'm driving around Central Park. Where are you?"

"I'm at the courthouse," Tom replied. "Why are you here?"

"Stay where you are. I'll see you in five." Click.

Tom peered at his phone in confusion. What was his sister doing here? He didn't need this distraction right now. He began to pace all the more impatiently while waiting for his sister to arrive.

Finally, he recognized the sound of his pa's twenty-year-old Jeep hum in front of him on the street. Jenny had barely stopped before she hopped out and scurried over to him.

"Tom!" she cried, throwing her arms around him.

"Hey, sis," he said, returning the hug. "This is a surprise."

Jenny quickly released him and held out a long envelope. "This is for you. It came in the mail today. It says urgent, so Ma told me to drive over here and give it to you right away."

Tom examined the envelope carefully. Afghanistan! "Could this be—" he said out loud. He tore the envelope open. The first thing he noticed was a big, fat check written to him in a scrawling hand. "No way!" he exclaimed.

"What is it?" asked Jenny.

Tom glanced up to look at his sister. "I...I wrote to Daphne's father in Afghanistan because she...she's in trouble. He sent me some money to help. I can't believe it got here so fast! Look at how much he spent on postage to make it priority mail." He pointed to the stamps on the envelope.

Jenny glanced at it quickly but didn't appear very interested in that particular detail. "What kind of trouble is Daphne in?"

Tom shook his head and opened up the letter to read it.

Dear Mr. Multon,

I am appalled at the news you have shared with me. My wife and I will get on the very next available flight to Brocksville, but we are having visa problems. I know you didn't ask for any money, but please use this for legal fees.

We hope to see you and our dear Daphne very soon.

Regards,

Zack Zollinger

P.S.: I know a superb detective in Brocksville: Phillip Ross. He's the quirkiest, most honest man alive. Look him up. He might be able to help.

Tom smiled as hope flooded him.

"Tom?" Jenny said a bit impatiently. "Are you going to answer my question? What kind of trouble is Daphne in?"

Tom looked up at his sister again. "Let's go for a drive, and I'll tell you about it."

***

Tom was sitting and waiting for Detective Ross in his huge, fifth-story office that overlooked Brocksville. He could see nothing but blue sky through the glass windows that stood tall from ceiling to floor. A half dozen foreign plants in big pots dotted the large space. His desk had nothing on it but a thick, leather-covered planner.

Abruptly, Detective Ross bolted into the room. Tom turned in his seat to see him. He was skinny and wiry with lots of moles on his bald head. His thick, circular spectacles made his eyes look like they were behind a magnifying glass. Without a word, he stared at Tom as he made his way around his desk. He plopped himself down in his black leather chair and noisily scooted it in. He interlocked his fingers and placed them in front of him.

"What can I do for you?" he asked, raising his eyebrows above his glasses. Tom was surprised the detective didn't offer any introductions.

"I'm Tom Multon," he said, deciding to introduce himself anyway. "I would like you to look into...into a person of rather high clout here in the community."

The detective's mouth turned slightly mischievous. "And who is that?" he wondered.

"Judge Bridges, sir."

Without out any warning, Detective Ross burst into a strange high cackle. "Judge Bridges!" he hooted with his head thrown back. "We don't need proof to know he's a bad egg!"

"But we need proof this time," Tom blurted out.

Ross glanced back at him as his laughs subdued. "Okay," he agreed, waving his fingers towards him as if he were beckoning to a child to come close. "Tell me everything."

Hastily, Tom told the detective everything: from the party at Daphne's dorm, to the bruised Daphne outside Delooté's dorm, to his chat with Laurel, as well as his work with Craig and the subsequent missing files. Tom was so furious inside after he had finished, he felt his heart just might explode right out of his chest.

Ross leaned back in his seat and folded his arms. "It sounds like you and Craig already gathered enough hard evidence to convict the little Delooté snake. We need to retrieve it and then find evidence Bridges was involved." By the twisting of his mouth and the spitting of his words, Tom was pleased to notice Ross already hated the Delootés, or maybe it was Bridges. Either way, Tom felt hope again.

Ross thrummed his fingers up and down on the desk for a long moment before he suddenly slapped his palm down hard. "All right! Let's get going!" he exclaimed, standing up.

Tom stood up with him. "Am I coming with you?" he asked.

"Well, you'll certainly be useful since you witnessed so much and can probably answer some questions that will come up along the way. Don't you want to catch the scoundrel?" he asked, raising his eyebrows high.

"Well, yes, of course!" Tom said.

Ross meandered to the front of his office and opened the door, gesturing for Tom to proceed. "Well, then," he said. "Let's get going."

Their first stop was the police station. Tom ended up having to fill out every form and write every statement he had already written again so Ross could get a search warrant for David's belongings, specifically his vehicle.

Warrant in hand, the two men walked back to the detective's modest Corolla. "You think we will find something in Delooté's car?" asked Tom.

"He's a filthy rich brat, isn't he?" Ross noted. "Probably has a GPS, at least."

"Probably. So?"

"We'll find something then," Ross said with a grin.

Detective Ross drove like a maniac. Just as Tom's head had stopped spinning from the ride, Ross had already jumped in and out of David's flashy red Beamer. "I got it! Let's go!" he declared as he let out his high cackle.

"You got what? And where are we going?" Tom questioned.

"To see Judge Bridges! Get in the car!"

"What?" Tom asked, confused. He had barely shut the passenger door before Ross was speeding off again.

"The GPS showed that the snake went to Bridges' office. I probably won't be able to get a warrant to search any of Bridges' files, so I am going to have a chat with him, see him squirm a bit."

"Will that help?" Tom asked skeptically. "You know he won't tell the truth."

"I know that," Ross said. "I'm good at reading people, though. He might give me another clue of what to do next."

Tom sighed heavily. He hoped Ross knew what he was doing.

***

Tom felt adrenaline pump through his veins as he walked into Judge Bridges' office with Detective Ross. It was smaller than Ross' office and quite bare by comparison. Not a single plant was in sight, only a shiny oak desk and a middle-aged man slouched over it. Judge Bridges had dark, black eyes and deep wrinkles that smothered his entire countenance. He said nothing as the two men walked in. He just glared at the detective for one penetrating minute.

"Shall we sit down?" asked Ross, finally. However, the question sounded anything but polite.

Bridges smirked. "Don't bother. I don't think this meeting will last long."

Ross sniffed and sat down anyway; Tom followed suit. The two older men didn't even seem to notice he was there as they stared each other down.

"I found on David Delooté's GPS that he's paid you several visits," said Ross. Although his tone was light, it sounded like a very pointed allegation.

"Why do you care about Robert's son?" Bridges asked him, a scowl crossing his face.

"Ah, yes, Robert Delooté," Ross said snidely. "I'm sure you two weasels are the best of friends."

Bridges rolled his eyes.

"How much did they pay you this time?"

"There you go again with your accusations," Bridges said with a wicked smile. "How dare you. I'm an honest judge."

Tom scoffed out loud at that.

For the first time, Bridges turned to face him. "Who is this lovely sunset boy?" he asked condescendingly.

"The one who is going to see you put in jail," Tom threatened coolly.

Bridges laughed out loud. "How cute."

Tom glowered back at him but said nothing.

"I have a warrant to search all of David's possessions," Ross announced. "So why don't you just let me see his files? Hmmm?"

Bridges put on a conniving smile. "As you very well know, Detective, your warrant doesn't include things in *my* possession." He grinned even wider to show his shiny, white teeth.

Ross shrugged. "Well, then, maybe I'll just go talk to all the waitresses at your favorite restaurant and see if they overheard any meetings you had there with David Deloôté. Surely they'll remember seeing such an infamous, rich young man there."

The judge's eyes bulged for a brief moment before he raised his eyebrows in feigned nonchalance.

Detective Ross nodded. "Good chat, Judge. I hope you don't break too many laws today." He stood up and made his way to the door. Tom took a moment to glare at the judge one more time before he did the same.

As the big double doors to Bridges' office latched shut behind them, Detective Ross leaned over to Tom, "Let's go to that restaurant," he whispered.

Tom nodded, and the two sauntered down a long corridor. Tom noticed Bridges' secretary stare at him wide-eyed as he passed her.

"Oh, excuse me!" she called to him. Tom turned around to see the short blonde scamper towards him in her thin high heels, her gray business suit swishing along with her. "Excuse me," she said again when she reached him. Her bright red lips were trembling slightly. She smiled a nervous smile. "I'm Wanda, uh, wha-what's your name?" she stuttered.

"This is Mr. Multon," Ross said as he put one casual hand on Tom's shoulder, "and he really needs to go now."

Wanda seemed all the more frazzled by this. "Oh, I...I was just hoping that...that you would call me sometime." She smiled anxiously and held out a shaking piece of paper to him.

Ross dropped his arm and laughed under his breath.

Tom rubbed his chin and smiled politely. "I'm very flattered, Wanda, but I sort of have a girlfriend." *Of course, "sort of" is the truest part of that statement.*

Wanda smiled rather forcefully this time and grabbed Tom's hand and placed the paper in it. "Well, take my number just in case."

Tom furrowed his brow as he felt something hard inside the paper. He glanced down to see what it was, but Wanda quickly put her other hand on top. *Shhh*, she said with just her lips, shaking her head the tiniest bit.

Confused, Tom studied her face, trying to discern what she was saying.

"Let's go, Mr. Multon," Detective Ross muttered, grabbing him by the shoulder and coaxing him to turn around. "Just walk out," he whispered to him. Ross must have noticed it, too. Tom turned his head and waved at Wanda. Wanda waved back, looking nothing but relieved he was leaving.

Tom tried to be discreet as he stuffed the hard thing into his pocket, burning with curiosity as to what it was. When they finally sat down in the detective's vehicle, Tom began to reach into his pocket.

"Don't get it out now!" Ross fiercely whispered as he surveyed the oncoming traffic. However, his expression was as casual as ever.

"Why not?" Tom wondered.

"Wait until Bridges can no longer see us from his office window."

"All right." Tom forced himself to be patient as he buckled his seatbelt.

Tom waited until they were two blocks away before he pulled out the strange object—small and gray and rectangular. Tom instantly recognized it as a voice recorder.

Detective Ross let his high cackle go free. "Ha! This is great! Let's listen to it!"

Tom pressed the playback button. A man was shouting angrily; he didn't recognize the voice.

"Ah, that Robert rascal." Detective Ross spit.

"Robert Delooté?" Tom asked.

Ross nodded but held a hand up to silence him. His driving slowed as the two listened intensely.

Robert was so angry his words were hard to understand, but Tom did hear him say, "You owe me one! You owe me this!" and "My son will not!" and "Just a silly girl!" and "My career will not be interfered with by this!" Judge Bridges' voice was also there but muffled by Robert Delooté's yelling. Then, the recorder went silent, and Tom heard a huff like someone had just sat in a chair.

"How good of you to sit, Robert." This was Judge Bridges' voice.

"Why aren't you listening to me, Ben?" asked Robert.

Bridges snorted in contempt. "You haven't been listening to me! I kept telling you to calm down so you could see I have already taken care of everything for you."

"Actually, I took care of most of it," said a new voice.

"Is that *Craig*?" Tom yelled at the recorder, utterly flabbergasted.

"That is true," Bridges agreed. *"I couldn't have done it without the detective here."*

"What?" yelled Tom again. "*Craig* did this to me?"

"Shhh!" exclaimed Ross, lifting his hand up again to silence him.

"We need to talk money," said Bridges. *"I need $50,000."*

Robert made a mocking sound. "Why would I give you that much?"

"Well, because it was expensive for me to convince Detective Lawson here to destroy all of the evidence he had just spent hours collecting for the Multon boy. I need you to give me double what I paid him."

"Or else what?!" Robert fumed.

"Or else *I will make sure all of the witnesses' testimonies will be just enough to convict your son."*

Tom's jaw tightened as he clenched and unclenched his fists.

"You can't do that," Robert seethed.

"I don't see another option for you," replied Bridges *calmly.*

"Fine!" Robert relented hotly, and there was a loud strik-ing sound on what must have been the table. *"This better not even make it to court!"* he spit in threatening tones.

Tom could hear the wicked smile in Bridges' voice. *"Sure thing."*

Tom clicked off the recorder and smacked the window with his fist. "How could he? How *dare* that Craig—!" He stopped short as he turned to see Detective Ross laughing wildly.

"Eh-heh, heh, heh!" Ross crowed as he slapped his thigh over and over and sometimes the steering wheel.

"*Why* is this funny?" Tom said, baffled. Tom waited for him to finish laughing, but it was another minute before Ross got one word out.

"Judge Bridges is going to go to jail! Imagine! A judge in jail! It's just too hysterical!" The detective let out another loud, obnoxious hoot.

Tom felt the side of his mouth twist into a smile.

"He didn't even know he was being recorded!" Ross' laughs were now inadvertent spurts of screeching. "It's too much!" he squeaked out. "It's just too much!"

Then it dawned on Tom. With this evidence, Judge Bridges would go to jail! And so would that lying, betraying Craig! And that devil David Delooté! Tom's heart soared with relief. He soon realized he was laughing just as hard and ridiculously as the neurotic detective beside him.

Chapter 26

Unblemished

Daphne lay on her bed and stared at her bright yellow walls. She used to love this room. It was cheery and reminded her of sunshine even during the dark winter months. Daphne's grandmother had stenciled a large aspen onto the wall along with some blue birds sitting on the thin branches. Framed cross-stitch pictures hung on the walls, some of which depicted red roses, violins, and ballet shoes. Daphne very much admired her grandmother's talent that had brought them to life. The beauty of these handiworks used to bring her such simple joy. *Where is it now?*

And then there was a soft knock on her bedroom door. "Daphne, may I come in?" her grandmother asked.

"Sure, Grandma."

The door creaked open, and an old, elegant lady poked her head through the door. "I have a surprise for you, dear," she announced.

"What is it?" Daphne wondered. Despite her dreary mood, she was still curious.

"Well, come into my sewing room and see."

Daphne groaned and put an arm over her eyes. "I don't feel like moving right now, Grandma."

"Oh, fiddle-dee-dee! Do you think I would still be alive if I stayed put just because I wanted to?"

Daphne frowned but said nothing.

"Come on. You've got to move those legs sometime," urged her grandmother.

Daphne stifled a groan and slid her feet off the bed and onto the squishy, blue carpet.

"That's a girl," said Grandma as Daphne followed her out of the room, down the hall and into a tiny, full-to-the-brim sewing room.

At first, Daphne didn't know where to look with all the bright, material clutter, but then her eyes rested on a fluffy dress laid across an ironing board in the center of the room.

"Is that for me, Grandma?" Daphne asked.

"Of course it is, dear."

Daphne walked over to where the dress lay and lifted it in front of her body. It was definitely the type of sundress Daphne used to love to wear. It was a perfect yellow with colorful flowers lining the skirt and white lace for a trim. It had a fluffy petticoat sewn underneath so it puffed out from the waist. The sleeves were also puffy with white lace. Even though it was out of style, it was as lovely as anything. It was something Grandma made, and Daphne had to admit such a thoughtful gift cheered her quite a bit.

"There's that smile I remember!" exclaimed Grandma.

Daphne looked up and realized she *was* smiling. "Thank you, Grandma. It is beautiful. You must have spent the entire week making it!"

"Oh, come, child. I can't speed-sew like that anymore. My eyes are too bad," Grandma confessed, batting a hand at her. "I started this at the first of the year. I knew you would come visit me some time after your semester ended, and I wanted to have something nice for you. I finished it last night."

Daphne was all the more touched by this and felt prickling tears behind her eyes. "You are too good, Grandma."

"Nonsense!" cried Grandma, batting her hand again. "Now go try it on, dear. Go on. Quick, quick," she urged, gently pushing Daphne towards the door.

A minute later Daphne came out of her room wearing the new sundress.

"Ah! You look beautiful! Absolutely *beautiful*!" Grandma exclaimed, placing her wrinkly hands together.

Daphne smiled shyly and looked down to smooth the dress with her hands. "It fits perfectly, just like everything you have ever made me."

"You're exaggerating. Now come over here, sweetheart, and sit in front of my rocking chair so I can brush your hair."

"Are you turning your home into a beauty salon?" Daphne asked as she walked into the living room with her grandma.

"Don't pretend you haven't always loved it when I do this," said Grandma as she settled herself into the rocking chair.

"Of course, I do," agreed Daphne. "My hair never looks better than after you fancy it all up."

Grandma laughed a tinkling laugh. "Well, it's been awhile. Let's see what I can still do."

Daphne sat, feeling strangely content as her grandma brushed through her long hair and then smoothly pinned all of it up into what Daphne knew was an elegant French twist.

"There is not a girl in the world who wouldn't give anything to have the shine your hair has, Daphne. Now go look in the mirror and tell me if you approve," Grandma ordered.

Daphne stood and walked a few steps to the large, oval mirror that rested on top of the mantle of the brick wall. She tried not to look at the bruises on her face. She turned her hair to one side and then the other to examine Grandma's masterpiece.

"You've still got the magic touch, Grandma."

Grandma laughed again as she slowly stood up from her chair. "Now, dear, come sit with me on the porch swing, will you?"

Daphne stifled a groan. "It sounds nice, Grandma, but I think I'll just stay inside."

"Now, why on earth would you do that?" Grandma asked. "It's an unusually beautiful, sunny day out there. Come on, now," she murmured as she grabbed her cane and made her way to the front door. Daphne did not follow. Grandma stopped and turned to face her before she opened the door. "Why are you just standing there?"

"I don't want people to see me, Grandma," Daphne admitted.

"Oh, who is going to see you on this old road?" Grandma said. "Even if they do, they will see a beautiful girl and her old grandmother enjoying a hearty swing."

Daphne cracked a smile at that.

"Ah!" Grandma said, pointing a knobby finger at her. "You keep that smile on your face, and all will be fine."

"Okay, Grandma, but I will do it inside."

"No, no, no. You're not staying cooped up in this house for another minute. Come on. You and I both need some air."

Daphne groaned audibly this time but submitted nonetheless.

"That's right," Grandma said with a smile, opening the door. "The sunshine will do you good."

Daphne sighed as she followed her grandma out into the bright outdoors. She only took a couple of steps before she stopped short. There, at the head of the wooden deck just past the porch swing, stood a redheaded man. He was facing the opposite direction looking out at the open field. He quickly turned around when he heard them exit the house. He paused when he saw her. His hair blew softly in the light breeze, as did his buttoned-up blue shirt. "Hi, Daphne," he finally said.

Daphne stared at him a minute longer and then turned to face her grandmother. "Did you know he was coming?"

"Of course, dear! Why else would I have gone through all that effort to get you cleaned up?" her grandma replied with a sly smile.

Daphne cocked her head, giving her a disapproving look.

"I'll let you two catch up," said her grandmother. "I feel like baking anyway."

"Wait, Grandma!" Daphne cried, catching her grandma's arm.

"What is it, child?" she asked in a low voice.

"I don't want to talk to him!" Daphne whispered severely.

"Then, don't talk," said Grandma. "Listen."

Daphne had no response to that, and her grandma smiled sweetly. "You'll be fine," she assured her, giving Daphne's hand a squeeze. With that, her grandmother slipped inside and shut the door firmly behind her.

Daphne sighed. This was going to be awful. She knew Tom meant well, but what did he expect from her? Daphne realized now she was still staring at the door her grandmother had closed behind her, but at the same time she couldn't get herself to move. She heard Tom's footsteps echo on the deck, and then he stopped. "Will you come sit on the porch swing with me, Daphne?" he asked.

Daphne took a deep breath. "Okay," she relented. Tom waited for Daphne to sit before he sat down beside her.

Daphne couldn't get herself to look at him, so she stared out at the empty, country dirt road beyond the front yard of the house. Tom moved the swing ever so slightly with his feet but said nothing. For several minutes, the two of them sat in silence.

"If anyone is going to say something, it will have to be you, Tom, because I have nothing to say," Daphne informed him.

"Okay," said Tom. Daphne sneaked a fleeting glance at him. He was swallowing hard. "Well, I do have a few things I want to tell you."

Daphne didn't respond, and so he continued. "First of all, I know you probably wanted more time to yourself, but I...I had to see you because...I've been really worried about you."

Daphne already felt tears coming to her eyes, and she wanted to curse herself for it.

Tom took a deep breath. "I also wanted to let you know I set up a court date with Judge Ruby next Tuesday for you and me to testify against...um—" Tom cleared his throat, "I'm hoping Laurel will also testify. I talked to her about it. If we're lucky, his bullish friend, Schatz, will talk, too. I'm pretty sure he knows about...what Delooté was planning."

Daphne leaned her head against the back of the swing and looked up at the sky. She was blinking hard, trying desperately to hold back the tears. Tom had already done the preliminary work for her. *What a friend!* All she had to do now was testify. It was the last thing in the world she wanted to do, but she knew she had to.

Tom scratched a hand through his hair; a gesture Daphne had discovered he did when he was nervous. "Wha...what do you think? Can you do that?"

Daphne bit her lip and nodded as she looked the opposite direction at Tom. She felt Tom shift in his seat. "I wrote a letter to your father in Afghanistan and—"

"What?" Daphne said, still looking away from him. "How did you get my parents' address?"

"Oh, well, remember when we made labels at the cabin for the packages you sent them? I still had the file on my laptop," Tom explained.

"Oh," Daphne said.

"Anyway, I'm praying they'll get here in time for the trial. But if not..." Tom swallowed, "if not, I'll be there."

Daphne spun her head around to look at him for the first time. "Why, Tom?"

Tom raised his eyebrows in surprise. He looked worried at her question. "I told you I would always be here for you, Daphne," he said simply.

"I appreciate all you have done for me, Tom, but I don't think I want you there in the courtroom."

Tom's worried expression became more pronounced, and he also looked a little hurt. "Why not?"

How was she supposed to explain this? Maybe not answering him would be easier. Yes, it was. Daphne turned her head to look back out at the road. Her breathing was getting ragged. She focused on breathing slowly.

Tom persisted as he leaned over to look at Daphne's face. "Why not, Daphne?" he repeated. Daphne looked back at his face, full of concern. She loved his face, and she loved the way he was looking at her right now. It made Daphne's heart burn and ache.

"It doesn't matter. I just remembered you have to be there anyway to testify about what you saw."

"Why don't you want me there?" he asked in an urgent whisper.

Daphne felt the tears coming again, but she couldn't stop them this time. "It will be hard enough to say what I have to in that courtroom, and it will be even harder to say it in front of you," Daphne confessed. Her tears turned into sobs.

Tom reached up and held Daphne's face gently in his hands. "Did he really do it, Daphne?" he breathed.

Daphne nodded and wept some more. Tom's already pained face completely changed and became more profound than Daphne had ever seen before. It was much more than worry. It was deep, deep sorrow. His face scrunched up, and his chin quivered as he began to weep with her. Despite everything, Daphne knew at that moment Tom was feeling this sorrow for *her*. Her pain was his pain, and for some reason, that knowledge made the pain seem a little easier to bear. Maybe she could go on if Tom were by her side. She desperately needed him but didn't want to tell him.

Tom wrapped his arms around her and buried his face in her shoulder. "I'm so sorry, Daphne." She could feel him shaking. Daphne buried her face in his chest, and he tightened his embrace and caressed her back with urgent gentleness. They remained in the same position for many long moments as they wept all the tears that could ever be wept.

Finally, Tom let go and rested his forehead against hers. "I love you, Daphne," he sniffed. "I love you so much. I will do everything I can to get you through this. I promise."

"I know you will, Tom, but I don't deserve you. Especially now," said Daphne, her voice choking.

Tom held Daphne's face in his hands again and looked straight into her eyes. "Don't you dare say that ever again, Daphne. This thing is awful, but you are just as beautiful and virtuous now as you have always been."

Daphne shook her head and looked down as fresh tears came once more. "Yes, you are!" cried Tom with urgency as he pulled her gaze up to his again. "Yes, you are. You'd better remember that...always."

Daphne just stared back at Tom's beautiful brown eyes. He was so good. So good. He turned away in shame. "If I had only come a few minutes earlier," he whispered as more tears spilled down his cheeks.

"It's not your fault."

Quickly he turned back to her. "It's not yours either. Delooté will get put behind bars and...and I wasn't going to ask you this so soon, but—" He glanced at Daphne as if in thought. "Never mind. That discussion is for another time."

"Yes," said Daphne.

"What?"

"Yes, I will marry you."

Tom raised his eyebrows. "H...how did you know?"

Daphne smiled a little. "I'm smart."

Tom smiled back. "Yes, you are. And to remind you, I'm a little more deserving of you now because I'm going to finish college and I have a plan for my life. You've always been part of that plan."

"I love you, Tom," Daphne breathed.

Tom smiled. "So, you'll accept me now?"

"If you will accept me."

Tom put his palms on her cheeks again and looked at her solemnly. He was crying again. "With all my heart," he whispered fervently, "and then some." He began to finger his hand through her hair and leaned in to give her the most gentle, tender kiss ever given. After the longest, loneliest, most horrific week of Daphne's life, she was now sure of one thing: Tom. Tom loved her.

Epilogue

Tom couldn't help his nervous leg from bouncing up and down as he waited anxiously in the courtroom for Daphne's case to come. His heart sped up rapidly when Daphne's lawyer finally stood to introduce it. The next few minutes proved to be the worst of his life. Daphne courageously sat on the stand with complete poise, voicing out loud the heinous things that devilish leech had done to her. Tom became so angry and so sick to his stomach with the scene she painted, it was all he could do to stay sitting down and not punch Delooté to a pulp right there in the courtroom. Tom kept glancing over at him, slouching next to his lawyer. His face was beet red, and his hair was drenched in sweat. His eyes dropped in shame as Daphne testified against him. He looked angry, too. Tom could see he was clenching and unclenching his jaw.

When Daphne walked off the stand, David stood up in rage and yelled, "She's lying everyone! She's lying!"

The judge slammed her gavel and said, "Don't give me cause to add fines to your charges."

David's lawyer pulled him down by the arm and gave him a reprimand Tom didn't hear.

Tom was happy to testify as a witness on Daphne's behalf of what he saw and heard Delooté say, but he hated Daphne had to listen to it. He made sure he did not glance at her while he spoke. He didn't want to see how it hurt her.

Tom, Daphne, and Laurel testified, as well as three kids from the party, the man who saw them at the gas station, and even David's supposed friend Schatz. The jury had no problem concluding Delooté was guilty.

Tom uttered the most fervent prayer of thanks. They had done it! It was over! It was the longest morning Tom had ever spent, but it was well worth it when he saw the devil get escorted out of the courtroom and off to jail. The two joined eyes as the court attendant handcuffed David. Tom couldn't help but smirk at him. David tried to glare back, but the expression was weak on his shamed face. The entire room stood up and stared at him as he bowed his head in disgrace while walking past all of their probing eyes.

An intense, momentary, silence suffocated the courtroom following David's departure, but soon the crowd began talking noisily and meandering toward the exit door. Tom scanned the room for Daphne and found her on the opposite side, wrapped in the tight embrace of an older gentleman. A woman with tear-stained cheeks was beside them. Daphne hugged her next. Her parents! He slowly approached them, not wanting to intrude.

Mr. Zollinger noticed Tom staring at them and took a few long strides in his direction.

"You must be Tom," he said, clasping his hand in a firm handshake.

Tom nodded. "That's right, and you must be Daphne's father. Thank you for your timely assistance, sir."

"Oh, no! Thank you!" Mr. Zollinger cried. "Thank you so much for taking such good care of my girl!"

"Yes," said Daphne's mother who had joined them now. "We are so grateful!"

"My pleasure," said Tom with a smile. "It's good to meet you both."

"So Mom, Dad, I see you have met Tom," said Daphne as she approached them.

"Yes. A fine young man," her father said to Daphne. "Let's give them a minute. Shall we, dear?" he murmured to his wife. She nodded and gave Daphne another tight squeeze before leaving her side.

Tom didn't waste any time before taking Daphne in his arms.

"Thank you, Tom," she whispered into his chest.

"You're the brave one," he declared. "I have something for you."

"I hope it's you," she replied.

Tom smiled at that. "Yes, you definitely have me, but I have a little something to make it official."

Tom felt Daphne's breath catch. Quickly, Tom snatched a diamond ring from his pocket and got down on one knee. Daphne gaped down at him in amazement.

Tom couldn't help but smile at her expression. "Daphne, you've had my heart ever since you came into my life. It will always be yours. I love you, Daphne. Will you marry me?"

Daphne laughed through her tears. "You already know I will, Tom Multon," she confirmed.

Tom smiled affectionately and kissed her hand and slipped the ring onto her finger. A perfect fit.

"Well, get up and kiss her, you idiot!" Tom heard Mr. Zollinger speak loudly from across the room.

Tom and Daphne glanced over to where he stood near the doorway with Daphne's mother. Their tear-stained cheeks were now wrinkled with smiles.

"Yes, sir!" He shot up to his feet and took Daphne's face into his hands and gently kissed her sweet lips. They tasted better every time.

About the Author

In the third grade, Brenda Hodnett won a trophy for writing a story about white unicorns and pink pansies. She has been writing ever since: novels, short stories, poems, and volumes of memoirs. She is also passionate about music and has performed in many venues including the Disney Concert Hall with the Los Angeles Master Chorale. Brenda holds a bachelor's degree in music education from California State University, Northridge.

www.ingramcontent.com/pod-product-compliance
Lightning Source LLC
Chambersburg PA
CBHW031102260626
47172CB00001B/181